THE JUBILEE PLOT

Esther & Jack Enright Mystery Book Seven

David Field

SAPERE BOOKS

Also in the Esther & Jack Enright Mystery Series
The Gaslight Stalker
The Night Caller
The Prodigal Sister
The Slum Reaper
The Posing Playwright
The Mercy Killings
The Lost Boys

THE JUBILEE PLOT

Published by Sapere Books.

20 Windermere Drive, Leeds, England, LS17 7UZ,
United Kingdom

saperebooks.com

Copyright © David Field, 2018

David Field has asserted his right to be identified as the author
of this work.
All rights reserved.

No part of this publication may be reproduced, stored in any
retrieval system, or transmitted, in any form, or by any means,
electronic, mechanical, photocopying, recording, or otherwise,
without the prior written permission of the publishers.
This book is a work of fiction. Names, characters, businesses,
organisations, places and events, other than those clearly in the
public domain, are either the product of the author's
imagination, or are used fictitiously.
Any resemblances to actual persons, living or dead, events or
locales are purely coincidental.

ISBN: 978-1-912786-39-8

Chapter One

'Before you pass sentence, my Lord, Detective Inspector Enright — the officer who investigated this case — wishes to be heard in the matter of clemency.'

Mr Justice Harrington raised both eyebrows as defence counsel Marshall Hall sat down, having had little to do except explain the reasons why his clients Harriet Crouch and Amy Jackson had killed the infants they had just pleaded guilty to having murdered.

'This is highly unusual, is it not?' the judge enquired of Marshall Hall. 'I've listened carefully to what you've had to say in mitigation of the sentence of your clients, and I take into account their pleas of guilty and expressions of remorse, both of which were delivered with your customary command over the English language. And yet now I'm being required to hear — from the defence end of the bar table, I assume — something further in their favour from the very man whose tireless and unceasing efforts brought these two murderous wretches to justice?'

'Indeed, your Lordship,' Hall confirmed as he rose for long enough to address the Bench, then sat down again heavily when the varicose vein in his leg protested at the new imposition being placed upon it.

'Very well,' the judge agreed, 'I'll hear from this witness, although there would seem to me to be but one possible disposal available to me, after what I was informed by Treasury Counsel. Inspector Enright, what can you possibly have to add, and what could possibly deflect me from the death penalty in this case?'

Having taken the witness oath, Percy cleared his throat, looked defiantly up and across at his Lordship, and began. 'Your Lordship, as you have been advised, it was my grim duty to investigate the series of deaths of young babies that led to these two ladies being arrested and brought before the Court, where they pleaded guilty as charged. They made no secret of the fact that between them they were directly responsible for the murders of ten helpless infants, and during my very first interviews with each of them they explained their reasons.'

'None of those reasons constituting a defence to charges of Murder, I take it?' the judge enquired.

Percy shook his head. 'Not "defences" in the legal sense, no your Lordship, which is why — on the advice of their counsel Mr Hall — they pleaded guilty. But before your Lordship passes sentence, I feel that it is imperative that you learn of the circumstances that led to these deaths, terrible though they are in the perception of those of us who are fortunate to have led comfortable lives without fear of hunger, without being abused by others, and without the stigma of being the unwanted produce of others.'

'You're about to employ the word "orphan", Inspector?' the judge demanded with arched eyebrows. 'If so, let me save you some breath. If I were to employ leniency in every case in which a miserable miscreant stood before me seeking to escape the hangman by claiming orphan status, we could use the gallows for firewood, and could convert Newgate into yet another Methodist chapel.'

'If your Lordship would hear me out,' Percy replied slightly testily, 'I merely refer to the orphan status of these two ladies as a convenient label to attach to the means by which they ceased to have any protection from the law, ceased to lead lives that were deemed to be of any value to those entrusted with their welfare, and indeed ceased to qualify for the most basic human entitlements of life, liberty and personal integrity.'

'A very strong claim, Inspector,' the judge replied with a frown, 'but what significance can it have in relation to the clear duty that confronts me? If their lives have been so miserable, why would they wish to prolong them?'

Percy went bright red as he fought with his anger. 'If you will forgive me, your Lordship, that perception of the cheapness of human life when it is led by those on the very bottom-most rung of our social ladder is *precisely* what has led to the appearance of these ladies before you, and precisely explains why they, in their turn, sought to mercifully end the lives of others before they could be led with such misery as they themselves had endured. The system has failed Harriet Crouch and Amy Jackson, my Lord, and it cannot now be allowed to sweep them away in order to prevent the public scandal that must be exposed through what they can attest to regarding what was done to them.'

'Do you speak as one of these Reformists, Inspector?' the judge said in an irritated tone.

'No, your Lordship, I speak as a committed Christian who joined the police service in order to protect the lives of those weaker than myself. To do my best to ensure that those living God-fearing lives in this society of ours could so without fear of the Devil in their midst.'

'Before this degenerates into a sermon, Inspector, you might wish to elaborate on what experiences can possibly have converted two women from what should have been their natural instinct to nurture infants into a wicked determination to do away with those left in their care. Then you might go on to explain to me why this should prevent their being hanged.'

'Certainly, your Lordship,' Percy continued as he raised his voice for the benefit of the newspaper reporters.

'Harriet Crouch and Amy Jackson were born in human bondage,' Percy explained as pencils passed hastily across notebooks, 'in the sense that they have no memory of mothers' arms, no memory of warm nourishing milk, and no memory of smiling faces looking down on them. Their memories came to consist of the gnawing and persistent sensation of slow starvation, interspersed with seemingly purposeless beatings — certainly beatings for which they can recall no cause on their part.'

'They were treated coldly and institutionally,' the judge interrupted, 'but that makes them no different from a thousand others like them. Proceed to something relevant, Inspector — and without any further displays of journalistic excess.'

'It has to be hoped,' Percy replied angrily, 'that daily — sometimes hourly — rape and sodomy are not also the recommended and authorised routine of our orphanages, for that is what they each suffered when, at an approximate age of eight, these two women were transferred to the so-called "Children's Ward" of the local Workhouse. In Harriet Crouch's case it was for stealing the food that her starving body craved, while Amy Jackson's sin would seem to have been sharing that stolen food with Harriet Crouch. They had already formed the sort of lifelong bond that can be forged only in the fire of utter despair and hopelessness, when any hand stretched out in friendship seems like a lifebelt. Since I can only assume,' Percy proceeded in a voice chilled like slaughterhouse ice, 'that Miss Crouch and Miss Jackson are the only persons present in this room who know what it's like to be treated as a sexual spittoon by every deviant who's sought employment in the Workhouse solely in order to be able to live out their sick fantasies on those in no position to make any formal complaint, then I won't even attempt to elaborate, except to invite your Lordship to imagine what it must do to one's self-esteem. For the rest of us, who enjoy our freedom, our rights under the law, there's always the comforting thought that if we are abused there is someone to whom we can complain, even if it *is* only to the police, who in many cases will fail in their half-hearted efforts to locate the culprit and bring him to justice.'

'The police force that you represent?' the judge reminded him.

Percy shrugged his shoulders. 'Probably not for much longer, my Lord, since this case has brought home to me, more than any other that I've handled in a period of service exceeding thirty years, that I've been wasting my time. I could have done nothing to prevent what these women endured, since there was no-one to whom they could turn.'

'When do you intend to get to the part which justifies what these women did to innocent babies, Inspector?'

'Clearly, it *cannot* be justified, my Lord, but it is my submission to you that the deaths of the ten infants, which have been described to us in horrifying detail by Counsel for the Crown, while they were at the hands of Harriet Crouch and Amy Jackson, should be attributed to an institutional failure of which we, as Englishmen, should be thoroughly ashamed. The moral blame for all those deaths must lie with our so-called charitable institutions, which created the women who stand before you. Those who generated in these two women such a fearful dread of what lay in store for any child that had the misfortune to be locked away behind the grim walls of these Halls of Evil that they chose, as an act of mercy, to end the lives of those children for whom they could find no alternative in the form of adoption.'

'And you suggest to me that society should express its guilt by way of a recommendation for clemency on my part?' the judge asked with evident amusement.

'It most certainly should not be allowed to hide its shame for what it has created in these two women by dropping them through a trapdoor on the end of a rope, then burying them in a pit of lime.'

'Do you have anything further to add?' the judge said testily as his hand reached for the black cloth.

Percy shook his head with sadness. 'No, your Lordship.'

'Very well, you may stand down from the witness box, since I've heard nothing to justify clemency in this case. Stand up, prisoners.'

Percy hung his head as he heard the all too familiar words of the death sentence being intoned without any indication of emotion or regret. He allowed himself a brief look at the faces of the two women. Harriet Crouch smiled.

'You're a good man, Percy Enright. Don't give up the fight.'

Percy caught the meaningful look on the face of the court usher who was waiting to lock the courtroom doors at the end of what, to him, had simply been another working day. But for Percy Enright it was a very significant day. It was the day on which he would go home and write out his letter of resignation. Thirty odd years defending the indefensible. Thirty odd years believing that he was somehow doing his bit to improve the society to which he was dedicated. During that time he'd been shot, knifed, kicked, spat on and punched. He'd been offered bribes, and his life had been threatened countless times. He'd returned home soaking wet, uniform torn from his back, boots covered in victims' blood, and utterly despondent. But he'd never given up. Until now.

For thirty odd years he'd apparently been wasting his time.

Chapter Two

'Uncle Percy's all over the morning paper!' Esther Enright told Jack excitedly as he threw his hat at the hook on the back of the scullery door and missed as usual.

It was the front page 'lead' story in that day's *Daily Mail*, which Esther would collect from the Post Office every morning on her return from accompanying their eldest daughter Lily to school. In two weeks time she'd also be handing over their second child Bertie, and not before time, given the restless boredom that caused him to be hyperactive and almost beyond Nell's control as she tried to keep him occupied while Esther took care of the two youngest. Miriam was now eighteen months old and staggering around on two wobbly legs like a drunken navvy on pay night, while recently born 'Thomas Percival' required a feed every three hours if he was to be prevented from bawling the house down.

Jack's mouth gaped open as he read the detailed report of what Percy had said in open court during the sentencing of Harriet Crouch and Amy Jackson at the Old Bailey the previous afternoon. He'd never known his uncle to be so eloquent but unfortunately it almost certainly meant the end of Percy's career as a police officer, a career that Jack had been sharing for the past ten or so years. Now a Detective Sergeant in the local Essex force, and based in its Chelmsford headquarters, Jack had joined the Metropolitan Police with both the encouragement and support of the uncle who'd taken over his upbringing when Jack's father Thomas had died shortly after Jack's fourteenth birthday. By then Uncle Percy had been drafted into Scotland Yard, the elite detective force that handled all the Met's more difficult cases, leaving uniformed constables like Jack to maintain the peace in 'lively' areas such as Jack's first posting, Whitechapel.

Even when Jack had moved out to Essex, where he was now a Detective Sergeant at the head of a detective force of precisely three, himself included, Percy had somehow found ways of involving, in the most complex and potentially deadly investigations, both himself and Esther.

Jack put down the newspaper article and looked up at Esther.

'So what did you think?' she asked eagerly. 'He was rather outspoken, wasn't he?'

'That's rather like saying that the Queen's a little on the plump side,' Jack replied. 'At least he won't experience any more indecision about resigning after this.'

'How do you mean?'

'Did you read what he said?'

'Only briefly, since I had to supervise Nell black-leading the fireplace in the sitting room, and Bertie was being a perfect pest as usual. Your uncle seemed to be criticising the orphanages and Workhouses for their lack of effective supervision of what goes on in there. That's nothing new, surely?'

'Not to people like us, in the know,' Jack reminded her. 'But the vast majority of the reading public want to rest assured that these orphanages are well supervised, and not likely to trouble their consciences. As long as what goes on in there remains a secret, and they don't actually have to look at, or even read about, what *really* happens to orphans, then Mr and Mrs Average are happy to remain ignorant. Uncle Percy certainly ruffled a few middle-class feathers there, at a guess.'

'But why will that affect his decision about whether or not to resign?'

'Because the decision will be taken out of his hands. Put another way, he'll be thrown out of the Met.'

'For speaking the truth?'

'Of course. The popular thinking inside the Met is that the public must be reassured at all costs that we have all the nastiness suppressed, buried, and out of sight, so that they can lead their self-satisfied lives without fear. Uncle Percy just announced that there are horror stories bubbling under the surface, and that we're losing the ability to hold the lid down.'

'Don't you think that's a bit of an exaggeration, Jack?'

'Is it? Have you forgotten how the East End reacted when the Ripper was doing his nightly rounds, and we seemed powerless to stop him? Don't you remember the vigilante groups, the outraged letters to the newspapers, the near lynchings of anyone who even vaguely resembled the bogey man of their nightmares?'

'Come to think of it, I had my own 'bogey man' experience the other day. I'm sure I was being followed,' Esther said thoughtfully.

'Followed by whom? And where?'

'It's probably nothing but my imagination,' she offered, realising at the same time that this would not stop the questions.

'Tell me what you imagined, then,' Jack countered, and she relented.

'Well, I was taking Lily to school the other day — Monday, it would have been — when I noticed this man standing under that large elm tree further down Bunting Lane, looking back up at the house. As I walked down the lane he seemed to be walking about a hundred yards behind me, always keeping well back, but always the same distance away. Then when I came out of the school he was there again, a few yards on the other side of the school. I was a bit nervous by this stage, so I ducked into the Post Office and pointed him out to Mr Duckworth. He told me that the same man had been in the Post Office the previous week, enquiring if there was anyone called "Jacobs" living in Barking. The only person he knew of that name was old Mrs Sybil Jacobs, the retired schoolmistress, and then the man asked if anyone had moved into Barking lately with mail being delivered from a forwarding address in Clerkenwell. Ted Duckworth told him no, although he obviously knew about us. But something about the man gave Ted the creeps, and that's why he hadn't alerted me to the man's enquiries. He fully intended to tell you about the man, since you're a police officer and you'd be able to sort him out.'

'And so I will,' Jack muttered with a darkened face. 'Nobody's going to spy on my wife and daughter with impunity. I'll stay home tomorrow and wait for him to lurk down the street. You can point him out, then I'll demand to know his business.'

'He'll probably stay away if he knows you're home,' Esther pointed out, and after a moment's reflection Jack nodded.

'You're probably right. Added to which, I'm up to my armpits in paper at work at the moment. But I'll send young Billy Manvers down here to keep an eye on you and Lily, and perhaps warn the man off. He doesn't sound like your usual lurker — it's almost as if he's looking for you specifically.'

'You saved me the trouble of sacking you,' Chief Superintendent Bray glared at Percy as he threw the envelope down on the desk in front of him. 'That *is* your resignation, I assume?'

'Naturally,' Percy growled, and the ensuing silence was uncomfortable for them both. Finally it was Bray who broke it.

'What were you thinking of, man? You only had three years left for a full pension retirement, and now you'll get only half. What in God's name got into your head?'

'A desire for justice,' Percy snarled back. 'As you reminded me, I was three years away from having devoted my entire working life to maintaining a system that grinds the very poor, the most deprived, and the most in need of our protection, into the ground, and then either locks them away or hangs them, in either case solely in order to hide the evidence of their very existence, and the way that our so-called Christian society has dealt with them. I wasn't required to protect the innocent all those years — I was being used as a convenient shovel for society's shit.'

'I once thought the way you do, Percy,' Bray continued in a softer tone, 'but I had the brains to keep my doubts to myself.'

'You call it "brains" — I call it "courage". Or at least, "honesty". As the reward for keeping your mouth shut about what's happening to the weakest in our community you've been rewarded with a bigger shovel, that's all. At least I'll be leaving with my integrity intact.'

The colour rose in Bray's face.

'In the circumstances, I'll ignore that insult. You can leave today, if that'll give you time to clear your desk. I wouldn't want you around the place for any longer than necessary, in case you pollute some of the younger officers with your revolutionary — some might say "anarchistic" — opinions. Talking of which, how's that nephew of yours reacted to the things you said in court?'

'No idea — I haven't seen him since. Hopefully he knows me well enough to appreciate that I spoke from the heart.'

'It's a pity you didn't engage your brain at the same time. What will you do for a living now, since I assume that you can't keep body and soul alive on a half pension?'

'The money I'll be receiving weekly would be joyfully accepted by a single mother in Whitechapel or Wapping and would feed her and her three children for a month,' Percy observed with an expression of distaste. 'But in answer to your main question, I had in mind going back to market gardening. That's what I did before joining the Met all those years ago, but hopefully I can go back to it in some sort of supervisory capacity — perhaps managing a greengrocery or something — since I'm a bit long in the tooth for wielding a shovel.'

'Good luck any way, Percy. We've had our differences over the years, and most obviously over your recent outburst, but you're one of the best thief takers in the Yard, and you'll be hard to replace. I thank you for your years of service, and I'm sorry to see them end in this way. That's all, and I'll let you get on with clearing your desk.'

Jim Bermingham wiped the condensation off the inside of the window of his watchman's office inside Brinsley's Gem Importers premises in Hatton Garden as he heard a coach stop outside. He never had to deal with deliveries on the night shift, so he was intrigued as to why the vehicle had halted by the front door to the premises he was guarding. Then through the veil of early autumn drizzle that was drifting down past the street gas lamp he caught sight of the conical police helmets of the three men who descended from the rear of the coach and walked up to the front door, sounding the bell.

He sighed and walked out of his office to the front door, then lowered the hatch through which he could communicate with the outside world. He found himself staring into the urgent face of a 'bobby'.

'Sergeant Cameron, "E" Division. There's a team of suspected robbers on your roof, and we need to come through in order to intercept them inside when our men chase them down through the skylights. Open up, please.'

Jim did as instructed and was about to accompany the sergeant and his two constables when a thought suddenly struck him.

'Them skylights don't lead nowhere once yer comes off the roof an' 'asn't done fer years. They was blocked off, so 'owdyer reckon them blokes is usin' 'em ter rob the place?'

The 'sergeant' treated Jim to a sick grin as he stuck the pistol under his nose. Behind him, several men ran down the hallway and into the strongroom area carrying large and apparently heavy carpet bags. Jim heard urgent instructions being shouted, and several minutes later, while he was still staring down the barrel of the pistol and trying not to wet himself, there was a massive explosion, and the door to the central strongbox sagged forward on its hinges. Half a dozen men wearing police uniforms gleefully raced inside and began filling the carpet bags with precious stones, then ran outside and threw them into the waiting coach before diving in after them.

'Thank you for your assistance,' the 'sergeant' told Jim before loosing both barrels into his face.

Chapter Three

'Now that Percy's made the sensible decision to get out, let's hope that Jackson follows his lead, like he did when he wasted his life by joining the police force in the first place,' Constance Enright pontificated from behind her teacup as the Enright family sat enjoying the last of the September sun in the room in the old Church Lane family home that had been grandly christened 'the sun lounge'. It was the traditional family gathering for Sunday dinner, and from where they sat they could watch Lily and Bertie fighting for possession of the swing on the lawn outside.

'I rather gather that Percy had that decision taken out of his hands,' Beattie replied icily. 'He always had a big mouth that went off at all the inappropriate moments.'

'Like when I proposed to you?' Percy fired back grumpily, and it fell awkwardly silent until Jack felt obliged to come to the defence of his lifelong hero.

'The day that a man feels that he's not free to express an honest opinion will be a sad one for English society,' he observed, slightly uncomfortable at the pomposity of his own words.

'You'd never make a politician,' Percy chuckled back bitterly.

'What was it all about, anyway?' Constance said, to a responding snort from Beattie.

'Don't get him started, please! I've heard nothing for two weeks except his attempts to justify throwing away half a pension. They're totally unconvincing, but they sound very grand.'

'I happen to agree with him,' Jack responded. 'Given the risks that we run, the dangers we confront, and the occasional unpleasantness that we have to witness, we're constantly relying on the belief, deep down, that in some way we're working for the benefit of society.'

'You mean that you're not?' his mother enquired. 'Please don't say that, since Esther and I can use that line every time some old snob in the Ladies' Guild looks down their nose at us as the wife and mother of a mere tradesman.'

'Of course we are,' Jack assured her, 'in the sense that, by and large, we keep crime off the streets. We can't stop it happening in the first place, of course, but when we catch the offender and have them locked up for a lengthy period, it deters anyone else from doing the same thing.'

'There was once a time when I believed that as well,' Percy replied sourly. 'That was a hundred years ago, before I began locking up the same offenders for the second or subsequent time. Before I'd seen my first dozen innocent corpses or gazed into the defeated and fear-ravaged eyes of the mother of three who'd just been beaten to pulp by the animal she'd vowed to honour and obey.'

'I *did* warn you not to get him started,' Beattie muttered. 'In the circumstances, the only decent thing I can do to make amends is to take him away with me.'

'Not before he's told us what life has in store for him next,' Jack protested, and was treated to a hollow laugh from the man in question.

'Not a great deal, if the first two weeks have been anything to judge by,' Percy advised the company. 'Despite several personal applications to a variety of enterprises, it seems that no-one wishes to imperil the future of their agricultural produce in the hands of a man whose last thirty odd years have been spent pouring shit onto the general public rather than onto vegetable rows.'

'I'm *definitely* taking him home now,' Beattie insisted as she collected her handbag from the side of her chair and rose to her feet. But Jack hadn't finished asking questions.

'Has *nobody* shown any interest in speaking to you about what you can offer, Uncle Percy?'

'Only the Home Secretary, and I doubt that he wants to ask my advice about how to get the best out of leek shanks.'

'He's asked to see you?'

'Twice, but only, I suspect, to kick my bollocks even harder than Bray did.'

'Percy!' Beattie all but shrieked. 'That was outrageous and unseemly! We're leaving now — immediately!'

'I'll send you a wire when I'm due for release.' Percy grinned at Jack as he rose to leave and was guided out of the house by Aunt Beattie steering his elbow as she continued to berate him regarding his language. A slightly red-faced Esther looked up at Jack appealingly, and he took the hint.

'I'm afraid we'll have to be leaving too, Mother. We left Nell in charge of Miriam, and Billy was expected to keep her company after scything the lawns. In the circumstances, we'd better get home, if only to preserve Nell's reputation.'

'That young man of hers — "Billy" — certainly makes an excellent job of my lawns, after I showed him how they needed to be done,' Constance told them. 'Perhaps as well that he came along when he did, because too much exertion leaves me a little breathless these days and seems to provoke those occasional pains in the chest.'

'You need to take it easier,' Esther advised her affectionately. 'I can always take over some of the Ladies' Guild correspondence from you — you only have to ask.'

'I wouldn't dream of burdening you further, dear,' Constance insisted. 'You have enough to do, bringing up four children, two of whom seem to have given up fighting with each other, and are now gazing forlornly through the kitchen window, no doubt hoping that Cook will let them back into the house.'

'I'll go and get them,' Jack offered, 'and then we must be off. It looks as if Tommy's settled down to sleep in Esther's arms, so this might be a good time to slip away, since the pram ride always seems to knock him out completely.'

As they walked slowly back up Church Lane towards the crossroads where they would be turning right into Bunting Lane, Lily and Bertie having opted to turn the journey home into a race, Jack was a little concerned at what he'd heard earlier.

'What was all that about Mother's health?'

'Nothing really,' Esther assured him. 'She's past her best, that's all. Most women her age find that they can't quite keep up any more.'

'She's only fifty-five,' Jack objected. 'Admittedly the soft life she's been leading has allowed her to put quite a bit of weight on, but she's no great age. But she was complaining of shortness of breath and pains in her chest, wasn't she? Has she seen Doctor Browning about it?'

'You know your mother,' Esther replied. 'And she accuses *me* of being over-proud, sometimes! She just waves her hand in the air when I suggest it and puts it down to "needing to shed a few pounds". I've given up with her.'

'Keep a watchful eye on her for me, all the same,' Jack requested. 'And talking of watchful eyes, Billy Manvers tells me that he spent every morning last week trailing behind you and Lily, with no sign of anyone following you. Perhaps you were imagining it after all.'

'Let's hope so,' Esther agreed as she steered the pram carefully round a muddy pothole in the lane. 'Why did the Home Secretary want to see Uncle Percy, do you think? Is he in even more trouble for what he blurted out in court that day?'

'Uncle Percy never "blurted out" anything in his entire life.' Jack smiled. 'He no doubt weighed and measured every word, and he clearly believed what he was saying. He was right, as well — London's going to the dogs, and I don't just mean the ones the Met uses. On the surface is a huge commercial success story, but underneath it's just a festering boil waiting to explode its puss over everyone.'

'Ugh!' Esther grimaced, screwing up her mouth in distaste. 'That was an *awful* expression to use, Jack Enright. Your language is no better than your uncle's.'

'Bad language is the only way in which to express what London's rapidly becoming,' Jack replied by way of justification. 'The decent folk on the surface are outnumbered ten to one by the ones underneath who're just ripe for some sort of revolution, and it's only a matter of time. You've presumably read in the newspaper all about these anarchists, as the editors call them?'

'Yes, but aren't they just foreigners trying to infiltrate our Government?'

'Some of them, certainly, but from what I read in the crime reports wired up from the Met, they're persuading ordinary London folk round to their way of thinking, trading on their poverty and resentment.'

'Perhaps as well you work in Essex, then.' Esther smiled as they approached the driveway to number twenty-six. 'Hello, what's going on here?'

There were two men rolling and wrestling on the front lawn, their clothing covered in the cut grass that Billy had clearly not raked up after scything it. The reason why he'd not got around to it was most probably the fact that he was one of those wrestling, while his opponent was a man twice his height and weight, although seemingly twenty years older. Lily and Bertie were watching their antics, entranced, as Jack rushed onto the lawn and separated the two, then grabbed the newcomer as he gave every indication of running off. On the assumption that Billy had a good reason for his actions, Jack asked for his assistance in pulling the man's arms up his back until he could slip, from his jacket pocket, the wrist restraints that he carried with him everywhere.

Once the man had been subdued, and as he stood panting and sweating in the late afternoon sun, Jack demanded to know what was going on.

'I were in the kitchen, 'avin' a cuppa wiv Nell,' Billy explained, 'when I sees this 'ere cove steppin' off the railway line over the garden fence an' then down the side o' the 'ouse. Then when I went outside, 'e were ferretin' through yer rubbish bin, so I chased 'im, an' caught up wiv 'im on the lawn 'ere. I reckon what 'e's a burguler or sumfin'.'

'We'll find out, shall we?' Jack said as he tightened the notch on the wrist restraints, causing the man to squeal like a piglet. 'Now then,' Jack leaned forward, 'not only can I release the pressure on those wrists, but I can also tighten it. First of all, may I take it that you're the slime who's been following my wife and daughter to and from school recently?'

The man nodded, and Jack released the restraints slightly.

'See? I'm a man of my word. Now, who are you, and what do you want?'

'My name's Herbert Shaw, and I'm a private investigator. If you'll free my hands, I have my business card in my pocket.'

'Later — perhaps,' Jack replied, 'when you tell me why a private investigator needed to follow my wife.'

'She's Esther Jacobs, right?' Shaw wheezed.

'She *was* once Esther Jacobs, but now she's "Esther Enright", because she's married to Jack Enright. That's me, by the way, and I'm a Detective Sergeant, so keep talking.'

'I was hired to find her.'

'Who by?'

'That's between me and my client.'

'And *this* is between me and you,' Jack hissed as he turned the wrist restraints up two notches, and the man screamed in agony.

'Jack, stop it!' Esther pleaded with him as she rushed across to join them. 'Lily's obviously upset to see her father behaving in such a brutal fashion, and she's started to cry.'

Jack jerked his head in Esther's direction.

'There's the lady you've been following at the request of your client, or so you'd have us believe. Start talking again, or you won't be able to use your hands for a week, due to the lack of circulation. You may even require surgery afterwards.'

'Esther Jacobs?' Shaw enquired, and when Esther nodded he continued. 'I was hired to locate you by someone who wishes to contact you again after a lengthy lapse of time.'

'Who?' Esther asked, totally at a loss.

'He gave the name of "Abraham Daniel Jacobs", and he claims to be your brother.'

As two men walked into his rear garden via the side path, Percy looked up from where he was removing the last of the trellis framework from the vegetable patch after harvesting the remainder of his crop of runner beans. The taller of the two men was in the lead as they walked across the lawn towards Percy.

'Detective Inspector Enright?'

'I was, until three weeks ago,' Percy replied sullenly. 'Who wants to know?'

'You're to come with us,' the man advised him.

'Really?' Percy replied defiantly.

'Really,' the man confirmed. 'The Home Secretary asked you nicely — twice. Now he insists.' He took a small folder from his inside jacket pocket, opened it, and held it high in the air. 'Superintendent Melville, Special Branch. This is my colleague Sidney Reilly. We're both armed, but hopefully we won't be required to demonstrate that fact on this sleepy Monday morning in a quiet street in Hackney.'

'Neither you nor the Home Secretary have any authority over me since I resigned,' Percy insisted.

Melville smiled. 'Even as a private citizen the Home Secretary can command your presence. And since he's giving up his morning off in order to speak to you, he'd be personally offended if you declined this third invitation. If we have to come back here, it's unlikely that we'd be bearing a fourth, and your wife's too young to be wearing black just yet.'

'This is an outrageous breach of my personal liberty!' Percy insisted angrily, but Melville simply smiled even wider.

'One of the aspects of my job that I particularly enjoy. Now, may I suggest that you get cleaned up, give your wife an excuse, and accompany us to the coach waiting discreetly at the end of the road?'

Three hours later, Percy was seated in a beautifully tended garden in a Buckinghamshire village, and Home Secretary Sir

Matthew Ridley was pouring the coffee and inviting Percy to help himself to the scones and jam.

'I must apologise for the means by which I eventually acquired your presence, Inspector, but it would seem that the first two invitations were not to your liking.'

'Neither was the third,' Percy replied gruffly, only partly mollified by the gift of scones, 'and I'm no longer an Inspector at the Yard. Presumably your trained ape knew that, since he seemed to know a lot more about me during our discussions on the way down here. Largely one way, of course, since Melville seems to enjoy the sound of his own voice.'

'It's thanks to my "trained ape", as you call him, that I knew of your attempted resignation,' Ridley advised him with a knowing smile.

'Attempted?' Percy queried.

Ridley nodded. 'You didn't seriously think that I'd allow such a staunch guardian of public safety to leave the team at a time when he's most needed, did you? Your resignation letter was forwarded to me at my request and has been declined.'

'After what I said in open court about the rotten state of society's arse?'

'*Particularly* after that, and for two reasons. The first is that you're perfectly correct and are clearly committed to wiping that arse. The second is that you now have a reputation within Scotland Yard for being a shit-stirring revolutionary.'

'And that makes it both safe and advisable to insist that I remain?'

'Absolutely. Help yourself to your fourth scone, and let me explain, since even I need to remind myself of why I'm taking such a radical course.'

While Percy spread jam half an inch thick on the largest remaining scone, Ridley began. 'If I were to say "Anarchist", what mental image would that conjure up for you?'

'Bomb-chucking lunatics bent on bringing down our government structure,' Percy replied with his mouth full.

'You would not concede that "Anarchists" might be ordinary folk who simply wish to see an end to the tyranny of government?'

Percy thought for a moment while he cleared his mouth of scone, then his brow creased in thought. 'As I well know from my years in the Met, if we don't have some form of government, then it becomes the law of the jungle, in which the weak get trodden into the ground by the strong, who are not predisposed towards attending to the needs, or indeed the continued existence, of those weaker than themselves. That was what I was banging on about in court when those two women were being sentenced. They'd been let down by a system that had allowed others stronger than them to take cruel advantage of their helplessness.'

'Precisely,' Ridley smiled. 'Which is why you're just the man for the job.'

'What job?'

'You would agree, I assume from what you just said, that we cannot for one moment contemplate an absence of government in this country? A state of affairs in which the powerful, or those with the biggest gang of hired thugs, rule the lives of the weak by terror and extortion?'

'Of *course* I agree,' Percy replied testily. 'I've spent my entire police career dealing with gangs of thugs, mostly by buckling them and sending them for trial, imprisonment and the gallows.'

'And on occasions you've been known to take the law into your own hands, like some form of licensed vigilante, employing actions that have led to the deaths of suspects before they could even be brought before a magistrate? "The Ripper", for example, or that East End enforcer who was torn apart by the mob in the street? Then there was that art dealer who went under a railway locomotive.'

'Those were all unfortunate accidents,' Percy insisted. 'I didn't set out to have them killed — well, perhaps in the case of Michael Maguire, but even so…'

'You don't have to justify yourself to me, Percy,' Ridley smiled, employing his Christian name to good effect at precisely the appropriate moment. 'But we're agreed that, despite its failings, you'd rather see a Government in place than have no Government at all?'

'Of course,' Percy agreed. 'The alternative is unthinkable.'

'And you'd be prepared to work in order to ensure the continued existence of some form of government within Britain? Commons, Lords and Queen preferably, but some form of government anyway?'

'Where is this leading?' Percy asked, intrigued despite himself.

It fell silent for a moment while Ridley maintained a dramatic silence by means of refilling his coffee cup. Then he dropped the bombshell.

'We have reason to believe that there's a concerted plot to throw England into sufficient chaos to allow a foreign power to move in.'

Percy stopped chewing in order to allow his mouth to fall open.

'You mean an enemy invasion?'

'Of sorts, yes. But not immediately, not directly, and not overtly.'

'Is this when you tell me that what you have to say must not be repeated?' Percy said with faint sarcasm, to be met by a most unpleasant smile from the Home Secretary.

'We passed that point some minutes ago, and I was relying on your innate discretion and integrity. You may have acquired a reputation recently for going off at the mouth, but I know enough about the *real* Percy Enright to feel secure in the knowledge that you won't repeat a word of what I'm about to tell you to any unauthorised person. Of course, if you do, you've already met Superintendent Melville and his deputy ape.'

'Before you disclose any State secrets,' Percy cautioned him, 'you presumably have some task for me at the end of it?'

'A task, a reward and what some would deem a bribe,' Ridley smiled. 'Now for the gory details. Perhaps laced with a little local history.'

'Will we need more coffee?'

'No, but perhaps some brandy to go with it.'

Ridley waved his hand in the air, and a uniformed manservant appeared from the shrubbery in which he'd been hiding. Ridley ordered a decanter of brandy and two glasses, then smiled at the unspoken question written across Percy's face.

'You're correct, Inspector. Manning makes excellent coffee, knows which brandy I prefer, and is an excellent marksman and bodyguard who can lose himself in the bushes. He'll ensure our ongoing privacy while we continue our conversation.'

Once the brandy was poured, Ridley looked Percy firmly in the eyes and continued.

'Of the various organisations dedicated to bringing Britain to its knees, you perhaps best know the Fenians, since you had to deal with them when you were investigating the untimely demise of Lord Stranmillis.'

'Only indirectly,' Percy conceded. 'They were simply the hired help of others when the time came to silence his Lordship because of what he could reveal about the sexual inclinations of a senior Board of Trade official.'

'For the record, that man is no longer in his former post,' Ridley advised Percy with a smile. 'We knew anyway. But you will at least have learned that a certain section of the Irish who've settled here in England are capable of extreme violence?'

'They did away with the Irish Secretary and his deputy in Dublin some years ago, I remember that,' Percy replied, 'but isn't their agenda simply an independent Ireland, free of English control? Why would they encompass the entire overthrow of the English Government?'

'Because they're stupid, hot-headed and easily manipulated,' Ridley replied. 'They can be persuaded that by throwing in their lot with others they can use a free Ireland as a bargaining counter. In reward for their muscle, and their talent with explosives, they'll be allowed to set up an independent Ireland when the English Government is brought down.'

'Persuaded by whom?'

'We'll get to that later. Now let's consider the up and coming trade unions. You've had trouble with those many times in the Met, have you not?'

'Mainly in a public order context.' Percy nodded. 'There was that Trafalgar Square riot a few years back, ostensibly in support of the Match Girls Strike, although we had it on good authority that this was just an excuse for a punch-up with uniformed constables. Are you saying that they were manipulated as well?'

'You've presumably heard of the Fenian Barracks?'

'Who hasn't, inside the Met?' Percy frowned. 'It's a block of tenements in Poplar that's sent more Met officers to hospital than any other comparable block anywhere else in the East End, and that's saying something. It's a good example of what we were talking about earlier — rampant lawlessness, no respect for authority, and almost impossible to police. In short, a small sample of what to expect if law and order breaks down in England. But what's the connection with the Trafalgar Square riots?'

'Over twenty of those Match Girls came from "the Barracks" area,' Ridley advised him. 'The Irish saw their chance to stir up a mob, ostensibly in support of downtrodden working girls, but in reality designed to test the ability of the Met to resist a mass riot in a public place.'

'I begin to see what you mean,' Percy frowned. 'One group of the disaffected and desperate whipped into a frenzy by another such group with a little more brainpower. At that rate, most of the East End could be considered a powder keg waiting for the match. Some revolutionary English loudmouth with sufficient powers of oratory to light the fuse.'

'And what makes you think it's confined to London, or even England?' Ridley said, to which Percy had no response other than polite silence. 'And why do you think that my Government is so opposed to such liberal immigration laws?' Ridley added by way of reinforcement. 'If you read any newspaper, you'll be aware that Europe has been the scene of dreadful outrages in recent years, mainly using this new dynamite stuff that's capable of blowing entire buildings apart. French cafes, Italian museums, a Spanish opera house, and

Swiss hotels. To add to the dramatic effect, several high-profile victims such as heads of state, assassinated by lunatics who weren't afraid to die in the process.'

'What does that have to do with Salisbury's anti-immigration stance?' Percy asked.

'Because we grant asylum to these madmen,' Ridley replied heatedly. 'Take a look at those who've been allowed to settle in London alone — Jews, Frenchmen, Russians, Italians to name but a few. How can we tell who they really are, and why they're really here? It was, after all, a Frenchman — Martial Bourdin — who managed to kill himself while attempting to blow up the Greenwich Observatory. Then there's that dreadful "Club Autonomie" off the Tottenham Court Road that Bourdin frequented almost nightly. We've had that under observation for some time, but it didn't stop Bourdin, and it won't stop the next lunatic who's prepared to die for a cause that someone else's given him.'

'You want me to work under cover among immigrant communities?' Percy asked sceptically, but Ridley smiled as he shook his head.

'We'll leave that to Melville and his ferrets. What I want you for is something much subtler.'

Chapter Four

'I knew you had a brother,' Jack said as he and Esther sat drinking tea and munching on slices of cheese toast that Nell had left out for them before going for a walk with her 'young man' Billy, 'because you told me about him when we first got together, but you haven't made mention of him since. Wasn't he in the army or something?'

'He was, the last I heard, in a letter from somewhere in Africa, but that was years ago, before we were even married.'

'So you weren't particularly close, even after your parents died in that river accident?'

'Not even *before* that. He was two years older than me, and a big strong boy who learned to fight because he was Jewish, in the days when there were all sorts of different families living in Spitalfields. Believe it or not, it was respectable in those days, and the older, more established, families, resented the "Yids" who moved in and began to make money, like my parents. Anyway, Abe used to delight in showing me how big and brave he was by pulling my long hair, which was usually done up in ringlets in those days. Then when my parents died he took off and enrolled in some sort of military school. He was seventeen by then, and presumably he fulfilled his ambition to be a soldier, because the last letter I got he was serving in some Guards regiment or other, and about to go into battle in some unpronounceable place in North Africa.'

'He obviously survived that,' Jack observed, 'since he appears to be back in London. That private investigator's office is in Aldgate, so presumably Abe was living in the City somewhere when he hired him. We'll no doubt get more information when he writes to you, as you gave permission for him to do.'

'Are you sure you don't mind?'

'Why should I? You've put up with my family for the past ten years, so it's the least I can do. He's your older brother, you said?'

'Yes, by two years, so I suppose he'll be in his mid-thirties by now, and probably ready to leave the army, if he hasn't already. I wonder what he'll do for a living.'

'A lot of former soldiers join the police,' Jack advised her, 'so assuming that he's got a clean record and a good discharge report from his regimental senior officer, I might be able to find him something in the Met, if he's interested. They've been known to bend the maximum age requirement for enlistment if a man's physically fit.'

'I'm not sure that I want *all* my family exposed to danger,' Esther frowned.

'Well, you can cross Uncle Percy off that list,' Jack reminded her, 'although it's going to seem strange for me, knowing that he's no longer down there at the Yard and only a wire away.'

'Better get used to it,' Esther said as she snuggled closer to him.

'A pity you dulled your appetite with all those scones.' Ridley smiled across the dining table inside the well-appointed country mansion.

'Not sufficiently to pass up this excellent salmon,' Percy all but purred, 'although the lettuce and tomato may prove to be something of a challenge. And I'll leave the potatoes to our fellow diners.'

William Melville smiled politely but said nothing, while Sidney Reilly appeared not to have heard. The butler poured the wine, and Ridley raised his glass in a toast.

'To Her Majesty.' As the others echoed his words, and hands were restored to knives and forks, Ridley took the toast as his cue. 'Appropriate, really, in view of what I have to say next.' It fell dutifully silent until Ridley looked directly across at Percy. 'You recall the fuss and pomp that surrounded the Queen's Golden Jubilee celebrations almost ten years ago?'

Percy nodded. 'It was just about my last job in Hackney. I'd been attached to the Yard for a year or two by then, but I'd been a uniformed constable in that area for several years, so they put me in charge of the detachment keeping an eye on the revellers in Victoria Park. We did a busy line in drunk and disorderly, public indecency, pick-pocketing and soliciting for the purposes of prostitution, but nothing dramatic.'

'You had a quieter day than me,' Melville observed bitterly.

'And me,' Sidney Reilly confirmed. Ridley regarded them with a tolerant smile, then let Percy in on the secret.

'It's not generally known, but there was a Fenian plot to blow up the Queen and all the assembled dignitaries during the 1887 Golden Jubilee ceremony in Westminster Abbey. Their "main man" was an Irish loony called Millen, but fortunately for us he'd been on our payroll for some years, and he was encouraged to continue with the pretence, for reasons which I'll leave Melville here to explain, since he was at the centre of it all.'

Melville cleared his throat somewhat portentously, then picked up the story.

'You'll be aware, of course, that for years Scotland Yard has maintained an "Irish Branch", since you yourself have crossed paths with them several times in the course of your work with the "Political Branch". I was a member of the Irish Branch, and I was the one who, shall we say, "cultivated" Millen, who was highly regarded by the Fenians because of his previously demonstrated talents with dynamite. I turned him into a paid spy for the Government, then encouraged him to become the leader of the "Jubilee Plot" as we named it. This was for two reasons, the first being to prevent anyone else being given the job, and the second being the opportunity to draw others into the net. Millen was highly regarded by other members of the Fenian Brotherhood, and one by one they stepped out of the shadows to join him.'

'Quite a haul,' Percy muttered respectfully.

Melville nodded. 'Also very risky. As you can imagine, there was fierce debate as to whether we should close down the entire operation days before the Westminster Abbey ceremony, or let it run until the last minute, in order to capture the conspirators from the United States who were bringing over the dynamite, along with two men delegated to detonate it. I argued strongly that we should let it continue until the very last moment and thank God I was proved right. We nabbed the lot of them, and the long-term consequence of our success, after much debate in Home Office circles, was the emergence of the "Special Branch" of which I'm now the head.'

'And the Queen had no idea what had been going on, probably literally under her feet?' Percy asked.

Melville shook his head. 'Not even to this day.'

'And therein lies the problem,' Ridley joined in. 'Her Majesty was so delighted with how the Golden Jubilee bunfight went that she's ordered another one for June of *next* year, to be called the "Diamond Jubilee", to mark the fact that a few weeks ago she became Britain's longest ever reigning monarch.'

'And you're worried that the Fenians will try again?' Percy said as he extracted a salmon bone delicately from his mouth with the aid of his fork.

Ridley frowned. 'If it were just a matter of Fenians, we're pretty sure that we could forestall any assassination attempts. But it's much wider than that these days, with Anarchists coming out of the woodwork daily. We now have to worry about the trade unions, these women who think they should be allowed to vote, some sort of revolutionary movement that recently took off in Russia, and God knows how many madmen with perceived grievances against the Establishment and access to a revolver.'

'So where do I fit into all this, apart from years of experience of keeping royal offspring from blotting the family copybook?'

Ridley and Melville exchanged glances, and Ridley nodded, leaving the next part to Melville.

'We have good reason to believe that certain — "interested parties", shall we call them? — have begun to infiltrate and corrupt the Met.'

'That's nothing new,' Percy pointed out, 'and that's a matter for you and the rest of Special Branch, surely?'

'Ordinarily, yes,' Melville conceded, 'but we've got our hands full keeping an eye on the foreign elements. Added to which, we don't want to alert the enemy that we've rumbled them by raising the hue and cry. What we need is a subtle internal enquiry.'

'Me?' Percy said with a cynical grin. 'The loudmouth who just got himself officially sacked from the Met? I'm about as subtle as Big Ben.'

'Precisely,' Ridley intervened. 'Remember what I told you earlier, in the garden, Percy? Half the Yard think of you as a potential troublemaker who doesn't think twice about shitting in his own nest in order to bring about radical political reform.'

'And how do you know I'm not?' Percy challenged him, at which point Melville pulled back his jacket to reveal the revolver strapped across his waistcoat and smiled unpleasantly. 'If you truly are, then there's your answer. But we can use the fact that folk inside the Met *think* you are.'

'How and why?'

'Because,' Ridley explained, 'we're hoping that those within the force who've thrown in their lot with those who we think are planning something for the Diamond Jubilee will approach you to join their team. If and when they do, then, like Millen before you, you pretend to go along with it and report back to Melville.'

'And what evidence do we have that the Met's been — "compromised" might be the appropriate word?' Percy asked, and all eyes turned back to Ridley.

'You will of course be aware that last week a considerable quantity of valuable gems were stolen from a Hatton Garden dealer in a brazen robbery involving explosives, during the course of which the nightwatchman was horribly murdered?'

'Of course,' Percy replied. 'It was all over the newspapers.'

'What was *not* all over the newspapers,' Ridley continued, 'was the fact that they seem to have gained entry to the premises by fooling the nightwatchman into letting them in because they were wearing police uniforms. Several local residents who heard the noise of the strongroom being dynamited have informed us that they saw men dressed as police constables running out of the premises carrying what were almost certainly bags of valuable stones and throwing them into what looked suspiciously like a Black Maria.'

'That's pretty serious,' Percy observed unnecessarily, 'since it suggests that either they were actual serving police officers, or they had access to the uniforms and coach.'

'Either way, a serious "compromise", as you would call it, of the integrity of the local Division. And it's by no means the only incident recently that has led to the horrible suspicion that Met officers have been suborned.'

'Go on?' Percy invited him, and it was Melville who obliged.

'The week before that, there was a break-in at a warehouse in Wapping that was being rented by the War Office to store Army uniforms destined for the Sudan. We have no idea if anything was stolen, although we're now alert to the fact that there may be Anarchists walking the streets of London disguised as soldiers. The significance of the break-in was more the fact that whoever was responsible set fire to the place. Thousands of uniforms went up in smoke, and you could see the blaze several miles away in Bow.'

'Again, a serious and brazen outrage against authority,' Percy agreed.

'But you haven't heard the worst part yet,' Melville advised him. 'The warehouse in question was located directly behind a fixed beat point for the local force. There should have been a constable on duty right outside the place, but for some reason he was not at his post.'

'Has he been questioned?'

Melville smiled unpleasantly. 'Clearly he will be — once we can find him, and if he's still alive.'

'But killing a beat constable in order to effect a break-in, tragic and appalling as it is, isn't unusual for that type of offence,' Percy objected, to a responding frown from Ridley.

'Break-ins are normally for the purpose of stealing something valuable. Our concern is that we may now have malcontents out to assassinate Her Majesty with access to military uniforms. There's also the defiant public gesture that such outrages can occur under our very noses, not to mention the possible corruption or murder of a police constable.'

'Presumably these two are not isolated incidents?'

Melville shook his head. 'How many more do you need? Name your police division.'

'Stepney,' Percy replied to the challenge, and Melville extracted a list from his inside jacket pocket and began reading.

'"Stepney, Seventeenth of August of this year, ten thirty am. Acting on complaints from neighbours regarding suspicious comings and goings at a terraced house in Ellerdale Street, Constables Greenway and Padley gained entry by force and located a substantial quantity of firearms. The occupier of the said house, Nathaniel Hiscock, was taken into custody, and officers from the Robbery Squad took possession of what had been discovered in the house." End of police report.'

'So?'

'So,' Melville replied, 'three days later the man Hiscock had mysteriously escaped from his cell, and some eighty military rifles were unaccounted for in the vault to which they had been consigned inside the Yard.'

'Let's assume for the moment that these are not just a series of unfortunate and coincidental examples of police incompetence,' Percy suggested, 'your explanation for them is that someone is corrupting officers within the Met?'

Melville nodded, adding sarcastically, 'They told me you were quick on the uptake.'

'And you believe that if I simply resume my duties, someone will approach me and try the same thing?'

'That's what we hope,' Ridley advised him, 'given that you are rumoured to treat the Metropolitan Police Procedures

Manual as if it were a book of helpful suggestions in doubtful cases. But we'll obviously need to justify your reinstatement, after your somewhat dramatic departure, so we're sending you back into the "Political Branch" with the ostensible special duty of liaising with Superintendent Melville on police readiness for the Diamond Jubilee security operation. Your Chief Superintendent Bray won't be told your real role and will be advised from a very great height inside the Yard that he's not to express any dissatisfaction with your reinstatement, is not to interfere with your duties, and in fact is to keep completely out of your face at all times.'

'And I just sit there, collect my pay and await any approaches from the baddies?' Percy said disbelievingly.

'Not entirely,' Melville corrected him. 'We also require you to instigate subtle enquiries into how, if our suspicions are correct, various officers within the Met came to be corrupted. Perhaps the best way might be to send in another officer of Sergeant rank who's ostensibly conducting a routine review of manpower and operational efficiency. Preferably someone from outside the Met, although we appreciate that this may not be possible, because it has to be someone you trust implicitly, whose integrity is beyond question.'

Ridley smiled. 'I'm prepared, at this point, to lay a wager of a hundred pounds on the prospect that Enright here comes up with the perfect candidate without the need for any further thought, and that his name's also Enright. Anyone care to take me on?'

'Don't either of you waste your money.' Percy grinned as he looked across at Ridley.

'You really *do* have an efficient intelligence network, don't you?'

Ridley inclined his head in recognition of the compliment and turned to advise the other two. 'Detective Sergeant Jackson Enright is currently the head of what passes for the Detective Branch of the Essex Constabulary. Prior to that he was attached to the Yard, and while on uniformed divisional duties he gained extensive experience in the East End — precisely where most of these incidents appear to be occurring. He's still quite young, but experienced and ambitious, while possessing a commanding physical presence. He's of exactly the right rank and experience to be conducting routine reviews of operational efficiency within local police stations. His integrity has never been doubted, and he comes with the final advantage that he's the nephew of Inspector Enright here.'

'Sounds like the man we need, but will he agree?' Melville asked.

Percy smiled. 'He most certainly would, but no-one's asked me yet if *I'll* agree to all this.'

It fell briefly silent, until Melville muttered, 'After what we've revealed to you this morning? Present arms!', and in a well-choreographed move he and Reilly drew back their jackets to reveal their Webley revolvers. Percy smiled laconically.

'That would seem to be decided, then.'

'So glad you could join us,' Ridley grinned as he sat back in his chair. 'Now, anyone for apple pie?'

Once the coffee and port had been served, Ridley looked across at Percy.

'There's just one thing more you have to learn about the operation you've agreed to become a part of.' When Percy raised his eyebrows above his port glass, Ridley nodded to Melville, who took over.

'The Diamond Jubilee celebrations next June will be attended by the invited heads of all the Imperial nations; Canada, India,

Australia, New Zealand and so on. The Queen needed no persuasion, because that used up all the diplomatic accommodation in London, not to mention all the seats at the official ceremonies, thereby excluding awkward members of her own extended family from just about everywhere in Europe.'

'Didn't that rather increase the risk of a foreign assassin?' Percy asked.

Melville shook his head. 'No, it considerably reduced it, since we believe that the greatest risk comes from one of her own relatives.'

Percy's face expressed his shock and disbelief, and Melville availed himself of the silence to explain.

'Thanks to the strength of our dear Queen's affection for Albert in her younger years, there's hardly a throne inside Europe that's not graced with the backside of one of her remote relatives, some more remote than others. But that's also given us massive headaches in Special Branch, since not all of those nations are necessarily friendly towards ours. Take Russia, for example, where the Tsar is grappling with a revolutionary groundswell of peasant resentment against the old Romanov regime. His wife, the Tsarina and Empress Alexandra, is Victoria's granddaughter, and has secretly written to her grandmother for assistance from Britain should there be any attempt to overthrow the monarchy. This fact is generally known in revolutionary circles, and we believe that there may be an initiative from Russian dissidents here in England to forestall that possibility by assassinating the Queen. For that reason, it was not deemed appropriate to invite Tsar Nicholas to London, where he might be assassinated at the same time.'

'But that's by no means the end of the possibilities?' Percy prompted him, and Melville shook his head.

'By no means. Other grandchildren are either already occupying, or destined to occupy, the thrones of Greece, Norway, Romania and Sweden. And that's not all of them. But you could appreciate how a well-placed bomb at the right time, for example during a photographic tableau of half the royalty of Europe on the steps of Osborne House, might cause sufficient chaos in Europe to allow revolutionaries to take over in the vacuum of power thereby created.'

'You haven't mentioned Germany,' Percy reminded him. 'Aren't we currently engaged in diplomatic squabbles with them?'

'On the surface, certainly,' Melville confirmed, 'but it goes deeper than that, and the reason why I've left Germany until last is because it's the one we're most apprehensive of.'

'For what reason, if I'm allowed to know?'

Melville looked towards Ridley for permission to continue, and Ridley nodded.

'As everyone knows,' Melville recounted, 'the current Emperor of Germany, and for that matter King of Prussia, is Wilhelm, grandson of our Queen. On the surface he enjoys a good relationship with her and is constantly craving her good opinion. But the reason for that is the fact that the rest of his European relatives regard him as a pompous idiot, a bloated buffoon, with a dangerous and unstable personality. That personality stems from a difficult birth that left him with a slightly withered left arm, and for which he blames his mother, Queen Victoria's daughter of the same name. Wilhelm regarded his father as a weakling and grew up cosseted and surrounded by flatterers who gave him an inflated sense of his importance in the world, towards which he displays a warlike and aggressive face while entertaining excruciating self-doubts that are fed by the scorn of his cousins, who include our own

Prince George. He also detests his uncle, our heir apparent Prince Edward.'

'So he's unstable, and to be avoided at all costs,' Percy observed, 'but how does that make him dangerous to England?'

'The constant contempt and belittling from his European cousins has bred in him an almost insane desire to prove himself as the greatest ruler in Europe — a sort of reincarnation of Charlemagne or Barbarossa. For a long time he was held in check by his Chancellor, von Bismarck, who is, from Britain's perspective, the best adviser we could have wished for, and who is constantly advocating peace and diplomacy with the other nations of Europe. But given his social awkwardness, his low self-esteem and his grandiose plans for European domination, Wilhelm will have none of it, and he ignores and decries Bismarck, who is on record as having summarised the Kaiser's personality as that of someone "who wishes every day to be his birthday".

'I'm still not getting the picture,' Percy complained, and Melville treated him to a look of sarcastic sympathy.

'The man is dangerously unstable, wishes to rule half the world, has cast aside all wise and diplomatic counsel, wishes to declare war on Russia because he's been snubbed by its Emperor, and hates the heir apparent of England with a passion. In short, a bomb waiting to explode, and a man who hasn't received the invitation to the forthcoming Jubilee celebrations to which he thinks he's entitled, when others such as the Prime Minister of New Zealand and the Maharaja of Kashmir have been. The brutal truth is that Wilhelm only has himself to blame for the exclusion of all the royal grandchildren, because of his volatile manner when amongst them. Her Majesty loves him dearly, but she doesn't want him to repeat behaviour such as that when he was a child, and he bit the leg of the uncle who will shortly become Edward VII.'

'So he's resentful, and I can't say I blame him,' Percy observed, 'but why does that make him dangerous?'

'He'd like nothing better than to see England reduced to a robber baron state. He loves his grandmother, but hates the rest of the English royal family, and resents England's pre-eminence in the world. He raised his true colours up the mast at the very start of this year, when he sent a congratulatory, and very well publicised, telegram to Paul Kruger after the failure of the Jamieson Raid on the Transvaal.'

'But wouldn't a bomb during the celebrations put paid to his beloved granny?' Percy argued.

Melville smiled condescendingly. 'You are presupposing sanity and a logical thought process in the mind of the person commissioning that bomb, are you not?'

'I can see that I'm going to be well out of my depth in certain aspects of all this,' Percy said, to which Melville replied tersely, 'A very good reason for sticking to your part of the arrangement, and not venturing onto my turf.'

In case Percy had in some way been dissuaded against continuing what he had been persuaded to undertake, Ridley had one last card to play.

'We must, with some regret, call this meeting to a close, since I have to be in the House by five pm. However, before you go, Percy, you remember that I promised you a bribe?'

'Wasn't that a return to my normal duties and salary?'

'No, they were what I called your "reward". Your "bribe" takes the form of a reprieve for those two ladies on whose behalf you made such a fuss at the Bailey several weeks ago.'

'Harriet Crouch and Amy Jackson? I thought that the crusty old judge declined to recommend clemency?'

'So he did, but that's not necessarily the end of such things. As we do in most cases in which the death penalty has been imposed, the Home Office has received a petition for mercy in both their cases, with over five thousand signatures. It came to me in accordance with normal practice, since I chair the committee that meets to consider all such petitions. It's popularly known as "The Hanging Committee", and it's never once disagreed with me. It meets on Thursday of this week, and I propose to urge a reprieve for both of them.'

'Simply because I agreed to play your games?' Percy said cynically.

'Let's just say that I was inspired by your oratory in court.' Ridley smiled.

It was beginning to get dark when the coach deposited Percy at his front door, from which Beattie emerged in her apron and rushed down the path to fling herself at her husband.

'Thank God you're safe! I've been worried sick, and I didn't for one moment believe you when you said that the Home Secretary had sent his coach for you. You're a rotten liar, Percy Enright, but I love you deeply and genuinely, and I've spent the entire afternoon wondering how I could possibly live without you. Come inside and have some tea — you must be starving!'

'Not really,' Percy grinned, 'but it's not been such a bad old day. I've had dinner with the Home Secretary, I've got my old job back, and Harriet Crouch and Amy Jackson have been spared the gallows. I wonder if I've still got time to put a bet on a horse?'

Chapter Five

'This is a long way from what I expected when I agreed to marry you!' Esther protested, hands on hips, as Nell scuttled diplomatically out of the kitchen and began dusting the living room carpet for the second time that day. 'I thought we'd be living quietly in rooms in London,' she continued as her face reddened further, 'while you worked harmlessly at the Yard and I spent my days waiting for you to come home and fold me in your arms. Instead you exiled me out here to darkest Essex, uncomfortably close to your mother, and filled me with four children. Now you tell me that you're deserting me and going back to live with your uncle, as if we'd never been married!'

'I'll be coming home at weekends,' Jack reminded her in what he hoped was a pacifying tone, but Esther was not in the mood to be so easily placated.

'If I don't change the locks on the doors!'

'You wouldn't do that, surely?'

'And why shouldn't I? Marriages are seven days a week commitments — not "I'll pop back at weekends to give you more babies!" You're seriously suggesting that there'll be a "welcome home" party every Friday evening, after you've spent the week getting into mischief with Uncle Percy, not to mention the danger that he always seems to involve you in? Forget it, Jack! I'm not one of those pathetic little wifeys you can push to one side when it suits you, and I'm bitterly disappointed that you were so weak that you allowed Uncle Percy to talk you into deserting me, leaving me defenceless and lonely, with a desperate feeling of abandonment.'

'I had no choice,' Jack argued. 'Uncle Percy was only the messenger — it was the Home Secretary who ordered me back inside the Yard to work with him, and the task I've been given may well stand me in good stead for promotion in the near future.'

'So your so-called "police career" means more to you that I do, is that what you're telling me?'

'No, obviously not. I'm just trying to explain that this is not another of Percy's devious schemes. It's a direct order from a senior Government minister, and a chance for me to prove that I'm ready to be promoted to "Inspector".'

'Well, when you deign to come home one Friday afternoon with your dirty laundry for washing, and that "let's go to bed" look in your eye,' Esther retorted, angry tears beginning to fill her own eyes, 'you may find that all you have to inspect is an empty house!'

Jack abandoned his efforts to talk Esther round, before matters deteriorated any further. He announced that he was going to walk in the garden before supper and let himself out through the scullery door. He kicked a few wilting cabbage stalks in the vegetable garden beyond the lawn and leaned on the boundary fence beyond which the rail line ran into Barking, as he considered his options in the vague hope that he might have any.

Two days previously he'd been sitting in his office in Chelmsford when Uncle Percy's familiar figure had appeared in his doorway with his customary cheesy grin.

'How did you get up here, past the front desk, as a mere civilian recently retired from the force?' Jack asked as he smiled at the prospect of a break from boring paperwork and a dinner companion downstairs in the "Dining Hall", as it was officially known, where the appetising and heavily subsidised meals were often the only bright spot in a dull day.

Percy held up his police badge and grinned even more widely.

'I'm so well regarded by the Home Secretary that he begged me to withdraw my resignation in order to assist Special Branch with the security arrangements for the Queen's Jubilee celebrations next June.'

'I thought she celebrated that ten years ago,' Jack objected, to a further smile from Percy.

'That was her *Golden* Jubilee. The one next June will be her *Diamond* one. Sixty glorious years at the head of the British Empire.'

'And why do they need Percy Enright to look after her security?' Jack smiled back. 'She's greatly loved by all her subjects, or so we're constantly being informed.'

Percy's smile faded somewhat. 'Not all of them — and certainly not some of her own close family, or so *I've* been informed. Added to which, a lot of foreign Johnnies have been invited to this one, and I've been asked to make sure that the Met's ready for the challenge of policing the thousands who're expected over here with little command of English, and some rather strange personal habits. That's where *you* come in.'

'Because of my familiarity with strange personal habits?'

'No, because you're a Sergeant with no current position within the Met.'

'Don't remind me — this place feels like some sort of desert island some days. But since I'm no longer with the Met, what makes you think that I'd be of any use while Her Majesty's being driven through the streets of London in her open carriage, waving at the great unwashed?'

'Prior to that, we need to assess the readiness of the Met to rise to the challenge. This requires a "systems" review by someone of appropriate rank outside the Met. I immediately thought of you, and the Home Secretary's approved your temporary transfer back down to Whitehall, working directly under me.'

'What about my duties here?'

'That's Essex's problem, but it goes without saying that your current position will still be available to you when you complete your temporary assignment.'

'Why me?'

'I need someone I can rely on, and it has to be someone of your rank who's not in the Met. The chances are that you'll emerge from it with the rank of Inspector, which should be sufficient to placate Esther.'

'And why would I need to do that?'

'Because you can't be expected to take the train in and out every day, and there may be days when you have to work late. I thought you might like to move back to your old room in Hackney.'

'So I can add Aunt Beattie's cooking to the normal hazards of the job?'

'Talking of cooking, what's on today's dinner menu?'

'Don't change the subject, but boiled beef and carrots.'

'Excellent. I'm glad we got all that agreed.'

'We agreed only on what's for dinner,' Jack reminded him. 'What will this special assignment involve, exactly?'

'Visiting each divisional lockup to make sure that they have sufficient men and other resources, that they're adequately trained in crowd control, and that they don't have any anarchists hiding in the woodwork, that's all.'

'Will I be able to go home at weekends?'

'Of course. Wouldn't want Esther to get all riled up, would we?'

'I'm not sure she won't anyway,' Jack frowned. 'I'll have to pick the right time to tell her.'

'Well make it soon, because we want you to start on Monday. Report to me, and if possible try to avoid Chief Superintendent Bray before you do, since he's likely to be a bit shirty about my reinstatement.'

'So we're not reporting directly to him?'

'No, to the Special Branch, who have overall responsibility for security on the big day.'

'And the Home Secretary asked you personally to get involved?'

'He certainly did. Over the dinner table at his country retreat in Chesham, last Monday.'

'And what was Bray's reaction?'

'I haven't actually told him yet.'

'So where in the Yard building will we be located on Monday?'

'No idea, at this stage.'

'You haven't actually shown your face in there yet, have you?' Jack demanded as several pennies dropped at the same time.

'Guilty as charged. I thought we might stroll in there together, armed with a letter signed by the Home Secretary.'

Jack sighed. 'I should have known that it was something not quite above board.'

'And what makes you think that?'

'The fact that you're involved, for one thing,' Jack smirked. 'And the fact that you're dragging me in with you. At least you can't involve Esther this time.'

'Don't make that sound so much like a challenge, or I just might,' Percy threatened him with a knowing smile. 'I suggest that you plan to arrive at our house in time for tea on Sunday, then we can re-enter the Yard together first thing on Monday morning. Remember to give Esther a lingering goodbye kiss.'

'It may be the last,' Jack replied ruefully, 'since I don't think she's going to be greatly impressed by my absences through the week, promotion or no promotion.'

The atmosphere in the Bunting Lane house during the days before Jack was due to depart for Hackney would have been sufficient to preserve sides of meat in a butcher's back room, and nothing that Jack could do seemed to thaw it to any degree. Meals were a dismal, silent affair in which he soon learned not to look across the table into the accusing eyes of the woman he dearly loved, who was behaving as if his mistress was seated next to him, and who responded to every polite question regarding her health, her happiness, her need for the salt to be passed to her, or the state of the laundry, as if it were a gross and offensive insult. As if he hadn't been feeling sufficiently undervalued at home, he was made to feel somewhat surplus to requirements when advised by his own superior officer that the Essex Detective Branch could well withstand his absence for an indeterminate period, and all in all it was a considerable relief as he pushed open the front gate to Percy and Beattie's house in Hackney — the scene of most of his teenage years — strode with his portmanteau up the rose bush-lined front path, and rang the bell.

'Come in, darling boy,' Aunt Beattie enthused as she wrapped him in a welcoming hug. 'It's going to be just like old times having you back here, and it compensates for not going to your mother's today for the usual Sunday dinner.'

'A kick in the arse would be adequate compensation for that,' Percy replied with a grin as he waved Jack towards the sitting room door. 'In there, Jack,' he requested, 'since we have a few things to discuss before your aunt cremates the sausages.'

Once inside the familiar sitting room with its heavy wallpaper and the picture of Her Majesty on the sideboard, Percy's face lost its eager grin. He opened a drawer to the sideboard with a key that he extracted from his waistcoat pocket, pulled out a bundle of soft files and handed the first of them across to Jack.

'Those are the stations we need to look most closely at, by way of priority.'

'Any particular reason?'

Percy nodded. 'Those are the ones we think are the most corrupted.'

'We?'

'Well, Special Branch at this stage.'

Jack stared back at him accusingly. 'This isn't quite as straightforward as you first led me to believe, is it?'

'I'm afraid not, but if I'd given you the full picture you wouldn't have been so keen to join me.'

'As I recall, I wasn't,' Jack pouted, 'and if you knew just how much trouble I'm in with Esther...'

Percy raised his hand for silence, and continued in a lowered tone, with a half glance towards the closed door. 'Not half as much as I'll be in with both Esther *and* your Aunt Beattie if they find out what we're really up to. But this is beyond any personal difficulties we may have to endure — it has to do with the personal safety of the Queen, and the future responsible governance of the nation.'

'You've joined Special Branch, haven't you?'

'Not officially. We're both still serving Yard officers with the usual authority over the Met in general, but in reality we'll be snakes in the grass. Foxes in the henhouse. Spies on our own colleagues.'

'Sent in by Special Branch?'

'Precisely. If our true missions are discovered, we'll be about as popular in police circles as a dose of the clap in a convent.'

'So who will we be spying on, and why?'

'Those police stations mentioned in these files are the first, but we may uncover information that leads us to others. In a few short words, we have reason to believe that "hostile elements" have begun to corrupt the Met from the inside, so that it won't be functioning at its best when called upon to police the city during the Jubilee festivities.'

Jack's jaw dropped open. 'I suppose it's too late to refuse?'

'Too late by several days. You're in this with me, Jack, and if it's any consolation I can't think of anyone I'd rather have at my back while I stick my front where it won't be welcome.'

'Are you going to share these investigations with me, or just send me in and watch carefully where the bullets come from?'

'I'm saddened to learn that you could think of me like that, Jack. Genuinely saddened and disappointed. Have I ever let you down at the critical moment?'

'I need time to think about that.'

'Well while you're thinking, take a look at these files, which simply stink of corruption. Either that, or a level of incompetence that demands dismissal from the force.'

He handed the first one over, and allowed Jack to peruse the front page, then raise his eyes to stare back at him in disbelief.

'Were these real police officers raiding a Hatton Garden gem dealer, or robbers posing as police officers? If the latter, where did they get the uniforms from?'

'Two very important questions that may be the strongest lead we have as to how deep the corruption goes already. I'll be investigating that one, posing as the head of a disciplinary team that's been sent in by the Yard. You'll be posing as one of my assistants — in fact my *only* assistant — and here's your first assignment.'

He handed over a thin buff-coloured soft file, which Jack opened with eager eyes. He read what it contained, then looked back up at Percy.

'At least I'm familiar with the location of this one. Those Wapping warehouses were a bleak sight at two in the morning when I was patrolling up and down the High Street on my very first foot beat. I was the most recent recruit in Leman Street, and it was traditional to send the newest bobby down that miserable lonely street. I remember just about pissing my uniform trousers when I passed each of those dark entrance passages.'

'More recently it had become a fixed-point duty,' Percy advised him, 'and the fixed point in question was right outside the premises of Bartrams where the uniforms were being stored. As you can read for yourself, the constable appears not to have been on duty when the premises were broken into and then burned almost to the ground.'

Jack was still reading and felt obliged to ask, 'Presumably the staff of Bartrams were able to tell us how many uniforms they were storing?'

'Regrettably not,' Percy told him, 'but the Army Office reckons that it was close to three thousand. The frightening fact remains that we don't know if they were all consumed by the fire, or if some were stolen first.'

'They wouldn't be worth much, surely, except as blankets on cold nights?'

Percy frowned. 'You're missing the point, Jack. How much would they be worth to an Anarchist group seeking to infiltrate an army detachment guarding the Queen? And you haven't asked the obvious question about the constable who was supposed to be on fixed-point duty.'

'I sought of assumed that he'd been murdered, so that the burglars could gain access without the alarm being raised,' Jack admitted. Percy remained silent but pierced him with a stare accentuated by raised eyebrows, and Jack continued working his mind through the possibilities, before adding weakly, 'That is, of course, assuming that he was there in the first place. In my day, even though we had a defined beat, it was rigorously timed, with the local Sergeant making "spot" checks to make sure that we were sticking to the times. The problem was that thieves and other ne'er-do-wells knew where we'd be at any given moment and timed their misdeeds accordingly. All that stopped after the Ripper, because they reckoned that this was how he'd managed to never get caught.'

'And if the constable was required to remain in the same spot all the time — the very spot where burglars needed access?' Percy prompted him.

Jack shivered slightly. 'Either he wasn't there at all, or they sneaked up on him and killed him. Neither possibility is a very pleasant one.'

'There's been no sign of his body since,' Percy advised him, 'so *you* work it out.'

'You said this was my first job?' Jack enquired. 'How much background information can you give me on this Constable Ainsworth who should have been on duty?'

'None whatsoever,' Percy replied with a sour grimace, 'since his Inspector in Leman Street — Inspector Ingram — refused to divulge it, even to Special Branch.'

'Can he get away with that indefinitely?' Jack asked, remembering his own days in the same police station, when his

Inspector had been Edmund Reid. 'And when was this Ingram first appointed?'

'When Reid retired recently,' Percy advised him. 'Previously Ingram had been a Sergeant in Stepney, which will be another of your stations of enquiry. It's in that second file I gave you, and labelled accordingly, since you need to find out what lay behind the unauthorised release of a prisoner who'd been found in a house full of military grade firearms. While you're at it, and by way of an encore, you can find out what happened to some eighty Martini Henry rifles that were being stored under the arses of the Yard in one of its Whitehall vaults, and which disappeared at roughly the same time.'

'This man Charles Ingram — previously the Sergeant at Deptford, and then and now Inspector at Leman Street — would seem to be the common link,' Jack observed in what he hoped was an intelligent contribution to the enquiry.

Percy smiled condescendingly. 'Funnily enough, I *had* thought of that. However, I haven't had time to pursue any sort of further enquiry in that direction, so be my guest.'

'You've only handed me these two files so far,' Jack observed. 'Are there any more for me?'

Percy shook his head. 'Not at this precise moment in time, no. But it's my optimistic belief that when you start digging into those two incidents you'll be led into other enquiries that can become new case files. As you already appear to have instinctively grasped, there may be links between seemingly isolated incidents of corruption. But don't lose sight of the possibility that some of the lapses you'll be investigating might be put down to simple incompetence — let's not jump into wild "conspiracy" conclusions without clear evidence that constabulary cock-ups can be eliminated. As you'll know from sad experience, the Met is not without its idiots in uniform.

Now let's follow the smell of burning, shall we? I'm quite hungry after all this talking. Oh, and by the way — welcome home.'

The following morning Percy took great delight in striding to the front desk of the Scotland Yard headquarters in Whitehall, accompanied by a very apprehensive Jack, and carefully unfolding a letter bearing the crested letterhead of Her Majesty's Government and the personal autograph of Home Secretary Sir Matthew Ridley at its foot. He placed it on the counter under the glass partition, smoothed it flat as if it were a dress handkerchief, then asked if it might be conveyed to Chief Superintendent Bray without delay. Jack smiled to himself as they took a seat where indicated, and Percy had barely whistled himself into his fifth rendition of 'Ta Ra Ra Boom De Ay' when a voice bellowed out from the first-floor landing as its owner hurried down into the lobby with a murderous look on his face.

'I don't know how you managed it, but don't expect any warm welcomes!' Chief Superintendent Bray warned them.

'Nice to meet up with you again too, sir,' Percy replied with a smirk. 'You remember my nephew, Sergeant Jackson Enright?'

'Not as well as I remember you,' Bray snarled. 'This letter orders me to provide the pair of you with office space and access to our facilities here, but one foot over the line and you'll both be back out in the street — understood?'

'Loudly and clearly,' Percy smiled back infuriatingly. 'Now, my man, if you'd be good enough to show us where we can begin work, we won't detain you any longer.'

Bray's face coloured a deep red from his neck upwards as he turned his head towards the front desk and yelled a command. 'Show these two up to one of the spare offices on the fourth

— preferably next to that smelly lavatory that keeps getting blocked. Only the one office between the pair of them — no need to afford them any luxury.'

'You were pushing *both* our lucks there, weren't you?' Jack said with a grin as the uniformed constable escorted them up the main staircase.

'Probably not — and in any case the pompous old fart had it coming,' Percy replied, grinning. 'Remember that we're about as welcome in here as a bacon curer in a synagogue. Eyes front, keep that smile on your face, and let's get on with what we came here for.'

Chapter Six

'Is the Sergeant expectin' yer?' the constable at the front desk asked Percy, who shook his head with a smile.

'It wouldn't be a "spot inspection" if he was, would it, lad?' he said, and the young constable smiled back politely in acknowledgment of the logic of that.

'Only he's down at the storage yard, conducting a stock check,' the constable advised Percy, who nodded and enquired if it was 'still up Shoe Lane, on the right?' The constable nodded. 'You've been here before?'

Percy smiled reminiscently. 'Many times, wearing the same uniform as you. And I'm bound to observe that this front entrance was much cleaner in those days, because we were ordered to keep it that way. To judge by the grit at the front door, you've allowed a good deal of Fleet Street to blow in since my days here. You might want to put a brush across it before I return.'

Uncertain whether to rush outside immediately with a broom, or remind Percy that he took his orders ultimately from Inspector Greaves and not some unknown middle-aged investigator from the Yard, Constable Bradford simply smiled weakly again, then breathed a sigh of relief as Percy walked back out into the noise and confusion of Fleet Street.

Percy turned right, then right again up Shoe Lane, where he carefully ducked under the archway a few yards up on the right that led up a narrow alleyway towards the 'E' Division equipment store. He tutted at the wide-open door and the lack of anyone guarding it, then strode into what appeared to be the main storeroom at the back, drew his 'special issue' service revolver, and stuck it under the startled nose of the grizzled grey-haired man who sat at a desk, his head down studying several ledgers in front of him.

'Jesus Christ!' he blasphemed and Percy grinned reassuringly.

'Not quite but thank you for the promotion. "Inspector Enright" will suffice at this stage, but it looks as if I got here not a day too soon. I could have been anyone and I was able to walk right in here and catch you unawares.'

'I were concentratin' on these stock records,' the man explained in a tone of justified irritation, and Percy put the revolver back in his inside jacket pocket as he allowed his grin to turn into a warning grimace.

'Trying to find several stolen uniforms, plus an entire paddy wagon?'

'Beg yours?'

'You *are* Sergeant Cameron, to judge by your stripes.' Percy nodded at the man's tunic sleeve. 'Or does "E" Division run to more than one Sergeant?'

'No, I'm 'im,' the man replied. 'Hector Cameron, Sergeant First Class.'

'First Class by rank, but Third Class by performance, it would seem,' Percy muttered to himself.

'Afore yer ask if it were me what led that raid on that jewellers, let me tell yer — like I've told every other nosey fellow what's enquired — that it were nowt ter do wi' me, an' I were at 'ome the night it 'appened.'

'Home being?'

'Twenny-seven Plough Court, up the road there. It goes wi' the job.'

'And one of the duties that goes with the job involves responsibility for this storehouse, correct?'

'Yeah — so what?'

'The "so what", Sergeant Cameron, is that while you were responsible for everything in here, someone managed to steal an entire police wagon and a selection of police uniforms, one of which, we can only assume, was adorned with sergeant's stripes. There can't be too many of those lying around, if you're the only sergeant attached to Holborn.'

'I'm not,' Cameron advised him with a smirk of triumph.

'Then who's the other one?' Percy demanded.

'There ain't none at the moment, 'cos we're waiting fer a replacement fer Dick Birkenshaw, what retired a couple o' months back. It were 'is uniform what went missin' a week or so afore it musta bin used fer that robbery.'

Percy's face set in a stern expression. 'How can you be sure that it was missing a week or so before the robbery?'

''Cos I were doin' me job proper, an' I made a note that it were missin' at the time. I've still got the note 'ere somewhere, if yer give me a mo ter find it.'

'You mean that it's still here?' Percy demanded in sheer disbelief, and Cameron nodded enthusiastically.

'Bloody right it is. I keeps proper records in 'ere, I'll 'ave yer know.'

'Did you by any chance pass on this vital piece of intelligence to Inspector Greaves?'

'No, why should I?'

'You mean that your Standing Orders don't require you to report any missing equipment to your superior officer?'

'Yeah they do, but I were already in trouble about that wagon, so I kept it ter meself.'

Percy nearly gasped in disbelief, then reminded himself that this man was so stupid that he was worthy of further interrogation.

'So what got you into trouble regarding the wagon?'

'Well, it weren't my fault if it were a cold day, was it? We'd given the wagon a new coat o' paint, an' rather than shift it back indoors while it were still wet, which would've meant gettin' our 'ands dirty, we left it in the yard out there. There were a stiff wind blowin', an' we figured it'd be dry by mornin'. 'Cept when mornin' came, some bastard 'ad nicked it. The way the Inspector went on about it, yer'd've thought I pinched it meself.'

Percy hastily converted his chortle into a cough, trying desperately not to allow the moronic loss of so much police property, with its tragic sequel, to appear to be an occasion of amusement. It was time he sought a more mentally endowed person to question, so he left Sergeant Cameron with a stern assurance that he'd be speaking more about this to his Inspector, before walking swiftly back up Shoe Lane with his head bent forward against the aggressive late October drizzle and returning to Divisional Headquarters in Fleet Street, where he demanded an immediate audience with Inspector Greaves.

'What possessed you to promote such an obvious cretin to the rank of Sergeant?' he demanded as he shook his head in response to the proffered tea. Inspector Greaves took his time pouring his own before looking back up at Percy.

'Are we talking about Hector Cameron?'

'How many sergeants have you got?' Percy fired back. 'Cameron told me he was the only one stationed here at present, although given his obvious lack of ability in the matter of stores record keeping, perhaps he can't even count up to two.'

Inspector Greaves looked puzzled. 'Sergeant Cameron is excellent at counting, and for that matter all the other duties that are devolved to him. Before the unfortunate events of recent weeks I would have accounted him the most intelligent man on my force. He had an exemplary record as a constable, and I didn't experience a moment's hesitation in promoting him when I did, almost two years ago now, since when he's done nothing to make me regret my choice.'

'You mean apart from being totally incapable of explaining the loss of an unspecified number of police uniforms — one of them that of a sergeant — and an entire paddy wagon?' Percy replied incredulously.

Greaves nodded. 'Inexplicable, I grant you. As I said, until those losses I would have ranked Hector Cameron as one of the most astute officers in "E" Division.'

'God knows what that says for the rest, if you're referring to the man I met earlier this morning,' Percy remonstrated, before taking the time to think it through. 'Can you think of any reason, short of corruption, why such an able officer could demonstrate such base incompetence in the most fundamental of duties?'

'Not really,' Greaves conceded, 'although I can't bring myself to conclude that it must have been corruption. Cameron's a dedicated officer, and I can only put it down to his son's ill health.'

'Tell me about it,' Percy said as he extracted his notebook, to a frown from Greaves.

'I hope this isn't going to go on record,' Greaves said in an almost pleading tone, 'given Hector's previous unblemished record, but he has a son aged about eight years old who was recently diagnosed with some sort of chest ailment that requires nursing, a special diet and certain medications. Hector Cameron married later in life, to a woman not much younger than him, and Jamie's their only child, and deeply adored by them both. They're desperate not to have to consign him to some sort of sanatorium, and I think that the constant need to ensure that the boy is properly nursed and looked after has led to mental strain that occasionally causes him to be lax in his duties.'

'You mean that there have been other incidents than the stores losses?'

Greaves shook his head. 'No, there was only that one unfortunate series, and I must plead guilty to having covered up for Hector at the time. Now that you're here to assess our readiness for the Jubilee celebrations next year, I have to bring to your attention our urgent need for another sergeant to replace one who retired recently. That way I can assign Hector Cameron to other duties that may enable him to spend more time sharing the nursing duties with Sarah — his wife.'

'We don't yet have the finalised route for the Queen's Jubilee procession,' Percy told him, 'but hopefully she won't be coming any further north than the Abbey, so you'll only need to maintain a full street presence to marshal the crowds that will be heading down through Grays Inn Road and Drury Lane. The poor bastards in "A" Division will, as usual, cop the worst of it, in return for the privilege of policing Westminster.'

'But you'll support my request for a new sergeant?' Greaves pressed him, and Percy gave him the benefit of a grimace.

'You might want to think in terms of *two* new sergeants, Inspector, because I have a sneaking suspicion that your existing one may be for the high jump when I submit my final report.'

As he stepped out once again into the clamour of Fleet Street, Percy gave serious thought to what he had just been told. An exemplary officer who'd been uncharacteristically lax in his duties *might* have had a lot on his mind regarding ill-health in the family, but he might also have been bribed or threatened. How else to explain how he'd managed to part with police property that had been put to good use in the brutal raid on a gem merchant's late at night? Had someone taken timely advantage of random acts of carelessness on the part of someone not known for their inattention to duty, or had the failure to adequately guard the police store on two separate occasions been pre-planned with a man on the 'inside' who'd been willing to assist, for whatever reason? And who was to say that the uniforms and the wagon hadn't been taken on the same occasion, given that the person responsible for their security couldn't account for their disappearance?

Plough Court was some way up Fetter Lane, with its bustle of wagons coming and going with deliveries in and out of the many newspaper and other publishing offices than lined its pavements. As he turned in through the narrow entrance to the Court, the contrast was remarkable. For one thing there was no vehicle noise, only the excited chatter of urchins playing some sort of street game in their ragged hand-me-downs. The dust of the urban laneway had been replaced by damp mud, and the faint smell of human waste that hung in the air suggested that the dampness might be coming from inadequate privies.

He found number twenty-seven on the second floor of a tiled tenement staircase, and as he approached its door it swung open, seemingly of its own accord, and a nervous looking woman appeared surveying him with suspicious eyes. She was in her early forties, so far as Percy could tell, and her clothes were best described as 'once stylish, but badly worn from incessant housework'. Percy tried his best smile.

'Mrs Cameron?'

'Who's askin'?'

He extracted the police badge from his pocket and held it high in the air, registering the sudden look of apprehension on the woman's face. She appeared to be as respectable as her circumstances allowed and should therefore have had no reason for discomfort at the arrival of a Scotland Yard Inspector, but from the expression on her face he might as well have been a murderer on the prowl.

'I'm Inspector Enright from Scotland Yard, and I'm visiting your husband's station for the day, assessing its readiness for the Queen's Diamond Jubilee next year. I spoke to your husband earlier today, and I learned that you have a sick child. It may be that the Yard could assist with any medical expenses by means of its Welfare Fund, if the circumstances are appropriate.'

'Yer just 'ere ter spy on 'Ector, aren't yer, like the others?'

'What others, Mrs Cameron?'

'Yer know damn well what others. Them as told 'im ter keep 'is gob shut.'

'I know nothing about that, Mrs Cameron — "Sarah", isn't it? — let me assure you.'

'It's "Mrs Cameron" ter you, an' yer'll get nowt outer me.'

'If I might come in for a moment and see your child?' Percy insisted in what he hoped was a persuasive tone, 'I can report back to the Yard, and we might then be able to make some money forthcoming...'

''E ain't in there,' Sarah Cameron advised him bluntly with a backward shake of her head towards the set of rooms behind her as she simultaneously stepped forward to prevent Percy proceeding any further. 'Our Jamie's wi' a neighbour what looks after 'im while I does the cleanin' afore the nurse comes durin' the afternoons. I were on me way ter see 'ow 'e's goin' when you turned up.'

'Please don't let me stop you,' Percy offered reassuringly. 'I'll just wait here until you get back, and then I won't keep you long. I just need to see Jamie, that's all.'

'Please yerself,' Mrs Cameron replied as she slipped past him on a faint cloud of stale sweat and headed down the staircase, looking up once on her way down, as if checking to make sure that Percy was honouring his undertaking not to enter her home. He stood there reflecting on what life must be like for a couple with an only child born late in their lives who was crippled by consumption, or something like it, then he came swiftly to attention as he heard a faint noise from beyond the open door.

It sounded like the plaintiff cry of a small child, and he strained his ears in the hope that it would be repeated. After a delay of some thirty seconds he was rewarded by the sound of a weak voice calling 'Ma!', and the realisation hit him that he'd been lied to. Jamie Cameron wasn't being looked after by a neighbour at all — he was here in the tenement, so why had his mother slipped downstairs on the pretence that she had to look in on him?

He learned why after waiting for fifteen frustrating minutes at the top of the landing outside her front door. His ears caught the sound of several footsteps entering the tenement from the lane, and Sarah Cameron reappeared, bustling somewhat out of breath up the second flight of stairs, accompanied by two men. One of them was tall and thin, and wearing a heavy waterproof coat over what looked like workman's attire, while his companion was noticeably much shorter, and barehaded, revealing a thin fluff of gingery hair that made his head look like an orange billiard ball.

'That's 'im,' Sarah Cameron advised the two men, and the taller of them approached to within a foot of Percy, who clenched his fists in preparation for a fight.

'Yer was askin' about young Jamie?' the man demanded, making it sound vaguely indecent.

'Indeed I was,' Percy reassured him. 'I'm from Scotland Yard, and it may be that we can make some financial contribution to assist in his care.'

'Never 'eard o' Scotland Yard doin' owt like that,' the man insisted, 'an' anyways, 'e's well provided fer. I'm the boy's uncle, so bugger off — now.'

'I have to see the child, in order to complete my report,' Percy insisted, and the man's face darkened as it became more menacing.

'I've told yer once ter leave an' my associate 'ere's very 'andy wiv 'is fists,' the man said as he gestured with a jerk of his head towards his diminutive ginger-haired companion.

'That right?' Percy asked the smaller man, who look puzzled by the words, but remained silent.

'Now — yer gonna go, or what?' the taller man demanded.

Percy nodded. 'As you insist, but I'm not sure that I'll be able to recommend any payment from the Metropolitan Police Benevolent Fund.'

'That's only fer widders,' the tall man advised him accurately, and Percy was still asking himself how this rough-looking scruff was aware of that when he stepped to one side, leaving a clear path between the two men that Percy was impliedly being invited to take, which he did, making a mental note to conduct further investigations into the Cameron family.

Jack experienced a strong sense of *déjà vu* as he stepped into the entrance hall of Leman Street Police Station, shaking the rain from his coat while he walked up to the Charge Desk, with its associated 'fish tank' to the left, already beginning to fill steadily as the morning drunks were unloaded from the wagons at the door, or carried in by grunting constables. The Sergeant on the front desk looked familiar, and Jack smiled as he was asked for his name.

'You don't remember me, clearly,' he told the Sergeant, who looked more closely at him, then broke into a grin of his own.

'Jack Bloody Enright! The last time I saw you was when we brought you up from the cells, charged with murder. Then we were told to release you 'cos you'd croaked the Ripper, even though you weren't officially one of us at the time. What ever happened to you after that?'

'A long story, Albert, but none of it would have happened if you hadn't loaned me your billy club to do it with.'

'As I recall you all but stole it from me. But what brings you back here — I take it you're back on the force?'

Jack extracted, and displayed, his police badge with a broad smile.

'You're not the only one who made it to Sergeant, as you can see. I'm normally based in Chelmsford these days, heading up a very small and totally inadequate Essex Detective Branch, but I've been selected for a special duty, assessing the readiness of Met. stations for the Diamond Jubilee next year.'

'That some sort of regatta on the river?'

'No, a bit more than that. The Queen will be celebrating sixty years on the throne, and we're expecting tens of thousands in the streets, all from different parts of the world.'

'Sounds like a normal day in Whitechapel,' Sergeant Preedy grinned, 'but I hope that means more manpower down here? Right now we're stretched like a hen's arse with a duck's egg in it.'

'That will depend on my report,' Jack advised him, taking early advantage of the manpower shortage he'd been relying on as his excuse to ferret through records. 'To begin with I'll need to see the beat rosters for the past few months — say, back to July.'

'You'll need Inspector Ingram's permission for that,' Preedy advised him. 'And he's a grumpy bugger at the best of times, although don't tell him I said so. Do you want me to send word upstairs?'

'This is somewhat irregular,' Inspector Ingram advised Jack from behind his narrow spectacles, his gimlet eyes reflecting his disapproval. 'But since the Home Secretary's commissioned it, and since it will hopefully mean more manpower for us, I'll authorise it. If you care to wander down into one of the Detective Branch offices — and God knows, we have enough of those empty at the moment — I'll have the rosters sent in to you without delay. In the meantime you might want to sample the tea room. It's one floor up, at the end of the hallway.'

'Yes, I remember it well.' Jack smiled as he rose from his chair, leaving the Inspector with a quizzical look in the eyes behind his spectacle lenses.

Shortly under an hour later, suitably refreshed with tea, Jack began his attempt to make sense of the duty rosters from recent weeks relating to the infamous 'Beat Four' that would place the constable allocated to it immediately in front of the Bartrams' warehouse that had been the subject of the arson attack some weeks previously, with the suspected loss of a quantity of army uniforms that the convenient fire had been designed to conceal. Evidently Beat Four was no more popular than it had been in his early days as a constable on the Wapping waterfront.

For several weeks prior to that in which the fire had occurred, the duty had been allocated, on the night shift, to Constable Michael Black, who Jack could only assume was new to Whitechapel, and therefore ripe for being allocated the worst beat in the Division. But at the start of the week in question he'd been inexplicably replaced by a Constable Edward Ainsworth, and it had been Ainsworth on notional fixed-point duty immediately outside Bartrams when the deed had been done. This clearly raised certain important issues that needed further investigation.

First, the obvious one of why Ainsworth had not raised the alarm. Either he'd been disabled, and possibly murdered, or he'd simply turned a blind eye to what was going on behind him, possibly at gunpoint, and too embarrassed afterwards to admit that he'd been rendered powerless. If the latter, there would have been a report from him in the incident file from Special Branch in Jack's possession on the desk in front of him, and there clearly wasn't. This left the uncomfortable possibility that Ainsworth had been murdered, or otherwise disposed of, but the quick answer to that would be found in the 'roll call' sheets for the following day, which would reveal whether or not Edward Ainsworth had reported for duty on the subsequent night shift. At the same time, Jack could search the roll call records for any clue as to what had kept Constable Michael Black from what should have been his regular beat.

Rather than distract Inspector Ingram from his no doubt onerous and varied duties, Jack went in search of Sergeant Devlin, now an ageing old warhorse who'd been holding down that rank when Jack had been a constable serving under him. Bill Devlin was now allocated 'Headquarters' duties following a near riot during the official opening of the 'Blind Beggar' public house in Whitechapel Road two years previously, when the brewery that owned it laid on far too much free ale, and poor old Bill had suffered multiple fractures to both legs as he led the police charge against a wall of drunks armed with chair legs.

Part of Bill's duties consisted of maintaining the manpower records, and he raised no objection when Jack collected the files he needed, claiming that he had Inspector Ingram's authority to assess manpower strength ahead of possible additions to the roster in time for the Diamond Jubilee. Jack was fortunate that he had already made a note of the home addresses of both Constables Ainsworth and Black and had noted the absence from duty of Michael Black for a week before Beat Four was reallocated — at his own request, Jack noted with suspicious surprise — to Edward Ainsworth, who had not reported back for duty the morning after the attack on Bartrams, or any day since.

Fortunate in the sense that he looked up with mild alarm as he heard a shout of protest from the doorway of the modest office in which he'd installed himself while examining records. There stood a steely-faced Inspector Ingram, who was clearly not seeking a quiet chat regarding Jack's progress thus far.

'What d'you think you're doing, ferreting through the roll call records?' Ingram demanded, and Jack went for the obvious excuse.

'If you wish to be considered for an urgent increase in manpower,' he explained in a measured and, he hoped, a reasonable tone, 'then I need to assess where you're most vulnerable, and I can see immediately that you've recently experienced difficulties with regard to men failing to report for duty.'

'I'm not letting you report back about lack of morale in Leman Street,' Ingram advised him icily, 'so hand those records over to me — now!'

'If you insist,' Jack returned pleasantly. 'As it happens, I've got what I wanted from them anyway.'

'Good — then you can bugger off back to Whitehall, can't you?' Ingram snarled back at him. 'Or do I need to have you escorted out?'

'Hardly,' Jack continued to smile, 'since I know the way out from long, and I may say bitter, memory. I thought Inspector Reid was a bit rough on his men, but you appear to have raised the bar a bit higher in that regard.'

'Out — *now!*' Ingram bellowed, and Jack did as requested, needing little encouragement to head downstairs to see if his favourite pie shop from 'the old days' was still in business.

'You weren't wrong about Ingram,' he grinned at Albert Preedy on his way out.

Chapter Seven

'Billy's doing a magnificent job of scything the lawn as usual,' Constance Enright observed as she moved back from the sun lounge window extension towards the table in the main sitting room on which Alice had laid out the tea and salmon sandwiches, and on which Esther had arranged the incoming correspondence for the Ladies' Guild for Constance's attention. Outside it was overcast, with the prospect of further rain, and Esther was hoping that it would hold back until after she'd been able to collect Lily and Bertie from the Board School that they both now attended.

'I think he's only too delighted to be able to live and work so close to Nell,' Esther replied. 'They make a really sweet couple, and Jack and I intend to give them a splendid wedding in what I suspect will be the near future.'

'How good is Nell, really?' Constance asked. 'I know you set your heart on giving her a good start after her unfortunate days in that orphanage, but have you been adequately rewarded?'

'It's not a matter of reward,' Esther told her. 'It's simply a matter of following your inner urgings to help people who deserve it. Nell was well taught in domestic duties at the orphanage, and she's a superb cook, if somewhat basic in her repertoire. She's also taken fully to the other jobs she's had to learn, like setting fires and cleaning fireplaces, and hopefully after they're married she and Billy will find a position as a married cook/housekeeper and handyman somewhere close by here, so that we can keep in touch with them.'

'You must be very grateful for Nell's company around the house while Jackson's away all week, irresponsible boy that he is.'

'I certainly am,' Esther confirmed, 'and I'm missing Jack already, after only a day, but I won't let on when he comes home on Friday. I'll keep it frosty, just to remind him that he has responsibilities at home that he's neglecting while he gets into mischief with Uncle Percy.'

'What are the two of them working on, anyway?' Constance asked as she bit into her second salmon sandwich.

Esther shrugged. 'Jack wouldn't say, but that's just typical of him, making his work sound all mysterious, when it's basically just a manpower review, as far as I can tell.'

'I'd like to think that it's a little more sophisticated than that, dear,' Constance replied. 'Anyway, let's get on with these letters, shall we? Is there anything from the Bishop's office about the Harvest Festival?'

'Not that I noticed when I opened them,' Esther advised her, 'although the Bishop *was* highly complementary during the tea party that followed, so no doubt he'll get around to writing to express his appreciation. Are you alright?'

Constance had winced, then turned pale. She was rubbing her left arm with a puzzled expression but smiled back weakly at Esther as she gingerly lowered herself into the vacant chair.

'Just a stab of indigestion, I imagine, although it seems to have quite robbed me of breath. Oh dear.'

Beads of sweat were standing out on her forehead, even though it was only moderately warm in the sitting room that day, with a low-burning fire, and little sun coming through the glass roof of the sun lounge. She continued wincing and grimacing, then fell backwards in her seat.

'Perhaps if I lie down this dratted pain will go away,' she suggested. 'Could you help me to the sofa, dear?'

Thoroughly alarmed, Esther held Constance under the elbow and guided her, doubled up, towards the padded sofa under the window, then helped her into a horizontal position. Esther banged heavily on the window glass until she had caught the attention of young Billy outside, to whom she waved with hand gestures to indicate that he should come into the house. A few moments later, minus his boots, he appeared in the sitting room doorway, and Esther called out urgently, 'The mistress seems to have been taken ill. Do you know where Dr. Browning's surgery is?'

When a nervous looking Billy nodded, Esther ordered him to run at full speed and fetch the doctor. Once Billy had disappeared, Esther did what she could to comfort Constance, who was white-faced and complaining of the worst indigestion she had ever experienced. The all-purpose maid Alice rushed in, equally white-faced.

'Billy says as 'ow the mistress 'as bin taken poorly. Is there sumfin' I can do?'

'Just keep an eye out for Dr Browning,' Esther instructed her, 'and bring him straight in here when he arrives.'

Some thirty nervous minutes later, Constance was beginning to complain about the unnecessary fuss while Dr Browning stood back up after sounding her chest with the aid of an instrument draped round his neck and addressed himself to Esther.

'Did you notice if she came out in a sudden cold sweat?'

'Yes, she did,' Esther confirmed, as Constance assured them both, yet again, from her prone position on the sofa, that it was just a touch of indigestion — no need for all this fuss.

'Did you get shooting pains down your left arm?' the doctor enquired, and when Constance shook her head vigorously, Esther confirmed that she had seen Constance clutching her arm.

'And I suppose you're going to assure me that you didn't experience any breathlessness either?' Doctor Browning said with a tolerant smile.

'Yes, I did,' Constance admitted, 'but I get that with indigestion.'

'You also get it with heart attacks, which is what you've just experienced in a minor form,' the doctor advised her as he took out his notepad and wrote something down before tearing the sheet from the pad and handing it to Esther.

'You're the daughter?' he enquired.

'Daughter-in-law.'

'Take this prescription to the chemist's. The tablets have to be taken three times a day, after meals, and your mother-in-law requires at least three days in bed with absolutely no stress or activity. After that, a little gentle exercise each day — perhaps a sedate stroll to the crossroads and back, but no further. And you won't appreciate me saying this, Mrs Enright, but you need to shed at least a stone in weight.'

After the doctor had gone, there was the predictable argument until Esther persuaded Constance into her bed upstairs with the promise of returning to her bedside the following day and going through all the abandoned correspondence with her. Then before venturing out into what had now become persistent drizzle in order to collect Lily and Bertie from school, Esther popped her head into the kitchen, where the cook was sitting drinking tea.

'Whatever you were planning for the mistress's supper, forget all about it and make it either a thin vegetable broth or a boiled egg. And only one slice of toast.'

'So how did your first day go?' Percy asked Jack as he leaned back in the armchair in front of the fire that Mary, their daily help, had lit before leaving for the day. Jack sat in the chair opposite his and protested yet again at Percy's insistence that they say nothing about their work until they got home. 'Every man and his dog uses the omnibus,' was Percy's excuse, 'and we don't want to be overheard. Added to which, we're supposed to be engaged on separate enquiries, and we don't want some genius to join up the dots.'

'I was doing fine until that pompous martinet Ingram threw me out of Leman Street,' Jack complained. 'He was very tight-arsed about the duty rosters that lay behind the beat allocations. As I already explained, "Beat Four" is the critical one — the one that covers the very location of Bartrams' warehouse. The constable who was normally allocated to it — a bloke called Michael Black — went absent from duty a week before the fire. I wasn't able to find out why, and it was while I was trying to find an innocent reason for it that Ingram threw me out. At the same time, I was curious to learn that the man who *was* allegedly on duty at that fixed point — a Constable Edward Ainsworth — had actually volunteered for it.'

'Seems suspicious, I agree,' Percy agreed, 'but perhaps he had a good personal reason for wanting to be at a fixed point — *other*, that is, than being in with the gang that did the raid.'

'That's the curious thing,' Jack insisted. 'That Number Four beat is like a punishment and is normally inflicted on the newest bobby into Leman Street. Believe me, that's what happened to me, and I didn't get free of it until the next bloke arrived, two months later. So why would Edward Ainsworth actually volunteer for it, and why hasn't he reported back for duty since the night of the fire?'

'I don't suppose you got any home addresses before you were chucked out of the station by Inspector Ingram?'

'I was well taught by an uncle of mine,' Jack grinned, 'and I got addresses for both Michael Black and Edward Ainsworth. That's what I'm going to be following up in the morning. So how about you?'

'Before I tell you,' Percy instructed him, 'remember to remind me again about Inspector Ingram when I've finished. He could be the second line of enquiry for me tomorrow.'

'And the first?'

'I need to check on the family background of that Sergeant Cameron from "E" Division. He doesn't quite add up. I interviewed him at the storehouse in Holborn from which the police wagon and uniforms disappeared before they were used in the Hatton Garden jewel robbery, and he did a fair impersonation of a total moron who should never have been promoted, and who wasn't capable of counting the fingers on one hand. But when I interviewed his superior officer, and the man who promoted him to sergeant — a solid looking bloke called Inspector Greaves — I was given a totally different picture of a man with a spotless record who'd made just one or two serious lapses of judgment at a time when he was distracted by family issues.'

'What family issues, exactly?'

'A sick son in need of special medical care, which suggests a need for money, and a potential for being corrupted.'

'Did you enquire further?'

'Of course. I went to his home address, but never got beyond the front door. The man's wife fobbed me off with the explanation that the boy was with neighbours, but that was just a ruse. While I was waiting for her to come back upstairs after checking on the boy, I distinctly heard what sounded like him calling from inside the rooms they were living in; then she came back upstairs with two no-nonsense blokes who assured me that the boy was being well cared for and invited me to bugger off.'

'And did you?'

'Do I strike you as a stupid hero? Of *course* I made myself scarce, but what makes me suspicious is that one of the blokes seemed to know all about the Met widows' pension scheme, while claiming to be the boy's uncle — the mother's brother. I'll be checking that out first thing tomorrow. Now, remind me about Inspector Ingram.'

'Inspector Ingram?' Jack responded, just as Beattie Enright poked her head round the door and advised them that tea was almost ready.

'What do you plan to poison us with this evening?' Percy asked genially, and his wife snorted.

'One of these days, Percy Enright, I really *will* poison you, and the only reason I haven't done so far is the fact that there'd be an obvious suspect.'

'I'll speak up for you, Aunt Beattie,' Jack said, to which Percy replied, 'You're just looking for a way to be excused her deadly dumplings, or her lethal lentil soup.'

'Five minutes,' Beattie advised them. 'Just long enough for me to sign the divorce papers.'

'Inspector Ingram?' Jack repeated. 'And keep it brief, because I'm hungry enough to eat even whatever Aunt Beattie's cooked.'

'It's pretty obvious, if you step back and look at the overall picture,' Percy pointed out. 'Ingram was a sergeant at Stepney when they found that cache of firearms in a local house. The man who occupied that house was released from custody a few days later for no apparent reason, and the weapons themselves went missing from a special store at the Yard shortly after that. Then Ingram gets promoted to Inspector at Leman Street, just in time to arrange the change in shift rosters that allowed the arson of Bartrams to take place right under our noses. Do I have to draw you a diagram?'

'So Ingram's corrupt,' Jack agreed, 'but someone else higher than him must have organised his promotion — his "reward", if you like.'

'And someone inside the Yard must have made it possible for those guns to be spirited out of the store at the Yard,' Percy added. 'You know how well guarded and supervised that is, so I have this horrible feeling that the corruption goes much higher than we had initially thought or hoped.'

'So where do we go from here?' Jack enquired.

'First of all, into the kitchen for an appointment with the Hackney Poisoner,' Percy grimaced. 'Then tomorrow, assuming I survive, I'll be making a pain of myself in certain quarters. I seem to have acquired a sudden taste for suicide.'

Jack dodged what looked suspiciously like an inflated pig's bladder that a group of ragged urchins were fighting for possession of as he ducked quickly into the gloomy entrance of a tenement yard in Lowder Street, Wapping. On his way up Raymond Street he'd passed the grim fortress-like outer wall of the local Workhouse, and he reminded himself that for families like the one he was about to visit, destitution and despair were only a missed week's wages away. Stepping carefully over the prostrate boots and stockings of a female drunk who'd clearly not quite made it up to her lodgings on her way back from the gin palace, he climbed one flight of stairs, then checked the room number that he'd written down hastily in his notebook the previous afternoon. He knocked on the door, and, as experience had taught him to do, he took a deep breath when he heard it about to open.

'Mrs Black?'

'That's me — Lizzie Black,' the exhausted looking drab confirmed as she gazed back out at him through eyes deprived of sleep. ''Ave yer found Mickey? Only I can't keep lyin' ter the kids about where 'e is fer much longer.'

'How did you know I was a police officer?' Jack asked.

Lizzie Black nodded towards his feet. 'Yer boots is clean, an' yer don't smell, so yer can't be from round these parts. Anyway, yer'll be the third this week.'

'You mean that other police officers have been enquiring about your husband?'

'Don't know who they was exactly, but yeah — suddenly every bastard in the world wants ter know where the lousy bugger's got to, but yer'd think 'e'd've told 'is own wife what 'e were about, wouldn't yer? Well, yer'd best come inside.'

'When did he first go missing?' Jack asked as he tactfully removed a child's wooden toy from the only available chair, while Lizzie Black perched her scrawny frame on the end of the unmade bed that occupied the centre of the only room that the tenement seemed to possess.

'Can't really tell yer, since 'e were sometimes missin' fer days at a time,' Lizzie told him. 'But it were a week or two back now, after 'e'd fallen in wi' that soldier.'

'What soldier would that be?'

'I weren't told that, was I? 'E never told me about 'is cardplayin' friends, like 'e never told me 'ow much 'e were losin'.'

'He lost money heavily at cards?'

"Owdyer think we come ter finish up in a shit'ole like this? We 'ad proper rooms at one time, down in Shadwell. Then Mickey took ter the gamblin', a' it were like it took 'old of 'is 'ole life. We 'ad 'eaps o' rows about it, an' 'e kept promisin' ter give it all away, but 'e never did. Then 'e come 'ome a few weeks since lookin' proper scared, an' eventually 'e got around ter admittin' that 'e'd bin playin' cards wiv a soldier bloke, an' 'ow 'e owed 'im lotsa money, an' 'e'd 'ave ter go inter 'idin' fer a while.'

'Is that when he disappeared?'

'Not quite. 'E come back a few nights later, wiv all this money, an' tried ter tell me 'is luck 'ad suddenly changed, an' that 'e'd be gone fer a while, but there wuz enough money ter keep me an' the kids fed fer a month. Well the month's bin an' gone, an' if 'e don't come back soon we'll all be in the Poor'ouse. Either that, or I'll 'ave ter sell me body, like some o' me neighbours. But who'd want a scrawny thing like me?'

'These other people who came enquiring after Mickey — are you sure they were police?' Jack asked.

'They said they was, although one've 'em looked too small an' skinny fer that. They was askin' why Mickey 'adn't turned up fer duty, an' I told 'em I didn't know. They asked me if I knew where 'e were 'idin' out, an' I told 'em I didn't know that neither, which were the truth. Then they went away, but another lot come only yesterday. Different blokes, but askin' the same questions. An' while I were down the street yesterday, I spotted one've 'em keepin' watch on the buildin', like 'e were waitin' fer Mickey ter come back.'

'If you feel threatened in any way, by these men who keep calling, or anyone else for that matter, you're to contact me at Scotland Yard. My name's Jack Enright — Detective Sergeant Jack Enright — can you remember that? And whatever you do, don't rely on anyone at the local police station where Mickey used to work — Leman Street, in Whitechapel.'

'Why not?'

'I can't tell you, but now I must be going,' Jack insisted as he got up from the chair. Just then the sound of a child crying became audible from what Jack had taken to be a cupboard of some sort. With an apologetic smile Lizzie rose from the edge of the bed.

'It's little Charlie — 'e's needin' a feed. Can yer show yerself out?'

Assuring her that he could, Jack made his way towards the doorway, then turned to make sure that she wasn't looking as he reached into his trouser pocket, extracted a couple of shillings and placed them carefully on the ledge near the door as he made his way back out onto the landing, and decided that he could resume breathing in at his normal rate.

There was a considerable contrast between the squalid room in which he'd spoken with Lizzie Black and the smart lodging house in Cable Street that advertised on its front window that it had 'clean rooms available for respectable business gentlemen', but that like many of its kind it was not prepared to open its doors to anyone who was Irish. Jack did the necessary with the heavy black knocker on the front door, and after a minute or so a comfortably padded middle-aged lady opened it with a broad smile.

'Good morning, sir,' she breezed. 'Looking for accommodation, are we?'

'No,' Jack replied as he raised his police badge high in the air, 'we're looking for Edward Ainsworth.'

'Haven't seen him for some time,' the lady replied. 'He's paid up a month in advance, so it's none of my business anyway. I'm Hilda Morton, by the way.'

'Detective Sergeant Jack Enright, Scotland Yard. I take it that he hasn't been gone a month, else you'd be re-letting his room, which I'd like to examine if I may.'

'Of course,' Hilda Morton replied as she stood back from the doorway to grant admission to Jack. 'He's the first floor back — number 5.'

Jack followed her as she led the way up the staircase to the first-floor room, which she opened with a key at her belt, and flung the door open.

'It's a bit musty after this while,' she advised him almost apologetically, 'but I'll leave you to it.'

'No, please stay,' Jack requested, 'since I need to ask you about your lodger. His personal habits, friends, tastes in food — anything you can tell me, really. Plus, I don't want there to be any suggestion afterwards that I stole anything from this room or planted something in it that doesn't belong.'

'As you wish,' she agreed. 'He was a very respectable gentleman, on the whole, and very punctual. But you'd know that, if you worked with him. He was a police officer himself, but I suspect that's why you're here. He's not been at work lately, has he?'

'And what makes you think that?'

Mrs Morton seemed somewhat offended by the question. 'As a landlady I make it my business to observe the comings and goings of my tenants, and I can tell you that "Teddy", as he invited me to call him, was normally very punctilious in his habits. Left for work every day an hour before he was due on, and always came home for meals when his shift hours permitted. He was staying "half board", which entitled him to two meals a day. He never once came home the worse for drink, although I know he liked to party.'

'"Party" in what way, exactly?'

'Well, young ladies, if you take my meaning. He was always eager to tell me about social gatherings that he went to, and the young ladies that he met at them. There was one in particular he often referred to — "Betsy" I think her name was. A publican's daughter, not that there's anything wrong with that, of course. I believe that he and she walked out a few times, and the last time I saw him was just down the road there, under the railway arch. He met up with this lovely looking young lady, all bonnet and feathers, if you get the picture, and she took his arm and steered him down towards St Katherine Dock way.'

'That was the last time you saw him, you say?' Jack took out his notebook in anticipation, and she nodded.

'Yes, that's right. That would be the day after that fire in that warehouse. I meant to ask him about that, since I think he was on duty somewhere near there. But he must have been late in after his night shift finished — no doubt held back by that dreadful fire — and he didn't come back for the breakfast he knew I'd cooked for him. Anyway, it was later that day that I saw him with the young lady I just mentioned.'

'I'd better set about examining the room, but don't go away.'

There wasn't much to examine, Jack soon realised. The bed was in the centre of the room, with a washstand and basin in one corner. The wardrobe revealed only a relatively clean and new-looking police uniform, a grey suit, various socks and undergarments, and two pairs of boots that clearly belonged to someone with large feet. This just left a set of drawers on the other side of the room, the top drawer of which was firmly locked.

Jack looked back across at Mrs Morton in the doorway. 'I don't suppose you have a key to this drawer?'

She looked slightly embarrassed for a moment, then nodded and reached inside her bodice to extract a key, which she brought over to him without refastening her top buttons.

'You understand that I respect the privacy of my tenants at all times, and that this key's just a duplicate for emergencies?'

'Yes, of course,' he reassured her as he opened the drawer, then stepped back sharply, as if he'd unearthed a live snake. He moved back cautiously and made a rough calculation of the bank notes to one side of the open drawer, arriving at a mental total of some two hundred pounds. Then he reached inside and lifted out the envelope that contained what proved to be a collection of postcards. Very specific types of postcards, all of which featured nubile ladies in their undergarments. And one at the very bottom without anything to cover her shame.

'My, my!' Mrs Morton cooed as she looked over Jack's shoulder. 'I knew he was a bit of a lad, but it seems that I underestimated him. If he comes back for these, I'll give him a red face and no mistake!'

Chapter Eight

Percy Enright gave a triumphant grin as he placed the selected records face up in front of him and confirmed a suspicion that had begun to form itself the previous day.

Sarah Cameron had been born "Sarah Mount" in Bow in 1854. Her parents had lived at the same address for some time, to judge by the census records compiled every ten years, and while she had two sisters younger than her, there was no brother, older or younger. The man who had warned him away from the staircase in Plough Court, whoever he might be, clearly had a reason other than a family one for ensuring that Sarah Cameron and her sickly child were not subjected to further scrutiny.

That reason might well be that Hector Cameron had been bribed in order to look the other way when police uniforms, and the wagon that went with them, had disappeared from his store. Bribed with either money or a promise that their sick child would be adequately provided for. Percy was in the process of mentally condemning Cameron for his weakness, and his betrayal of the law and order that he had been sworn in to uphold, when he thought of Jack, the nephew who had become like a son to him. What would he have done had he been in Cameron's place, and the sick child had been Jack? 'Walk a mile in my shoes', as he'd once heard somebody say, so perhaps he should go easy on Hector Cameron until he knew all the facts.

Of more concern was the admission by Inspector Greaves that he'd covered up Cameron's lapses. It could have been simply a matter of loyal sympathy for the unfortunate family circumstances in which a fellow officer with a previously unblemished record now found himself, or it could be something more sinister. An Inspector in any police station was in a perfect position to organise cover-ups, and indeed to instigate corrupt practices of his own. But insofar as Percy could judge from his own extensive experience of fellow officers, Greaves was a straight character — a bit on the weak side, perhaps, but straight. Which is probably more than could be said for George Ingram, the Inspector who'd thrown Jack out of Whitechapel police station when he began getting too close to what might prove to be an embarrassing set of truths regarding the inexplicable change of night duty allocations on the occasion of the Wapping warehouse fire.

Thoughts regarding Ingram's almost certain involvement in corrupt practices sent Percy in search of the man's service record, held centrally by the Yard ostensibly as a convenient means of centralising all manpower records, but in reality designed to give them an overview of the performance and efficiency of every man in the Met. Fifteen minutes later Percy was examining what to all intents and purposes was a splendid service record. George Ingram had been recruited as a constable in 1884 after a brief spell as an infantryman in the Rifle Corps during the First Sudan Campaign. He'd been allocated to Shoreditch, where following exemplary service as a constable, he'd been promoted to the rank of Sergeant and transferred to Stepney.

While holding down that rank, Ingram had been the man who had led the investigations following the discovery of an arms cache in a local house; investigations that had mysteriously culminated in the unexplained release from custody of the man who'd been occupying the house in which they'd been discovered, quite by accident, by two uniformed constables who'd entered the house in response to complaints regarding suspicious comings and goings. Percy consulted his notes and reminded himself that those two constables had been named Greenway and Padley, and the man who'd been released for no obvious reason had been one Nathaniel Hiscock.

Within two weeks of that bungle — further aggravated by the disappearance of many of the discovered weapons from the Scotland Yard vaults in which they were supposed to have been securely locked — Ingram had been promoted to Inspector and reallocated to Whitechapel's Leman Street Station, just in time to have become involved in whatever dark deed had replaced Constable Michael Black with Constable Edward Ainsworth, both of whom had now conveniently disappeared.

If Ingram wasn't corrupt, Percy concluded, then the moon was made of cream cheese. But since Jack appeared to have hit a brick wall when attempting to dig out more facts regarding the shift change on the night of the Bartrams fire, mainly due to the obstruction of Ingram himself, then Percy might be able to undermine Ingram's authority in one of two ways. The first would be to call in Special Branch over the man's head, but Percy was reluctant to take that course at this early stage, thereby blowing his own 'cover' and admitting his own inability to flush rats from sewers. The second option was to find some 'dirty linen' from Ingram's former days as a sergeant in Stepney, and it was in any case high time that he began investigating the worrying business of the missing arms stash.

Just over two hours later he was sitting in an office on the ground floor of Stepney's Arbour Square Police Station, talking with Ingram's successor, Sergeant Thomas Parker, a fussy little man who was clearly overawed by the sight of the letter from the Home Secretary that Percy had placed on his desk, in case there should be any doubt regarding his authority to ask questions.

'Without wishing to be disloyal in any way to my predecessor,' Parker told Percy with a worried frown, 'I have to admit that the records for Ingram's last few weeks as Sergeant here are a bit of a mess, and I haven't really had time to sort through them. Inspector Tomkins is well aware of the difficulty, but even so…'

'I may well be able to assist you,' Percy interrupted him, recognising a golden opportunity. 'My reason for being here is to assess your readiness for what may well be a considerable increase in crowd numbers on the day of the Diamond Jubilee celebrations, and if I can report favourably to the Home Office regarding your urgent need for additional manpower, then of course it would be of considerable assistance to you. The last thing I need to have to do is to report that your records are in a bit of a mess, so why don't I see what I can do to sort them out for you? It would be in both our interests, clearly.'

Sergeant Parker exchanged his frown for a smile of relief and gratitude.

'That would be magnificent, provided of course that there would be no adverse reflection on my own ability in that regard.'

'None whatsoever, let me reassure you,' Percy oozed back, and by the time that he returned from a substantial celebratory dinner at a local chop house, a room had been made available for him, and the desk was strewn with disorganised paper that Percy lost no time in sorting into piles, first by function and then by date.

He began with the cell records but could find no authorisation for the release from custody of Nathanial Hiscock, the man whose house in nearby Ellerdale Street had been used as the storage dump for what had been an alarming number of military issue rifles. Percy had a note of the date on which the discovery had been made — the seventeenth of August, barely two months ago — but when he checked the custody admission records for that date he quickly realised why no-one had been alerted to an unregistered release of a prisoner. The stark fact was that Nathaniel Hiscock had, according to the custody records, never been a prisoner in the first place. A gross piece of incompetence? A dreadful act of corruption? Or an inexcusable lapse in procedure on what had no doubt been a very eventful evening?

Percy needed to speak to one of the two officers who had brought Hiscock into custody in the first place, or the person on duty at the Charge Desk on the evening in question. The second question was answered as soon as Percy got the duty rosters for the past few months into some semblance of order, and he was far from surprised to learn that the Sergeant on duty at the Charge Desk had been none other than George Ingram himself. Since he would also have been in charge of the adjoining 'fish tank' in which all arrestees were first lodged before, in most cases, being transferred down to a cell, it would have been the easiest thing in the world for Ingram to release

Hiscock on the pretence of escorting him down to a cell, then quietly slipping him out of a side door.

That was, of course, assuming that Hiscock had made it as far as Stepney Police Station in the first place. The incident report for that night was conveniently missing from the morass of disorganised paper on the desk in front of him, so he would need to speak to the two officers who'd allegedly brought the man in. They were Constables Greenway and Padley, according to the far more reliable information in Percy's notebook, care of William Melville of Special Branch.

Percy was disappointed, but not entirely surprised, to hear what Sergeant Parker had to tell him as he handed over the records that he'd managed to sort into some semblance of order.

'I'm mightily obliged to you,' Parker told him with a reverential smile, 'and that makes it even more embarrassing for me to have to advise you that neither of the men you wish to speak to are available.'

'Have they *both* been subsequently murdered?'

'Only one of them — Greenway,' Percy was advised. 'He was found in the alleyway alongside a tanners' yard in Barrett's Court, where according to bystanders he'd gone to investigate a woman's screams for help.'

'Let me guess — no sign of said woman, but every indication that he'd been lured up there to his death?'

'How did you guess?'

'Years of bitter experience,' Percy grimaced back. 'No man on my shift would have been allowed up there on his own, but then again I gather than you're short of manpower — even shorter now that Greenway's been done in. What about Padley?'

'Promoted to the Yard at about the same time that George Ingram went to Whitechapel.'

'It figures,' Percy nodded sadly, 'but at least I think I can work out how the rifles came to be stolen afterwards.'

'They were transferred to the Yard, on Sergeant Ingram's instructions,' Parker told him. Percy raised both eyebrows at him and waited or the penny to drop. 'You don't think that…?'

'Don't I?'

'You mean that Jim Padley … that is … I mean, he wouldn't. Would he?'

'Would, and probably *did*, Sergeant. But don't worry — you've done nothing to reproach yourself for. Which makes you stand out somewhat in this place.'

Jack hung around on the pavement outside Leman Street Police Station until he was certain that it was Albert Preedy on duty at the Charge Desk, then shuffled in with his head down before raising it again with a friendly grin as he reached the counter.

'You chancy bugger!' Preedy grinned back at him. 'If the Inspector catches you back in here, I'll be the one instructed to put your arse back outside on the pavement.'

'All the more reason for me to keep this brief.' Jack grinned back at him as he cast a cautious eye up the staircase just in case. 'When are you due your meal break?'

'Half an hour or so, why?'

'Fancy a meat pie?'

'Better than the cheese sandwiches the missus packed me this morning. Where?'

'"Jimmy's", around the corner. My treat.'

'It's a deal,' Preedy replied with another smile. 'Now bugger off, before we both get caught.'

'So what are you really after, assuming that it wasn't just the pleasure of my company?' Preedy asked as he smiled his thanks for the brown paper bag containing a mutton pie that Jack had just handed him.'

'Information.'

'So what do you need to know?'

'Any unidentified stiffs pulled out of St Katherine's Dock lately?'

'How lately?'

'Any time since that warehouse fire on Beat Four. Probably hammered into a state that made it unrecognisable before it went for a swim.'

'Funnily enough, we sent one to the mortuary last week some time,' Preedy advised him with a shudder. 'It was stinking to high heaven, so we ordered it down the road on a handcart.'

'How was it dressed?'

'From memory, like it was going to church, why — what's this all about?'

'I take it that Edward — or "Teddy" — Ainsworth hasn't shown up for duty recently?'

'No, why?'

'I think he may be your stiff.'

'Far from "stiff", as I recall,' Preedy replied as he all but dry-retched. 'Running all over the place would be a better description — it must have been a fortnight old, at a guess. But do you *really* reckon it was Teddy Ainsworth?'

'That'd be my guess,' Jack replied. 'I suppose he was too far gone to recognise his face?'

'I don't recall the poor bugger having any face left, to tell you the sickening truth.'

'And none of you undressed the corpse?'

'What do you think?'

'So the body went down to the mortuary fully clothed?'

'Yes. We didn't even search it for personal possessions, since Inspector Ingram wouldn't let it through the door.'

'Perfect!' Jack whispered, almost to himself, but Preedy was curious.

'You might at least tell me what this is all about.'

Jack thought briefly and decided to risk it. 'I was puzzled as to why Ainsworth didn't report back for duty the night after he seemingly allowed a warehouse to go up in flames a few yards from where his arse should have been parked for the entire shift. So I made enquiries of his landlady and learned that he was last seen heading towards St Katherine Dock with a floozy on his arm. I reckon she was some sort of decoy.'

'If she was an acquaintance of Teddy Ainsworth's, she was probably more than a decoy, if you get my meaning. Did you search his lodgings?'

'Naturally.'

'Find anything significant?'

'You're referring to his dirty postcards, aren't you?'

'It was just a thought,' Preedy explained. 'Now that you clearly know what Teddy was like, you won't be surprised to learn that he may have been lured to his death by a tottie, will you?'

'Not half as surprised as he probably was.'

Later that afternoon Jack pushed open the rubber doors to the local mortuary, with its pervading smells of carbolic and formaldehyde, consoling himself that at least it covered the much worse smells that assailed his nostrils as he picked his way gingerly through the belongings that had come in here with the corpse from St Katherine Dock. With a muted grunt of triumph, reluctant to open his mouth to the sickening miasma by which he was surrounded, he located what looked like a set of solid silver cufflinks.

On one side were the engraved initials 'EA', which he hoped denoted their owner as Edward Ainsworth, while the reverse had a silversmith's mark that he believed revealed the manufacturer as having been 'Mappin and Webb'. If he was right, then it was a simple process of confirming the purchaser for whom these cufflinks had been manufactured — someone whom the silversmiths had no doubt believed to be a wealthy man about town, when in fact he had been a police constable with expensive tastes and a lifestyle that made him ripe for corruption.

'So what have we got?' Percy asked as he and Jack lowered themselves into the facing armchairs in the sitting room, ahead of a Tuesday supper that threatened to be another of Aunt Beattie's culinary experiments designed to test their gastric fortitude.

'I went back to Leman Street and traded on an old friendship. That was of course after I'd been shown the door by Inspector Ingram, but not before I'd been able to confirm that Michael Black — the constable who was originally allocated to Beat Four in Wapping, right outside Bartrams — had a gambling problem, fell in with some unidentified soldier, then claimed to have had a substantial win at cards before disappearing over a week before the warehouse was set on fire. No idea where he's got to, but his replacement Edward Ainsworth was living a high old lifestyle way beyond his means, was fond of the ladies, and was decoyed down to St Katherine Dock, where I believe his corpse was found in an unidentifiable state some two weeks later. However, among his possessions was a set of solid silver cufflinks, and I showed my police badge to the mortuary attendant — who thank God hadn't realised how valuable they were — and brought them home with me. Tomorrow I hope to confirm that they belonged to Edward Ainsworth. Not bad for a day's work.'

'You were thrown out of Leman Street by Inspector Ingram? That seems to confirm what my investigations have revealed, and it all seems to come back to George Ingram, whichever way you roll the dice. You might want to take a note of what I've discovered, because it gets a bit complicated.'

Jack extracted his notebook and pencil, while Percy leaned back in his chair, blowing pipe smoke lazily into the air in between snippets of acquired knowledge.

'As we agreed,' he began, 'I began looking into the phony story I was fed by Mrs Cameron regarding her son. She never had a brother, so the man who turned up was clearly sent to warn me off any further investigation. I'm now all but convinced that Hector Cameron was bribed to look the other way when certain persons up to no good stole the police uniforms and wagon that were used to rob the jewellers in Hatton Garden. But at this stage I've no reason to suspect his Inspector of anything other than misguided loyalty in covering up for him. Which is more than can be said for that arsehole George Ingram, as I discovered when I made enquiries at Stepney police station.'

'In connection with those rifles found in a local house?' Jack recalled, and Percy nodded.

'Indeed. There's a new Sergeant down there, and he seems to be an honest enough cove. From what he could tell me, and what I worked out for myself when I went through the paper explosion that passes for records in Stepney, the weapons were discovered when two constables called Greenway and Padley gained entry to a house occupied by this bloke Hiscock. That's when it gets a bit murky, since according to the records, Hiscock wasn't even taken into custody, which perhaps helps to explain why there's no record of his release. And lo and behold, the Sergeant in charge of custodies that night just happened to be our old friend George Ingram, who, far from being disciplined for his laxity in record keeping, was promoted with indecent haste to his current position as an Inspector at Leman Street.'

'So Hiscock went free?'

'So it would seem.'

'And the rifles?'

'Transferred to the Yard, from where some of them subsequently disappeared, of course. But there was another transfer out of Stepney at the same time as Ingram's. Constable Padley can now be found somewhere inside the Yard, where I strongly suspect I'll discover, when I ask some pointed questions tomorrow morning, he was allocated to stores duties.'

'A bit blatant, surely?'

'Not if someone higher up is covering for you.'

'Inside the *Yard*?'

'What makes you think that the Yard is any less open to corruption than the rest of the Met? And hadn't we already begun to suspect that the rot starts high up? William Melville warned me that I might be approached from within the Yard to join the conspiracy. I don't think it will be long before the waves I'm about to make threaten to rock the boat. But therein lies a risk, since you haven't asked me what happened to Constable Greenway.'

'Something tells me that it wasn't good,' Jack grimaced.

'And you'd be right. Lured up an alleyway by the screams of a woman no doubt amply rewarded for her vocal talents, then done to death in the course of his duty.'

'And we could meet a similar fate?' Jack protested. 'I'm the father of four children, let me remind you.'

'They'll come for me before they even consider you,' Percy assured him. 'But at least you'll be left to point the finger.'

'I'm about to point *two* fingers,' Jack replied sternly. 'Both of them in your direction.'

Chapter Nine

The following morning Percy frowned in disbelief as he read the file on Constable James Padway's duty allocations since his transfer to the Yard following his discovery of the arms cache in the Stepney house. At least he'd not met the same fate as his colleague Walter Greenway, done to death in a back alley, but he'd no doubt proved to be the only one of the two who was open to corruption, and his immediate allocation to 'stores management' was so blatant that someone within the Yard must have been covering up.

In only the second week of Padway's night shift in the 'Stolen Goods Repository' that he was supposed to be guarding, seventy-eight Martini Henri rifles had gone missing. This would not have come to light had his day shift opposite number not taken it upon himself to conduct a stock-take in order to relieve the boredom, and Padway had got away with it by pointing out that the previous stock-take had been a month earlier, two weeks before his allocation to the stores duty, and therefore no-one could confirm that the rifles must have disappeared during his period of duty. This conveniently overlooked the fact that the rifles in question — well over a hundred and fifty — had not been delivered to the store by the date of the previous stock-take, but had been stacked against the far wall, still in their boxes, a week before Padway was entrusted with their security.

At the same time, Percy was puzzled as to why the rifles had been allowed to be transferred to the Yard in the first place. Assuming that Sergeant Ingram, as he then was, had been perfectly capable of arranging for Nathanial Hiscock to escape from custody without having ever been officially in it in the first place, why could Ingram not have had the rifles stolen long before they reached the Yard? The slightly encouraging answer was that someone within Stepney police station had alerted the Stolen Property team within the Yard, and they had lost no time in doing the right thing. There were, it seemed, at least some officers in the Met who played by the rules. Then Percy reminded himself that he had a reputation for doing exactly the opposite, and that he shouldn't be so judgmental.

'I might have known you'd waste no time in crossing even the broad and uncertain lines of operation that you were given,' Chief Superintendent Bray glowered from Percy's doorway. 'And to judge by the written complaint that just landed on my desk from Inspector Ingram in Leman Street, you've passed the disease on to your nephew.'

'Your point being?' Percy said coldly.

'My point being that your remit from the Home Secretary was to review manpower and readiness within Met stations — not to do the same at the Yard, or to hint at corruption *anywhere* within the Met.'

'Should you not be concerned to learn of the potential corruption that we *have* uncovered?' Percy demanded huffily. This seemed to galvanise Bray into entering the office and taking a seat uninvited as he glared across the desk at Percy.

'I've been ordered to tolerate your shit-stirring outside the Yard, Percy, but don't fool yourself for one minute that I'm prepared to tolerate it on my patch. No doubt you believe that Jim Padley was responsible for the loss of those rifles from "Stolen Property", but I've already conducted my own investigations into that, and there's no evidence of his involvement, so put that file on your desk back where it belongs.'

'I'm not convinced that you were correct in absolving him from any involvement...' Percy began, only to be silenced by Bray bringing his fist down heavily on the desk.

'That's an *order*, Inspector! If I had my way, you wouldn't even be back in here like a bad smell in a flower vase! You've only got your arse behind this desk on the direct authority of the Home Secretary, but that cuts two ways. You'll stick rigidly to the conditions of your reinstatement, or else you'll be out of here. And those conditions do not permit you to cast aspersions on the way I run my own particular corner of the Yard. One more step over the line, and you'll be stepping out of the door for good and proper. Got that?'

'Loudly and clearly,' Percy muttered as he locked eyes with Bray. Without a further word being exchanged between them, Bray removed the file from the desk in front of Percy, rose from the visitor's chair and stormed out of the office.

'I really think I should be back on my feet, dear,' Constance Enright complained yet again as Esther plumped up the pillows behind her head, then tutted. 'And don't tut like that — it's not ladylike,' Constance added. 'The doctor clearly said — in your hearing as well as mine — that I could get up after a couple of days.'

'*Three* days,' Esther reminded her, 'and today's only Wednesday — the second day. We've got all this correspondence to sort through, and you can supervise that equally well from your bed, so let's get on with it.'

'I can't write while I'm sitting up in bed,' Constance grumbled, 'and I hate to burden you with all the replies.'

'It's no burden,' Esther assured her, 'and it gives me something to do apart from listening to Nell trying to stop

Miriam from staggering into furniture or wandering into dangerous places like the kitchen.'

'If I follow the doctor's orders and stay in bed until tomorrow,' Constance wheedled, 'could I come for a leisurely stroll up the road, like he recommended, and walk to your place for morning tea or something?'

'I don't think that would be a very good idea. Doctor Browning suggested that the limit of any leisurely stroll should be the crossroads, and it's another quarter of a mile or so down Bunting Lane from there. I couldn't forgive myself if something happened to you on your way to our house.'

'But surely you'd welcome the company?'

'I have your company in equal measure when I come here, don't I?' Esther pointed out. 'So let's not hear any more unwise suggestions about you over-reaching yourself and disobeying doctor's orders. Now, where do you want to start with all this lot?'

Jack opted to celebrate his latest discovery at 'Jimmy's Tea House', around the corner from Leman Street Police Station, waiting for Albert Preedy to at some stage slip out for a meat pie, as they had vaguely agreed at the end of their first assignation there. Then Jack would be able to report that according to Mappin and Webb, the cufflinks on the corpse pulled out of St Katherine Dock in a very ripe condition had indeed belonged to Teddy Ainsworth, suggesting that the rest of the gruesome find was also him. Jack was also hoping for an additional 'lead' on the missing Michael Black.

The early middle-aged lady who reminded him of his mother stood looking down at him for a moment from the other side of the table that he was occupying alone, before enquiring, 'Is this seat vacant?' Jack nodded, and she added, 'It's just that one can't be too cautious these days, and with you being a police officer I'd feel safer in your company.' She put her mug of tea down on the table and slid into the opposite seat.

'How did you know that I was a police officer?'

'You *are* Detective Sergeant Jack Enright, are you not?'

When Jack nodded, open-mouthed, she smiled reassuringly.

'Perhaps as well, because I'd hate to have been following the wrong person.'

'Following for how long — and *why*, precisely?'

'All the way from the West End, when you came out of that jewellers with a big smile on your face. You obviously didn't spot me, which is good, but I have a message for your uncle from William Melville.'

'You mean Melville from...?' Jack blurted but stopped himself as the lady shushed him to silence.

'"Careless lips", and all that, but you're correct. He wants Percy to be on the Thames Embankment, under Cleopatra's Needle, at noon tomorrow, reading tomorrow's *Daily Mail*. There'll be someone there to meet with him. Now, since you appear to have finished your tea, you'd best be getting along before we're seen together. If anyone asks, I'm your aunt.'

'Assistant Commissioner Doyle would like to see you,' the uniformed constable advised Percy through the open door.

Five minutes later Percy tapped tentatively on the half open door that revealed on its glass panel that it gave access to the office of the fourth most senior officer within Scotland Yard. The long head that appeared to be carved from granite inclined upwards, and Doyle smiled.

'Inspector Enright, do come in. I don't believe we've ever met, but I'm Brian Doyle. I came up through the West End and Westminster, whereas I'm told that you're an East End man, so that probably explains it. Tea?'

Percy nodded with a smile of his own, and took the seat indicated by the wave of the age-spotted hand while the Assistant Commissioner raised the receiver from the telephone on his desk and ordered tea and biscuits for two.

'Bray giving you a hard time, is he?' Doyle enquired, almost casually. When Percy's face registered surprise, Doyle smiled reassuringly.

'Not much gets past me up here. He roasted your arse earlier this morning, didn't he? Why was that?'

'I'm not at liberty to say, sir, I'm afraid.'

Doyle frowned. 'If you're working on something important, and Bray's blocking you, I can easily pull him from out of your hair. You must realise that.'

'I'm aware of your rank, obviously,' Percy replied guardedly, 'but I'm afraid that I report elsewhere.'

'Special Branch?' Doyle enquired with a broad smile, but Percy remained tight-lipped as Doyle added, 'Your face just said it all, Percy. Just relax, there's a good man.'

The tea and biscuits appeared, and Doyle poured for them both while pushing the plate closer to Percy.

'I respect and admire your integrity and confidentiality, Percy, but if you're to penetrate the brick wall that operates in this dump of a place, you're going to need friends in high places. I can open doors that you can only kick against.'

'I'm well aware of that, sir, but even so...'

'It must be very frustrating for a man in your position,' Doyle continued without any seeming annoyance at Percy's stubborn intransigence. 'You're well known as a crusader for social justice, whereas most of the idiots occupying the ranks between you and me seem dedicated only towards climbing the ladder and preserving their pensions. It's time for the wind of change to blast through this place, and men like you will be well placed when it does. What you might call a "new order" in policing the Met. That must surely appeal to you?'

Percy chose his words carefully. 'I joined the Met to protect society, sir, and nothing in the past thirty years has dented that ambition. The day that the strong are allowed to rule the weak is the day we can all dig a hole in the ground and attempt to hide in it. As for what you call a "new order", isn't that what those who're currently trying to undermine the Russian royal house claim to be promoting?'

'And what makes you think that they're wrong?' Doyle enquired, the smile fading slightly.

'They aren't, necessarily. What I object to are the methods they're employing.'

'And what do you know about those, precisely?' Doyle challenged him. 'Whatever corruption you find in the Met, or for that matter the Yard, you report directly to me, understand? Underlings like Bray are just seeking to feather their own nests and preserve their own pensions. The real authority begins on my level, and don't ever forget that.'

'Certainly not, sir. May I get back to work now?'

'You may, Percy, but be careful of the questions you ask, because you may not like the answers you get.'

'It was a very definite warning,' Percy told Jack that evening as they sat awaiting supper, 'and a far from friendly one at that. Thank God that Melville's finally back in touch, since I'd have needed to report back to him without delay anyway, and I had no idea how to do it without alerting suspicion. That lady you had tea with must have been one of his undercover ferrets.'

'She reminded me more of Mother than a ferret,' Jack smiled, 'but you're sure that it's safe to follow the instruction?'

'Do I have a choice?'

Jack slowly shook his head. 'I suppose not. How do you intend to pass on everything we've learned so far, including the obvious murders of Constables Greenway and Ainsworth, not to mention the possible murder of Constable Black?'

'Tomorrow morning I'll put it all in writing, along with my strong suspicion that corruption in the Yard runs as high as Doyle. Then hopefully there'll be an opportunity to pass it to whoever I meet with at noon.'

'Do you want me to follow behind you, just in case?'

'So that you can be followed in your turn?' Percy smiled. 'That lady you met today managed to trail you without you being aware of the fact, and I don't want Melville to gain the impression that we don't trust him.'

'And do we?'

'We have no choice, at this stage. Although the further we stick our heads into this ants' nest, the less confident I am about anyone or anything.'

'I have a horrible feeling that I've got as far as I can with my side of the investigations,' Jack said. 'Between us we've confirmed that certain corners of the Met have been corrupted, and all of it seemingly to the same end. Whoever's behind all this has acquired military uniforms and guns with considerable ease, that's obvious. But we're no closer to finding out *who*, or *why*.'

'Perhaps that's all that Melville wanted from us,' Percy speculated. 'I'll be able to report our findings tomorrow, and that may be the end of it. But if Special Branch wants us for anything else, no doubt I'll be informed.'

'Do you think it would be in order for me to go back to Barking?' Jack asked hopefully. 'I'm not sure what sort of reception I'll get, but if this really is the end of our appointed task, then I see no reason for staying here and incurring more of Esther's displeasure.'

'Leave it until I've contacted Melville's messenger tomorrow,' Percy suggested. 'Tomorrow's Thursday, and you can slip back home with a clear conscience on Friday morning unless we have some additional urgent work to do.'

'And in the meantime?'

'In the meantime you'll be facing more danger; your Aunt Beattie's cooking another of her special dishes from that menu book she must have acquired from the local undertaker's.'

On the Thursday morning, just as Big Ben boomed out midday, Percy approached Cleopatra's Needle carrying his newspaper and hoping that he wouldn't be kept waiting in the cold October wind that was blowing up the Thames, all the way from Southend by the feel of it. Discarded newspapers and food wrappers blew in gusts past his feet, and he extended silent heartfelt sympathy towards the tramp who sat perched on the top step of the plinth on which the Needle was mounted, seeking shelter from the icy blasts as his layers of old clothing flapped around him. The man had the right idea, however, Percy concluded as he mounted the steps himself and attempted to open that day's copy of the *Daily Mail* that stubbornly refused to lie flat in his hands in order to disclose its inner contents.

Ten minutes later he'd read, for the third time, the lead story about the latest leg of Tsar Nicholas's grand tour of Europe following his coronation earlier that year. He tutted with irritation, extracted his fob watch, flipped open its metal cover and reminded himself that he'd spent almost fifteen minutes wasting his time and risking influenza.

'Patience is a virtue, Percy,' said the tramp.

Percy whipped round in disbelief at the grinning face of the elderly vagrant seated with his back to the base of the plinth. 'You?'

'Did you expect me to approach you holding up a placard bearing the name of my department? What can you tell me?'

'It's all written down in a report tucked safely inside my overcoat,' Percy assured him, 'but how can I hand it over without alerting suspicion?'

'When we've finished talking, go down into the Gents by way of that staircase just ahead of you, place the report inside the newspaper, come back up, then throw the newspaper into that rubbish bin by the embankment wall. I'll pick it up when I leave. But don't go just yet — just step up to my level, as if you're trying to get a better view over the top of the retaining wall down into the river, then I can speak more softly.'

Percy did as instructed, and the man continued.

'Our friend wishes you to concentrate your efforts on the Westminster police stations, particularly the 'A' Division office in Bow Street. Find what links you can to the Wellington Barracks in Birdcage Walk, which will be the headquarters of the Foot Guards who'll be the Queen's first line of defence on her parade next year. Report back your preliminary findings a week today, at the same time, but not here.'

'Where, then?'

'Westminster Abbey, next to the baptismal font. On that occasion I'll be a priest in holy orders.'

Chapter Ten

Jack hummed happily to himself as he alighted from the train and began to swing his portmanteau eagerly through the darkness of late-evening Barking. The occasional gas lamps with their arcs of light cast a shimmer over the pools left by the sleet shower that had taken itself further south-west towards the northern outer suburbs of London, and as far as Jack was concerned they deserved it. He'd devoted the past four days to the people of the capital, and now it was his turn.

Uncle Percy had returned from his somewhat surreal encounter with the man briefed by Special Branch bearing the good tidings that they had finished with the East End but were now to concentrate their efforts on the far more salubrious environs of the West End. A hasty counsel of war over a pot of tea in a Whitehall tea shop across the road from the Yard had ended with the conclusion that the West End would still be there on Monday morning, and that since Percy had no burning desire to remain in their begrudged office, exposed to further verbal violence from Chief Superintendent Bray and further dark warnings from Assistant Commissioner Doyle, he could hardly expect Jack to do so either. The attractive alternative for which they had opted was that Percy would spend Friday digging in the last of the runner bean foliage that would fertilise his vegetable patch for the spring, while Jack would take his laundry on a late train from Fenchurch Street and return to the bosom of his family.

As Jack approached the house he reminded himself that his welcome home would be likely to be of the chilled variety, unless Esther had missed him so much that she was prepared to forgive him. He looked up eagerly for the anticipated welcoming glow from the house lights but saw only darkness. He would have to wait until tomorrow to greet his family.

The following morning as Esther sat warming her hands on a cup of tea, she grumbled, 'Some warning would have been nice.'

'I didn't know myself until around mid-afternoon, then I had to collect my things from Hackney and run for a late train.'

'The "things from Hackney" can go into the copper after breakfast, while you remind the children of the father they're in danger of forgetting.'

'I realise that I'm still in the bad books,' Jack sighed with resignation, 'but that's rather an exaggeration. I take it that everyone's fine?'

'The children are, although Bertie's going down with a sniffle that he probably caught when he got his feet wet through splashing in puddles all the way home from school on Tuesday. And your mother took a funny turn the day before.'

'By "a funny turn", I take it you don't mean that she's finally succumbed to a sense of humour?'

'A mild heart attack, according to Dr Browning. She was confined to bed for three days, and I managed to keep her there, but now she's threatening to walk up here every day, allegedly on doctor's orders, since he told her to lose weight and take some gentle exercise.'

'But she's OK?'

'She seems to be now, but it was quite dramatic at the time. Anyway, to forestall her coming up here you might want to call in on her this morning. That sounds like Lily and Bertie in the opening salvos of their daily warfare, so I'll leave them to you while I see to your laundry.'

'Daddy!' was the collective cry of delight that rang through the house, and even little Miriam was able to chortle 'Doddee' in her throaty style as she smiled up at him from the living room floor. After two hours supervising the democratic utilisation of the backyard swing by Lily and Bertie in equal turns, Jack announced his intention of wandering down the road to the family home in Church Street to surprise his mother.

'She's on a diet imposed by Dr Browning,' Esther advised him, 'so dinner will probably only be a cold salad.'

'At least it'll be warmer than the welcome home I got last night,' Jack muttered as he pecked Esther on the cheek and warned the children to be good.

'I didn't think you were coming back until tomorrow,' Constance told him as she wrapped her arms around him and shouted an instruction to Cook to put more potatoes on to boil. 'Esther must have been delighted.'

'If she was, she kept it well hidden,' Jack grimaced. 'I was made about as welcome as a burglar.'

Constance smiled. 'Shows how little you know about women. She feels neglected, that's all. You men are all the same; career minded, and family comes second. Your father was like it, and the stress took him to an early grave.'

'So, assure me that you're not headed in the same direction,' Jack looked down at her with a mock sternness. 'Esther told me all about your heart attack.'

'Even the doctor said that it was a *mild* one,' Constance protested, 'although I wouldn't let *him* loose on my canary. It was indigestion, that was all, and I only stayed in bed to please Esther, who was *so* bossy all last week. A far cry from the shy young thing you first brought home.'

'Esther's *never* been shy in all the time I've known her,' Jack protested. 'And if she *was* being firm then it was for your own good.'

'She clearly enjoyed seeing me confined to bed, anyway. And she positively refused to let me walk up to your house when the time came for me to take some gentle exercise — almost as if she had something to hide up there.'

'What, you mean a lover or something?' Jack joked, and Constance frowned again.

'Don't be vulgar, Jack. No-one could ever accuse Esther of anything like that. But she certainly didn't want me around in your absence. Would you like sherry before we eat? So good for the digestion, I always maintain, and the last thing I need is another dose of indigestion that some quack can pass off as a heart attack.'

By the time that Jack had his portmanteau packed ready for his Sunday return to London on the mid-afternoon train, Esther was clearly edgy about something. She barely spoke a word over Sunday dinner, and was picking at her food in that way she had when something was bothering her. Jack opted for silence, rather than provoke more recrimination about the fact that he was going back to stay with his uncle and aunt, and it wasn't until he reached down towards the hall carpet to pick up his luggage that Esther finally cracked and flung her arms around him as tears rolled down her face.

'Sorry for being such a miserable cow this weekend, Jack, but I love you and miss you so badly when you're away that it somehow makes me angry with you when you have to go. I know you have an important job to do and wouldn't be leaving us if it was something you could possibly avoid, but just know that I love you and I always will. Stay safe, darling man.'

She kissed him, then tore herself away and raced into the sitting room, bawling her eyes out. Nell rushed out from the scullery where she had been drying the dinner dishes, a huge question written across her broad freckled face.

'Is the mistress sick?'

'No — just sick of having to say goodbye to me. Go in and comfort her, if you can, then make her a pot of tea.'

'So how do you suggest we tackle Bow Street?' Jack asked Percy as they sat in their usual seats on either side of the fire, awaiting the ill tidings from the kitchen. Percy thought deeply for a moment as he sucked on his pipe.

'All my experience has been in East End stations, the same as you, so we'll need time to adjust to the rhythm and atmosphere of a West End establishment. My preliminary thought is that we go in together, ostensibly doing a full manpower audit, and that if possible we get to know the officers in there on a personal level. The word from Special Branch is that they've formed some sort of unhealthy association with the soldiers from the nearby Wellington Barracks, and if there's to be any risk to the Queen's personal safety during her triumphant progress up the Mall towards Westminster Abbey or wherever, then it may well come from the infantry walking on either side of her open coach, or the bobbies holding back the loyal crowds.'

'So all our efforts in the East End were a waste of time?'

'Of course not. We at least confirmed that elements of the Met have been corrupted, and by that means whoever's behind all this gained access to guns and uniforms. But it's unlikely that the Diamond Jubilee procession will go anywhere near the East End, so the next stage in our investigations is to try to find out if they have anything planned for the West End, and if so — what?'

'Wouldn't it be simpler just to do without a procession?'

'Then what sort of Jubilee would it be? The people want to see their Queen, Jack, and God knows they see little enough of her these days.'

'Do we know precisely where the procession will be staged?'

'*We* don't, and I doubt that anyone does, at this stage. But if we're able to get some useful intelligence on any plot, then we may be able to change the route at the last minute.'

'I must admit,' Jack said smiling, 'that when I first joined the police, I never thought that I'd be involved in the protection of the Queen from would-be assassins.'

'From what I can gather,' Percy told him, 'she may not be the main target. What they're seeking to achieve is chaos, and there's obviously more than one way of generating that. The assassination of the Queen is perhaps too obvious, but if they can disrupt the normal working of what passes for national security, they may be in with a chance of imposing a form of "order" of their own.'

'And who exactly are "they"?'

Percy shrugged. 'Who knows? There's no shortage of disaffected groups here in London. Jewish refugees from Russia, for one. As Esther can testify, they've been given a hard time in our so-called English "society". And talking of Russians, we read in the paper every day of the unrest being fomented against the Tsar by the great unwashed of his country, downtrodden for generations by the royal family, a bit like our own East Enders, who could easily be persuaded to unite with them in some sort of "world order" of the working class. I was also advised by Melville that Kaiser Wilhelm of Germany would love to see a Europe of which he's the big boss, and popular uprisings against the existing ruling classes of nations such as England would be right up his street.'

'It's a long list,' Jack agreed. 'We only have to hope that they don't all get their heads together. If they do, and law and order as we know it breaks down, what happens to people like you and me, who've dedicated our lives to the maintenance of the current system?'

Percy looked meaningfully across at him. 'I don't care to think about that, Jack, but since you've raised the subject you should keep in the forefront of your mind that what we're doing isn't simply in order to protect an old lady with a large family and an even larger waistline. She symbolises the society that we're striving to maintain and uphold; when and if she goes, then so do we, and if they taught you any history in that posh school of yours, then you may recall that when the monarchy fell in France just over a hundred years ago now, a lot of heads were chopped off people whose only sin was that they *looked* like the old order.'

'So we're doing this for ourselves as well?'

Percy nodded. 'Ourselves, and those we love, such as Esther, your children, your mother, and everyone else who's dear to us. Including your Aunt Beattie, who even now is trying to subvert the existing order from the inside, poisoning her nearest and dearest. If she doesn't achieve that, then there are plenty out there who'll happily do the job for her by more direct means.'

The next morning they were welcomed into Bow Street Police Station, rather over-effusively, Percy noted, by Chief Inspector Lionel Markwell, who Jack thought more closely resembled a tin soldier from Bertie's collection than a career-hardened senior police officer. He was straight-backed, moustached, and dressed in the most immaculate police uniform Jack had ever seen. Jack wasn't sure whether to shake the proffered hand or salute as Markwell waved them into chairs ranged in front of his impressively clear desk.

'Assistant Commissioner Doyle advised me that you were coming,' Markwell told them with a thin-lipped smile, 'and I feel sure that you'll find everything in order.'

Advised you, or warned you? Percy asked himself as he replied for them both. 'I'm sure that we will, Chief Inspector, but we're not here in any disciplinary capacity. It's just that the Home Secretary is very keen to ensure that you have sufficient manpower to allow a safe route through the crowds lining whichever streets are chosen for the celebratory procession. I don't suppose you've been advised of the final chosen route?'

'It hasn't yet been fully agreed, but we can be assured of sufficient manpower, since this station is always the first choice of men leaving the armed forces, as I did myself in my day. The Met is anxious to recruit the best of those who prefer to fight on the home front against crime and disorder in our own streets, rather than prop up some unworthy Heathen tribe in a far-flung dung heap.'

'Yes, the British Empire *is* rather over-extended,' Percy agreed with a wry smile, 'and it's nice to meet someone with a well-developed sense of priorities when it comes to the best interests of Queen and Country.'

'I can see that we're going to get along famously,' Markwell smiled broadly, 'and I'm very proud to be able to afford you every courtesy and facility as you learn just how well prepared we are here in "A" Division, and most notably here in Bow Street. I've allocated you your own office on the second floor, Inspector, from which you can run your own show. As for your Sergeant here, I thought he might best benefit from sharing an office with one of my finest middle-rankers, Sergeant Brennan. Liam had a fine record with the Coldstreams out in the Sudan, and within only a couple of years of his transfer into a police uniform he'd proved his mettle in the streets as well. As you'll be aware, some of our late-night revellers around Piccadilly Circus can get a bit out of hand, and Liam Brennan's our first choice to send in with a diplomatic request to go home and sleep it off.'

'The sort of late-nighters we encountered in the East End usually required a billy club to move them on,' Percy replied, and Markwell smiled condescendingly.

'I think you'll find that we are able to handle matters more diplomatically here in the west, Inspector. You may wish to allow your Sergeant here to go out on patrol one day with some of our finest, in order to get the flavour of things in our Division. He's tall enough not to look out of place among so many ex guardsmen.'

'I'm sure he'll look forward to that,' Percy answered with a sidelong glance at Jack before he had time to say anything to the contrary.

Constance Enright was tired to the point of frustration of being cooped up in her own sitting room day after day. After all, she had a position to maintain in the local community, and if she were not seen in public for over a week, there were some in the Ladies' Guild who might take that as a sign that there was a need for change in its committee, and that would never do.

It was at least a dry day, if a somewhat cold one, and she donned her best leather walking boots, adjusted her feather hat with the aid of the mirror hanging by the front door, shouted a last instruction to Cook that since she was about to indulge in a little healthy exercise, something other than chicken salad might be justified on the dinner table. Then she opened her front door and struck out boldly in her return to civilised society.

The doctor had suggested that she go no further than the crossroads, but that old fool probably knew nothing about real medicine, else he'd be practising in Marylebone rather than stuck in some country practice like Barking. Besides which, no-one could assess her health better than she could — it *was* her own body after all — so where would be the harm in turning right at the crossroads and walking all the way down to Esther's? That way, she could not only prove *her* wrong as well, but also check for herself whether or not there had been a letter from the Bishop's office, praising Constance's management of the recent Harvest Festival arrangements that Esther had kept hidden from her in a misguided but well-intentioned belief that the excitement might be too much for her.

She nodded regally to those of her acquaintance who were worthy of acknowledgement as she moved sedately up Church Lane like a galleon in full sail. She wasn't even out of breath by the time that she reached the crossroads and noted with concern that the windows of the bakery were in dire need of a good wash. If the inside was kept as clean as the outside, she concluded, then it might be a good idea to transfer their order elsewhere, before food poisoning was added to her gastric difficulties. She then became aware of the tall handsome young man who walked eagerly across her line of sight to continue his brisk progress from what had no doubt been the local station, on into Bunting Lane.

He strode like an army general leading his men into battle, Constance noted with approval. Just the sort of man that she had hoped her daughter Lucy would have met and fallen for, rather than that rather drippy architect Edward Wilton, although his income was most acceptable. The man was striding so strongly, and with such purpose in his step, that Constance was well behind him, and losing ground on him rapidly, as he approached the driveway to Esther and Jack's house. Then Constance stopped dead in her tracks from sheer shocked disbelief.

As the man neared the driveway, Esther ran out with a very broad smile of welcome, and threw her arms wide open and ran into the man's arms as he swung her round and round, her feet inches from the ground.

That was enough walking for one day, Constance assured herself as she lowered her head and turned back the way she had come in a very disturbed frame of mind. No wonder Esther had not wanted her mother-in-law around.

Chapter Eleven

'You'll find that we're a pretty friendly lot,' Liam Brennan assured Jack from the desk opposite his in the office that they were sharing.

Jack raised his eyes from the sheets of manpower records that had been brought down to him from the all-purpose Repository on the top floor of the impressive three-storied building that was the headquarters for over one hundred men of assorted ranks. 'I'm told that quite a few of these live in a special accommodation block down the road,' he replied. 'That must make it easier for them to get to know each other.'

'Indeed it does,' Liam confirmed in the faint lingering brogue that betrayed an Irish ancestry. 'But even those who live elsewhere can mix outside work, because we have a social club that we're all members of.'

'Sounds very cosy,' Jack responded in a slightly disinterested tone that he hoped would provoke further confidences.

'And so it is,' came the responding assurance. 'If you're free one evening I'll take you along there. We have a bar, and we play cards. Some of the men bring along their ladies, which is pretty unusual for a social club, you must admit, so all in all it's a fine place to relax off duty and forget the stresses and cares of life on the beat.'

'Your Chief Inspector Markwell suggested that I might go out on patrol with some of your men, although I suspect that it's a bit quieter than what I got used to in Whitechapel. But for now I really should get down to examining these roster lists before I can even consider knocking off for dinner. Are there any decent chop houses in the vicinity?'

'Heaps, but the best is "Marco's", around the corner in Broad Court. Most of the blokes go there, rather than eat in our canteen in the basement. It's run by Italians, and they seem to know how to handle food — you soon get used to all the oil. But around here there are plenty of fancy tea houses and suchlike, because this part of London gets so many visitors from all over the world. It's a bit of a pain really, 'cos they're always asking us for directions and expecting us to speak their language. Someone must have told them all that if you're in doubt you can always trust a London bobby.'

'I'd like to think you can,' Jack replied rather shortly. 'Now, if you'd excuse me…?'

'Yes, sorry,' Liam replied, then went back to reading his newspaper while Jack put his head down into the files he'd been loaned and made a big display of taking notes.

The detailed muster rolls with which he'd been supplied were of far more interest to him than the shift rosters that had accompanied them. Jack had been briefed by Percy to keep an eye open for links with the army, and they were not hard to find. Every other man enrolled into the ranks of Bow Street seemed to have begun life as a member of the armed forces, and a significant number of them had served in Guards regiments in North Africa. It was as if a police recruiting sergeant had been out to Cairo, or wherever, and persuaded entire companies of soldiers to exchange red coats for blue ones, rifles and bayonets for billy clubs and whistles. In many ways the stern training that these men would have undergone, plus the ease with which they would accept discipline after their discharge, and the natural camaraderie that came with army life, was reassuring in police recruits. But on the downside it made them more easily subverted by their 'mates', and more useful to an illegal organisation devoted to violent revolution.

Sitting in front of the fireplace in order to exchange notes ahead of Monday supper, Jack passed on what he'd learned to a concerned looking Percy.

'Obviously I'll pass that on to Melville when I make contact again on Thursday,' Percy told him, 'but just what proportion of the station do you think have abandoned the khaki for a police uniform?'

'I didn't keep exact numbers,' Jack admitted, 'but around a third, at a loose estimate.'

Percy frowned. 'That's a real worry, and you can bet that Markwell came by the same route. He's got "Khartoum" written all over his face, and I wasn't sure whether or not to click smartly to attention when we entered his office this morning. If there's an unhealthy connection with the Wellington Barracks, you can be sure that he's the driving force behind it.'

'That Sergeant Brennan is far too keen to let me see the inside of that little club of his. I think it could be some sort of trap.'

'You may be right, but it's also a golden opportunity to get a closer look inside what Melville believes to be a hotbed of corruption involving both soldiers and police officers. Even if "they" know what we're really up to in Bow Street, their intention towards you may well be to corrupt you in order to find out how much *we* know.'

'And if they suspect that we know too much, won't they try to do away with me?'

'So we pass up this gift horse because it's too dangerous, is that what you're saying, Jack? Didn't you face danger every day when you patrolled the dark alleyways of the East End? Wasn't everyone you arrested someone who potentially wanted to do away with you? Have you gone soft over the years?'

'That's unfair!' Jack protested. 'In those days I didn't have a wife and children to think about. I'm not scared for myself, but if anything were to happen to me…'

'It won't,' Percy assured him. 'For as long as they think they can get information out of you, you'll be safe. You have to play a double game, that's all.'

'If you say so. But in the meantime, you sit safe and secure inside Bow Street?'

'I'll be in Bow Street most of the time, certainly.'

'And what about the rest of the time?'

'On Thursday I have to turn myself into a sightseer and explore Westminster Abbey in order to meet up with Melville's messenger. Hopefully by then I'll be able to advise him what we've learned about this club that seems to be the centre of the action.'

'And what will you be able to tell him about *your* enquiries? Or is it all down to me?'

'I need to find out if Markwell and his cronies know anything about the proposed route for the Jubilee procession, and if so what arrangements they're making to police it. If I can match their proposed allocation of men to those with dubious backgrounds, then we can get Melville's ferrets to keep a close watch on them, and who they associate with. You can help with that by finding out the identities of those Met officers who're regular members of this club.'

'I take it you suspect Markwell?'

'Wouldn't you? He fits the picture perfectly — ex military, in a position of authority in Bow Street, and clearly not happy at the way the British Empire's being run. What about your Sergeant Brennan?'

'Again, a bit too obvious if anything. Even his name's Irish, and he makes no attempt to hide an accent that suggests that he's not long off the boat. I wouldn't be surprised to learn that he has a special skill in planting explosives.'

'You may be right about him being a little too obvious,' Percy replied thoughtfully. 'He might just be a decoy, to throw us off the scent of those who're *really* calling the shots. Anyway, that'll be for you to decide, since you're clearly going to be working with him.'

'If I go ahead and risk my neck in this club of his, can I have Friday off?' Jack said hopefully. 'I thought I'd go back to Barking on a morning train and call in to see Mother on my way home. I mentioned that she's had a mild heart attack that she's writing off as indigestion, but I want to look in on her and make sure that she's recovering well, and not misbehaving and ignoring the doctor's orders. Also, if I call in on her, it may prevent her waddling up to our house during the weekend.'

Percy thought for a moment, then smiled. 'I'll do you a deal, then. You get yourself inside this club of Brennan's, report back all you see and hear, and then you can leave for home on the Friday morning train.'

'You must be bored out of your mind, staring at all that paper,' Liam Brennan commented as he placed the mug of tea down on Jack's desk. 'It *was* two sugars, wasn't it?'

'Yeah, thanks,' Jack replied in imitation of a man whose mind was distracted by what he was reading. 'From what I can see here,' he continued, 'we're not likely to be making any serious recommendations for additional manpower. You must be the best manned station in the Met; there hasn't been a resignation or a transfer since May, and now it's November.'

'It's a popular billet, right enough,' Brennan confirmed. 'We don't get many hardened criminal types up this west end of town, and most of our work consists of keeping a watchful eye on sightseers. Then of course we get the big ceremonials to police, when we get to parade in our best uniforms, alongside our army mates, while the Queen, or the Prime Minister, show their faces to the mob. The best duty of all's outside the gates of Buck House when the Queen happens to grace London with a visit, usually for the State Opening of Parliament. All the girls cheer us on, and occasionally one of them will give us a kiss or pass us a sandwich or a cup of tea.'

'Very different from life up the sharp end, down in Wapping or Whitechapel,' Jack agreed. 'You must be one big happy family.'

'And so we are. Have you given any more thought to popping along to our club one evening?'

'Why not?' Jack smiled with fake enthusiasm. 'It's a bit boring in the evenings, with only my uncle and aunt for company. I miss my wife and kids too, so an evening's distraction would be very welcome. What's your club called, and where exactly is it?'

'It's called "The Home Front Club", and we obviously took that name from what soldiers call England while they're fighting abroad to support the Queen's lost causes. On long hot nights, while we were waiting for Abdul to come at us again, a group of us dreamed of being back on what we took to calling the "Home Front", and promised ourselves that if we survived to go home, we'd start a club to remember our comrades in arms who'd given their lives so that Her Majesty could hang a few more camel skins on her Palace walls.'

'You sound very bitter,' Jack observed diplomatically as Brennan's eyes blazed fervently at the far wall.

'Sorry, Jack, it just gets to me sometimes. All those good men lost — and for what?'

'I can sympathise, in my own small way,' Jack lied. 'Every time I had to tell a woman with a roomful of kids that her breadwinner in uniform had been knifed to death and thrown into the nearby canal, I used to ask myself if it was all worth it. It certainly taught me what matters most in life.'

'You have a problem with the way the country's being run?' Brennan asked eagerly, and Jack saw his chance.

'I certainly agree with you that it's time that the politicians were forced to go and look at real dead bodies or explain to distraught and desperate widows how their policies have taken their life and happiness from them.'

'Some people might call you a revolutionary,' Brennan suggested, and Jack allowed himself a wry smile.

'I don't know about that, but there's a lot about our country that I'd like to see changed.'

'You'll find a lot of people with similar views in the Home Front Club,' Brennan assured him. 'I'm off duty at two today, so I'll pick you up here at six, if that's convenient.'

'I have reason to believe that the celebrations will be spread over two days,' Markwell advised Percy as they sat sharing a pot of tea in the former's spacious office on the third floor. 'The first day will be marked by a service in the Royal Chapel at Windsor, then she'll come into town by the western route, arriving at Buckingham Palace in time for a State Banquet worth a Queen's ransom, and attended by all her hangers-on from around the world.'

'And you'll have all your men on duty around the Palace and its immediate surrounds?' Percy asked with raised eyebrows. 'If so, then they'll be pretty stuffed by the second day to which you referred. What happens then?'

'Pretty traditional stuff which we've handled without difficulty before,' Markwell assured him. 'A full open carriage turn-out, through Trafalgar Square, then down through Whitehall onto the Embankment, and "all stations" to St Paul's for the Thanksgiving Service. The main worry will be dumped onto the poor buggers in the East End, since we're informed that the old dear can't walk up the steps anymore and will remain in her carriage while the Archbishop does his bit from the steps themselves. Makes her a sitting duck for any loony with a gun or a bomb, but some idiot in Special Branch appears to have given the go ahead.'

'You got this from Special Branch themselves?' Percy said as casually as he was able, and Markwell nodded.

'Friends in high places, let's say. But clearly we had to be informed as early as possible.'

'It would seem that we're concentrating on the wrong end of town, if your information's correct,' Percy muttered. 'The real risk will be outside St Paul's, and that involves just about every police division in the East End.'

'I sincerely hope that you won't recommend drafting any of my men over there,' Markwell frowned. 'We'll be at full stretch covering two days of sweaty mobs lining the streets and craning their necks to get a glimpse of Her Royal Hugeness.'

'Rest assured,' Percy replied. 'From what I can tell, you have a very loyal contingent at your command here, and I wouldn't want to disrupt that in any way. But I must look again at the East End, since whichever crackpot organised these Diamond Jubilee arrangements clearly didn't know his arse from his elbow when it came to matters of security. As usual, the boys in blue will have to save the day.'

'I won't mention the unauthorised use of a police wagon,' Jack grinned as the driver flicked the reins and the horse set off at an even pace in the general direction of Green Park.

'It's actually authorised,' Brennan smiled back from the opposite seat. 'We're allowed to use the wagon whenever we want to visit the club immediately after work.'

'Chief Inspector Markham must be a very generous boss,' Jack observed as he made a mental note that they were turning left into St James's Street.

'He's also the Treasurer of the club.'

'Where exactly is the club located?' Jack watched the carriages coming and going down the wide and luxurious thoroughfare.

'Dead ahead, half a mile or so,' Brennan advised him. 'Number Twenty, St James's Square Gardens. A fine set of rooms on the ground floor, with a couple of actresses resident with their "gentlemen admirers" on the upper floors. They're usually out in the evenings, giving their all up the West End somewhere, so they don't mind the racket we make on some nights. But tonight's Tuesday, so it should be fairly quiet in there.'

It certainly seemed quiet enough as Brennan led Jack down the heavily carpeted hallway into what was presumably the main lounge. A few couples in casual dress sat drinking at tables, while a solitary pianist tinkled out popular melodies from the music halls as Brennan led the way to the bar and indicated for Jack to take a seat alongside him.

'I'll take a guess that you're a beer man?' he said, and when Jack nodded Brennan turned to the barman in his smart white jacket. 'A glass of beer for my friend here, and a double drop of the crater for me — on ice, but no water.'

The barman handed over Jack's foaming tankard, along with the large whisky that he'd poured from an Irish malt bottle, and Brennan smiled as he gestured lightly with his hand at the early evening scene before them.

'It'll liven up a bit later on, when the dancing starts, and the single ladies come in. One of the attractions of this place, and if your eye comes to rest on one whose beauty appeals to you, just let me know and I'll effect the introductions. A few drinks and you should then be well on your way to a memorable evening.'

'*One* of the attractions?'

Brennan nodded. 'As you'll be aware, we're supposed to wear our uniforms even when off duty and can be heavily disciplined if we don't. It's the same for the soldiers, and for all of us one of the real attractions of this place is that we can get out of those scratchy trousers and into something more comfortable. Another attraction is the card game that starts in the next room after nine o'clock, and sometimes goes on all night. No limit on the stakes, and very often some of the ladies drift in to watch and are *very* attentive towards anyone who wins a pile, if you get my meaning. Anyway, relax and take a good look round, since there's a lady over there who's beckoning for my attention. If you want a meal, you can order at the bar, and it'll be served in the dining room to the left of the front door.'

He wandered off, and Jack allowed his eyes to roam the half empty room. The few men in attendance were dressed fashionably in civilian clothes, so it was difficult to tell whether they were soldiers or police officers, but they all had the same look about them — the airy confidence that comes with being over six feet tall and trained for dealing with assailants. As for the women who were sharing carafes of wine with them, no doubt some of them were prostitutes carefully vetted for the occasion, but none of them looked as if they were.

His eye lit upon one woman in particular, who stood out because of her lustrous jet-black shiny hair and the penetrating blue eyes that glittered even across the few feet between them. When Brennan returned Jack made appreciative noises and enquired about membership.

'You have to be proposed and seconded by existing members,' Brennan told him, 'but before that happens you have to answer a few questions regarding your loyalty to the Queen.'

Or lack of it, Jack conjectured mentally.

'You're the only member I know so far,' Jack objected, and Brennan smiled.

'After a few visits here you'll get to know more, and by then we'll have a pretty good idea of whether or not you're membership material. Anyway, I have to go now, since I have to be back on duty shortly after five tomorrow morning. I can give you a ride back to Bow Street if that's convenient for you.'

Percy was waiting up as Jack let himself in quietly shortly after eleven, after the late evening bus ride across the city and past his former residence in Clerkenwell, provoking further reminders that he'd rather be home in Barking with Esther and the children. Percy beckoned Jack into the sitting room with an obvious expression of relief and enquired as to how his evening had gone. Jack smiled.

'One of the most salubrious establishments I've ever had the pleasure of attending. A very smart sort of club located in a very wealthy part of the West End. If it's financed solely by membership subscriptions, then clearly I'm in the wrong half of our profession, but I got the distinct feeling that someone is putting money behind it in order to attract bobbies and soldiers, then either blackmail them or get them into so much debt at the card table that they'll do what they're told.'

'Blackmail them on what grounds?'

'If you could have cast your eyes over some of the high-class whores in there, you wouldn't need to ask. For a working copper, or a non-commissioned grunt in a Guards regiment, they'd be irresistible.'

'And for a police sergeant with a wife and four children?' Percy said with a mischievous grin, and Jack's smile disappeared.

'Forget it. I'm considering applying for membership, but if someone's required to investigate the whorehouse benefits of membership, you'll need someone else. So how was your working day?'

Percy grimaced. 'Somehow or other, Markwell seems to have got hold of the detailed plans for the Jubilee procession. That's a big enough worry, but the real headache is that the Queen will be sitting stationary, fully exposed in an open carriage, at the foot of the steps of St Paul's while the Archbishop conducts the service in the open air. If what Markwell says is true, then the sooner we get back into the East End and make sure that everything's in order, the better. I'll need to ask to speak directly with Melville when I meet with his messenger on Thursday.'

'Can I still have Friday off?'

Percy nodded. 'But don't count on being able to visit your mother every Friday from now on, because I have a sneaking suspicion that, like that story I used to read to you about the little Dutch boy with his finger in the dike, we're going to be required to plug quite a few holes in security in coming months.'

Chapter Twelve

Percy took the seat at the very end of the pew in Westminster Abbey that lay directly across the aisle from the baptismal font, then sat patiently awaiting the man who was his only line of communication with William Melville. All around him he could hear muted conversations between sightseers in different languages, together with the rustling of guide books to this ancient citadel of God that had witnessed so much British history. Up ahead, in the choir stalls, a group of far from reverend young boys dressed in grubby surplices tussled and competed for the best seats ahead of their daily practice under the wavering baton of an elderly choirmaster who had seemingly given up the struggle to call them to order.

'Peace be upon you, my son.'

He didn't bother looking sideways, but from the corner of his eye he could make out a dark shape that resembled a man in clerical robes sliding into the seat across from his in the aisle, and he decided to risk it.

'Tell your superior that someone's got hold of the proposed procession route. Also tell him that the greatest risk will be when the lady in question sits outside St Paul's.'

'More detail, please.'

'It would take too long. I need to see your boss.'

'If you wish to speak with the organ grinder rather than his monkey, then the best place would be Tower Green, next Tuesday at two o'clock. *Pax vobiscum* and all that nonsense.'

The form slid out of the seat, and Percy made his way outside before the choir boys could render further violence to a wonderful chorale by Thomas Tallis. Outside in the warm winter sunlight he shook off the gloom of the interior he'd just left and hopped on a bus that took him all the way down to Stepney, where he knew that he could probably count on a reasonable reception.

'What brings you back?' Sergeant Parker enquired nervously. 'Have you got more information about those stolen rifles? Or are you here to render further assistance in bringing our records up to scratch?'

'Neither,' Percy smiled. 'I was just wondering if there'd been any circular regarding the processional route for the Diamond Jubilee celebrations. Only some stations in the West End seem to have got theirs.'

'Typical!' Parker muttered. 'It's always those posh buggers up west who get to know things first. Do you happen to know if the Queen will be coming this way, or will it all be confined to Buckingham Palace and Westminster Abbey?'

Percy frowned. 'At the risk of depressing you further — and bear in mind that I haven't been able to confirm this, which is why I was hoping that you could — it seems that there'll be a church service of some sort on the steps of St Paul's.'

'That'll be Whitechapel's worry, won't it?' Parker said hopefully.

Percy shook his head in sad denial. 'From what I could make out regarding their current manpower, I reckon they'll be calling in men from all over the East End. Even if your blokes aren't required at the Cathedral itself, you're going to have folks tramping your streets on their way towards it.'

'Can you get me more men? Isn't that why you were down here in the first place — to assess manpower, and recommend any necessary increase?'

'How many "specials" could you call in, if pushed?' Percy asked.

Parker thought for a moment before replying. 'About a dozen worth having, and a few more who'd come out for the money or the free food and drink, but won't they want to be attending the celebrations with their own families?'

'Good point,' Percy conceded. 'At any rate, we'll have to give serious consideration to boosting your numbers somehow or other. Perhaps with troops from the Tower Barracks — who knows? But now I'm aware of the full extent of the problem, I can make suitable noises in appropriate places. Thanks for seeing me, and I'm sorry that I couldn't be the bearer of happier tidings.'

'We're having a musical evening at the club this evening,' Liam Brennan announced as he slid behind his desk in the office he was sharing with Jack. 'You're invited, and there are a couple of chaps I'd like you to meet. But before that, since it's a bright sunny day out there, why don't we go and take a stroll through Green Park and inspect the men on patrol? The boss said that you wanted to see how we do things up west.'

'Yes, I'd be delighted,' Jack replied despite himself, and less than half an hour later the police wagon deposited them at the north gate. As they walked down the main drive they passed several uniformed constables on fixed point duty, who gave every appearance of being alert, and saluted smartly as they saw their Sergeant strolling towards them with the plain clothed visitor. One of the constables appeared to be surrounded by chattering school children accompanied by a young lady who was presumably their teacher, and Jack smiled to himself at the sight of a London bobby trying to make himself understood in the most elementary French, while the teacher put him to shame with her superior English.

'It's down that way, missus — mamzell,' the constable advised her as he pointed down the main path and received an entrancing smile of thanks from the pretty teacher.

'Everything in order, Pascoe?' Brennan enquired, and the constable nodded as he saluted.

'Yes, Sarg. Jenkins an' Bishop buckled a pervert down near the lavatories, but that's bin all this mornin', so far as I knows.'

'Very good, carry on,' Brennan instructed him in a manner no doubt well practised in his army days.

'There seems to be no shortage of manpower, anyway,' Jack observed as they walked on. He'd already seen more constables on duty directing foreign visitors through a pleasant park that he'd ever seen walking the dark streets of Whitechapel on a foggy night. Brennan seemed to read his thoughts as he pointed through the winter foliage towards the imposing facade of Buckingham Palace visible beyond the southern perimeter.

'We'll need every one of them when Her Majesty comes home for her big bash next June. There'll be a twenty-one-gun salute from the Royal Horse Artillery towards Constitution Hill down there, and we'll need to stop the sightseers from distracting the gunners, some of whom you'll probably meet this evening. It's normally formal dress for the musical evenings, by the way, but by tradition we allow visitors to wear mufti, so you'll be OK as you are.'

As the clock on the steeple of a distant church chimed seven, Brennan stepped out of the police wagon with Jack immediately behind him. There was, as usual, no doorman as such, but the door that gave access to the billiard room immediately inside the premises was wide open, and two pairs of inquisitive eyes surveyed them carefully from over a table that contained only a pink and black ball lying at the opposite end from the white, indicating a close game of snooker nearing completion. Brennan waved back in silent acknowledgment as they made their way down the hallway and into the bar, where he ordered the same drinks as on their previous visit together.

This time it was easy to distinguish the army types from their police colleagues because they were all wearing their formal Mess outfits, the preponderance of red frockcoats broken only by the coloured flashes at shoulder and wrist that denoted the individual regiments, and the gold down the front of one dark blue dress jacket being worn by a tall man seated at a table with a somewhat haughty looking lady who was so plain that she must be his wife, Jack concluded.

The rest were in 'black tie' order, and Jack assumed that they were police officers, one of whom he recognised as the man who had been directing schoolchildren in Green Park. There were only three women present at this early hour of the evening, one of whom Jack recalled immediately when he caught sight of her luxuriant black hair as she leaned over the pianist's shoulder pointing at something on his music stand.

Brennan beckoned to the tall, distinguished looking man with the gold braid all down the front of his dark blue jacket, who left the plain looking woman at his table after a brief aside and walked with a smile to where Jack and Brennan were leaning on the bar.

'Jimmy,' Brennan said, 'allow me to introduce a potential new member, Jack Enright, Detective Sergeant at the Yard. Jack, meet Captain James Britton, Royal Horse Artillery. He'll be in charge of part of the battery firing make-believe shells at Her Maj. on the morning of her drive to St Paul's.'

'Delighted to meet you,' Captain Britton told Jack as he attempted to stop the circulation in his extended right hand.

'Are you chappies going to stop the plebs from getting too close to our popguns on the big day?'

'Something like that,' Jack replied, 'but I'm glad to hear that the shells won't be real. I'm helping to assess the Queen's overall security for the day.'

'Two days,' Brennan corrected him, 'but I take it you were joking about the shells? If they were real, they could reduce Buck House to a pile of rubble in as little time as it took to fire them.'

'Of course I was joking,' Jack chuckled. 'I came down here once before, during your "Trooping the Colour" ceremony, and my little daughter at the time was terrified when all those cannon went off. But from memory that was in Horse Guards Parade.'

'To begin with it would have been,' Britton agreed, 'but if you were close to where we fired the guns, that would have been in Green Park.'

'Where we were today,' Brennan reminded him. It fell silent for a moment before Britton took up the conversation again.

'So are you one of these proud subjects of Her Majesty who loyally turns out with his family to wave your cheap little Union Jack at the old lady?'

There was something about the scornful way in which the question was posed that alerted Jack to the fact that he was being tested, and his reply was suitably guarded.

'We don't really see enough of her for that, do we?' he replied with a sight sneer. 'And I'll be damned if I'm going to holiday on the Isle of Wight, just to see where all the nation's money's being spent on ornamental gardens.'

Britton smiled back appreciatively, and the atmosphere grew noticeably more relaxed.

'Nice to have met you, old chap,' Britton beamed as he held out his hand for another crushing attack on Jack's. 'If you'll excuse me, better see to it that the memsahib's got enough alcohol to see her through yet another performance from "Lady Mary". Nice chatting with you too, Liam.'

As Britton made his way back to his table, the pianist rattled a glissando from his keyboard in order to command attention, and the lady with the long dark hair took up a pose in the curve of the grand piano as a somewhat grizzled individual in full evening dress walked into the centre of the room.

'That's Sergeant Pultney from "F" Division,' Brennan whispered in Jack's ear. 'He looks after all our musical activities, and he's got a fine baritone voice when we let him show it off. Hopefully Mary will be singing my favourite, as per my request, before they launch into duets.'

'Ladies and gentlemen,' the master of ceremonies announced, 'welcome to another of our musical evenings. We begin with our own Mary Carmody, who informs me that she's had a special request for one of her own favourite songs from her home country. Ladies and gentlemen, Mary Carmody.'

The polite spattering of applause faded as the pianist rolled through the introduction, then paused for dramatic effect as the lady closed her eyes, opened her mouth and let the opening line glide out as if propelled by a light breeze.

'Oh Danny boy, the pipes, the pipes are calling.'

Jack was no judge of music but took his cue from the reaction of the audience, the vast majority of whom appeared spellbound as the light contralto notes rolled effortlessly round the room. A swift glance at Liam Brennan revealed tears at the corners of his eyes as the song came to its sad ending of 'And I will sleep in peace until you come to me', and the applause burst out with enthusiasm at a level much louder and more heartfelt than its predecessor. Mary bowed her thanks, wiped a tear from her own eye, then launched into several other maudlin ballads before thanking her audience, taking a final bow, then moving to a table at which she joined a group of recently arrived men whose red jackets and white belts denoted them as officers of the Grenadier Guards.

Then it was the turn of the master of ceremonies to regale the assembled company with a selection of light classics from the currently popular operettas of Gilbert and Sullivan. It was noticeable that the ones that drew the loudest applause were those that appeared to mock either the monarchy or the forces of law and order. A particular favourite proved to be a song entitled 'A Policeman's Lot', and even Jack was forced to snigger at some of the innuendo regarding timid constables who were hesitant to perform their constabulary duties. The evening ended with the baritone sergeant being joined in front of the piano by Mary Carmody for a trio of duets on a patriotic theme, concluding with a lusty rendition of 'Rule Britannia' that drew the entire company into its repeated final chorus.

It was well after eleven before Jack crept silently through the front door of the Hackney house in which he was lodging, to find all the lights out in the front hall, but a note pinned to the kitchen door to advise him that there was a pan of soup on the stove and fresh bread in the bread bin. Silently he thanked Aunt Beattie for her kindly concern and ate his supper while his head was still ringing with the final chorus of 'Rule Britannia'. He was sure that the members of the Home Front Club sang it in some sort of sarcastic parody of the loyalty they were sworn to display when in their daily uniform, but which they could deride and belittle in their off-duty hours.

'We may as well travel into work together,' Jack suggested as he joined Percy at the breakfast table the following morning. Percy looked up from his kippers and nodded.

'However, I plan to be in the East End for most of the day, assessing how we can possibly even begin to guarantee the Queen's security at St Paul's. The damned idiot who dreamed up that particular folly obviously had no experience of life on the streets of the East End. Add to that a bunch of anarchists only too eager to assassinate the old bat, and we don't stand a rat's chance in a kennel.'

'It may well have been "the old bat" herself who asked for whatever it is you're complaining about, Percy Enright, and don't let me hear you referring to our Queen in such terms again,' Beattie said tersely as she all but slammed the jam pot down on the table next to the toast rack. 'And don't get jam on the tablecloth — it's clean on this morning.'

'What do you want me to do?' Jack asked.

'No idea, during the day. But how did you go in the anarchist playpen yesterday evening?'

'Interesting, if somewhat depressing. From various things said in conversation, they obviously have no love for the Queen and the existing political set-up, yet they're all men sworn to defend both. There's a distinct Irish flavour about the place, and they're probably being used by Fenians; the really scary thing is that they'll be the ones the Queen will look to for her protection on the big day, and they'll obviously be armed. At least, the soldiers will, and with enough corrupt police officers in strategic positions along the ceremonial route they could easily hide an assassin in their ranks.'

'Do they suspect you, do you think?'

Jack shook his head. 'Far from it. Just the opposite, in fact — I think they're testing me out for membership. Which is all very well, in one sense, but I have two serious problems. The first is that I can't, with any continuing credibility, hang around Bow Street like a bad smell, doing a job that could have been completed by now, even working at half speed. The other is that those traitorous bastards in that club make my skin crawl, and it's all I can do keep my hands off their throats.'

'You're just going to have to grin and bear it, Jack,' Percy advised him as he loaded jam onto his third slice of toast. 'It's the best possible lead we could have into what those anarchists are planning. As for your daily work, Bow Street isn't the only police station that's going to be heavily involved at the western end of the festivities. There's Mayfair and Soho in "C" Division, and Kensington in "F" Division, for a start. We also need to look at the possibility of drafting men across from one station to another, like for example Marylebone and Hampstead. You could do us all a valuable service by visiting all of these stations in turn, assessing how many men they'll need on the day to patrol their own patch, given the predicted increase in pedestrian movement down to Westminster, then seeing how many, realistically, could be drafted across to the East End for the St Paul's service.'

'That's a huge task!' Jack objected.

'And you've got slightly over six months,' Percy told him. 'Unless Melville can come up with a better plan when I meet with him on Tuesday, then a "master plan" of available manpower across the whole of the affected parts of the Met will be the key to holding the lid down on two hectic days next June.'

'Can I still have tomorrow off?'

Percy smiled reassuringly. 'Of course you can. But make the best of it, because it may be your last free working day for some time. If you can clear your desk in Bow Street today, all to the good, but make sure that you keep in touch with Sergeant Brennan even when you're on a tour of other police stations. We need you inside that club, sniffing out what's being planned. I'll make my excuses to Inspector Markwell and leave him believing that all my focus will now be on the East End.'

Thursday went according to plan for them both, and by supper time they were able to congratulate each other on having begun to expose what was undoubtedly some sort of plan to disrupt the Diamond Jubilee, possibly by assassinating the Queen. Based on what Jack had observed for himself, the main impetus for this seemed to be an Irish one, but Percy reminded him that while the Fenian Brotherhood might well have been recruited to do the dirty work, the dark forces behind the plot might come from anywhere. Even within the nation there were plenty of subversive resentful groups who viewed with bitter contempt the large chasm between the 'haves' and the 'have nots', whereas nations such as Russia and Germany also had a longer-term interest in throwing England into chaos.

These thoughts occupied Jack's mind so fully that he almost forgot to get off the Southend-bound train from Fenchurch Street when it rattled and huffed its way into Barking on Friday morning. At the last moment he jumped from the carriage with his portmanteau and walked through the barrier into the roadway that led to the crossroads. Instead of continuing across into Bunting Lane, he turned right down Church Lane, and within minutes he was being embraced by his mother and invited to stay for dinner. After what was almost certainly a larger meal than was medically advisable for Constance, who was clearly using Jack's presence as an excuse to cock a snook at Dr. Browning, they sat drinking tea in the sitting room.

Constance looked slightly uncomfortable as she opened up a line of conversation that for once was not inspired by goings on in the Ladies' Guild.

'I don't suppose you're allowed to tell me what you're involved in with your uncle down there in London?' she asked. 'Knowing Percy, it won't be anything safe and cosy, but the sooner you're back here in Barking, the better.'

'And how's your health, Mother?'

'Don't try to change the subject. You're neglecting Esther and the children. Particularly Esther.'

'So she reminded me when I came home last week,' Jack smiled ruefully. 'I hope I fare better this afternoon.'

Constance's eyes dropped down to the tea cup in her hand. 'There's something I feel obliged to tell you, Jackson. I feel *so* disloyal doing so, and believe me I've been grappling with my conscience all week, knowing that I'd have a moment at some time or other to talk to you in private this weekend, but...'

'What?' Jack pressed her, lines of faint amusement around his mouth.

'Well, it's just ... well, it's about Esther. I think she may be seeing another man.'

'*What?*' Jack spluttered, as tea sprayed down his shirtfront.

'Well, it was last Tuesday, when I decided to take the doctor's advice and go for a gentle stroll to the crossroads. Except, as Fate would have it, when I got to the crossroads I decided that I felt perfectly fine, and that I'd like to walk a little further, so I decided to call on Esther.'

'And she had a man with her?' Jack demanded, now on the edge of his seat with a dreadful anticipation.

'No — and in a way, yes,' Constance continued, confused. She saw the pleading anguish in Jack's eyes and hastened to clarify her meaning. 'As I was walking down the lane towards your house, there was a young man ahead of me. Very tall — even taller than you, but with broader shoulders — and from behind he looked very handsome. Then, when he reached your front gate, he was met by Esther, who ran out of your front drive looking *very* pleased to see him. I got the impression that she'd been expecting him, and she threw her arms around him, and he swung her round and round, with her feet clear of the ground.'

'Then what?' Jack asked in a doom-laden voice.

Constance shrugged. 'I just turned around and walked home. To tell you the truth, I was badly shaken by what I'd seen, and I didn't want to see any more. I desperately hope that I misread the situation, but I felt that I *had* to tell you. I hope you'll forgive me for being the bearer of such grim tidings.'

'Of course I forgive you,' Mother,' Jack reassured her as he rose swiftly to his feet, putting his tea cup down heavily on the side table. 'But whether or not I forgive Esther will depend upon what I discover when I get home. Thank Cook for an excellent dinner and tell her that I may be back for tea.'

Chapter Thirteen

Jack's mind was whirling with possibilities as he walked slowly down Bunting Lane, less keen on his return home than he had been when alighting from the train. At the entrance to the driveway he paused briefly, recreating in his mind a scene in which Esther threw herself into the arms of another man, who swung her effortlessly round in a circle. Then he looked down towards the house itself, wondering what dark secrets it already held, and whether or not Nell had been sworn to silence. After all, she owed everything to 'the missus' who'd plucked her from the uncertainty of her final year in an orphanage into her first domestic post.

For once he didn't hurl his hat at the peg on the back of the door as he stepped inside the scullery and listened to the sounds of the house. Lily and Bertie were fighting somewhere as usual, and the faint smell of kindling suggested that Nell was lighting the sitting room fire as a protection against the dank November afternoon. The kitchen door opened without warning, and there stood Esther with a pail full of nappies for soaking. Her arched eyebrows expressed surprise, but not necessarily any great pleasure.

'You're early,' was her only comment.

'Is that a problem?' Jack said tersely.

Esther managed a weak smile. 'Of course not, except that I like to know when you're arriving, because it helps with meals.'

'I had dinner with Mother.'

'Perhaps as well, because we finished an hour ago. A bit delayed as it happens, because Tommy's still teething, and spat everything back at me.'

'Who was here during the week?' Jack said bluntly.

Esther looked back at him quizzically before answering. 'Me, Nell, your four children — and Billy came over to fix that fence by the railway line before any of the children crawl through it to their deaths. You know — the one you never seem to have had time to fix?'

'Any other men?' Jack demanded.

'Of course. There's always a line of suitors at the front door, drawn by the ravishing beauty of a housewife in her mid-thirties boiling nappies.'

'I'm serious,' Jack insisted in a stern tone. 'Mother told me that she'd seen you welcoming a man at the front gateway.'

'Very well, since you ask. Yes, there *was* a man. On Tuesday. I had no idea your mother was spying on me.'

'She wasn't. She happened to be on her way to call in on you but turned back when she saw what was going on.'

'A pity she didn't come in, then she might have been better placed to peach on me.'

'Did the man come into the house?'

'Yes, why?'

'The bedroom, by any chance?'

'We were briefly in the bedroom, certainly.'

'I can't believe that you're so blatant and blasé about the whole thing!'

'We've been married for seven years, Jack Enright, and in all that time I've never once given you cause to suspect me of being unfaithful. You clear off every Sunday afternoon, God knows what you get up to in that wicked city, and all you can do by way of recognition of the way I keep house for you, look after your children, and wait patiently for the end of each week is to come trouncing in here and all but accuse me of adultery.'

'The facts speak for themselves,' Jack insisted, and Esther's face tightened in mounting anger.

'I'm not one of your criminals! The only "fact" you have is that a man visited the house on Tuesday — on my invitation, I might add — and from that you create some ludicrous accusations that belong in one of those disgusting books that you can buy in cheap and tawdry shops in the East End, where you spend your weeks in the company of thieves and prostitutes!'

'Why did you invite another man into the house?'

'Because he's my *brother*, you idiotic pratt!'

'Your brother?'

'Yes, my brother. Abraham Daniel Isaacs — remember him? The one who sent the private investigator to find me; that man you tortured on the front lawn in front of the children? I hope you treat Abe kindlier, although let me warn you that he's bigger than you. Anyway, he's coming for Sunday dinner, along with his lady friend.'

Jack smiled shamefacedly at Esther, as she fought back.

'How *could* you think that of me? Being separated like this every week is clearly not good for our marriage. Do you imagine that I don't think things like that about *you* while you're back in the city? You forget that I lived there once, too, and I know how those totties operate, with their fake smiles, their loud clothes, their cheap perfume and their gin-soaked kisses. A man alone for a few days is an obvious target, and the East End's full of them. Every pub, every street corner, every...'

He cut off the flow of her misery with a kiss, at the end of which he continued to hold her with a hand on either side of her still slim waist and looked deep into her eyes.

'You need *never* suspect me of anything like that, and I apologise from the bottom of my heart for what I suspected you of. Let's start again, shall we? "I'm home, darling!"' he called out to the kitchen door over her shoulder, and she giggled.

'Welcome home. Will you settle for tea and muffins? Nell just made some.'

An hour, and several muffins, later, they remained at the kitchen table, Miriam leaning against Esther's knee and Tommy nestling asleep on her chest as Nell responded to the war that was being waged in the sitting room by the remaining Enright siblings.

'So Abe wrote and asked to come and see you?' Jack asked.

'Yes. It was *so* wonderful to see him again, after all these years. He fell in love with Lily on the spot, and he kept Bertie amused by showing him how to arrange his toy soldiers in proper battle order. Miriam chuckled every time he tickled her under the chin, and Tommy slept through most of it.'

'It's a pity that Mother misread the situation, but don't be angry with her,' Jack requested. 'She was only acting in what she regarded as my best interests, and you'll get your own back by not going to Sunday dinner with her. You *did* say that Abe was calling round then, didn't you? And with his lady friend?'

'That's right,' Esther confirmed. 'They've known each other since they met out in Egypt, apparently, and I think, from what he said, that they're quite serious about each other. I got the impression that they're living together as man and wife, even though they're not married, but we don't mind, do we?'

'Of course not. It'll be good to have another side to the family. Is Abe still in the army?'

Esther frowned slightly. 'He was a bit vague on that when I asked him how long he was home on leave for, but no doubt we can ask him all about that on Sunday.'

The remainder of Friday, and the whole of Saturday, passed off quietly as if there'd been no misunderstanding. Jack played with the children until their bedtime on the Friday evening, then for the whole of Saturday morning, before strolling down to his mother's house for a frugal dinner, during which he was at pains to explain to her that the man she had seen had been Esther's brother, and that since he was visiting them for Sunday dinner, the family would not be down for Sunday dinner at her house the following day, as was the long-established custom. Constance advised him rather coolly that she quite understood their priorities, and that she'd be able to enjoy a peaceful Sunday dinner on her own for once, since Lucy and her family were on holiday, and Aunt Beattie had written a polite letter offering her own apologies, and those of husband Percy, for missing the weekly ritual.

As the morning drifted towards noon, and with the lamb safely installed inside the oven while Nell peeled potatoes and carrots, Esther seemed to spend more and more of her time in the sitting room, notionally peace-keeping between Lily and Bertie, but in reality glancing out through the window towards the driveway. Finally she scuttled into the kitchen, where Jack was reading Friday's newspaper in the middle of Nell's attempts to set the table and advised him excitedly, 'They're here! Do come to the front door and help me welcome them.'

Jack stood behind Esther as she pulled open the front door to the sight of a giant of a man, with closely tonsured black hair that was greying at the temples, standing on the top step in the act of reaching for the door knocker.

'Abe!' Esther gushed enthusiastically, 'it's *so* good that you could come! Come in and meet my husband Jack.'

The two men shook hands, and for Jack it was a rare event to be looking up into the eyes of another man. He was struck by how like Esther Abe was in his general features, and he was still absorbing this information when Abe turned back towards the woman who had sidled in through the front door behind him.

'This is the lady I told you about, Esther. Say hello to Mary. Mary, this is my sister Esther and her husband Jack.'

The lady in question appeared from behind Abe's shoulder, and Jack froze. It was the singer from the Home Front Club.

Their eyes met, and although her beautiful smile was one of serene sociability, her blue eyes dilated in uncontrollable surprise as she shook Jack's hand through her silk glove.

It was a very uncomfortable meal for Jack, but fortunately for his presence of mind it was Esther and Abe who did most of the talking, catching up on lost years.

'So where, when and how did you and Mary first meet?' Esther asked.

'In Cairo, earlier this year,' Abe answered. 'My battalion was on "stand-down", and we were encouraged to socialise with other battalions and their wives. I was introduced to Mary by my subaltern, and we danced all evening, because her normal dance partner was back on the front line.'

'Abraham's being tactful,' Mary advised them quietly, 'but you may as well know the truth from the very beginning of what I hope will be a lengthy acquaintance. The partner to whom Abraham was referring was my husband, and when your brother and I couldn't prevent our feelings for each other spilling over into … well, into something more physical, we ran away together and came to London.'

'What was the reaction from your battalion commander?' Jack enquired tactlessly. 'He's not likely to have given his blessing to your home leave in the circumstances, I wouldn't have thought.'

It fell silent again, and Abe's eyes dropped to the remains of the main course in front of him as he all but whispered, 'We never sought that blessing. I'm afraid you're having dinner with a deserter.'

It was Esther who recovered first from the shock, and she smiled unconvincingly as she tried to make light of what they'd just been told. 'At least you won't be risking your neck out there on the battlefield. You're the only brother I've got.'

Abe looked solemnly across at Jack. 'Esther tells me that you're a police officer, Jack. I hope you won't be running me in. They shoot deserters.'

'Why would I peach on someone who follows his own convictions?' Jack replied with a smile. 'Whether convictions of the heart, or convictions regarding the best way in which the laws of this nation should be applied, it's all the same. You take a stand on what you believe in.'

'And what exactly *do* you believe in, Jack?' Mary asked.

Jack gave her what he hoped looked like a cautious smile. 'A nation in which free men are allowed every opportunity to realise their true vocation, to strive for their dreams, and to do so without oppression from those less worthy of preference.'

'You almost sound like one of those Marxist types,' Mary prodded him.

Jack shook his head. 'All that philosophy stuff's over my head, I'm afraid. Let's just say that I'm all for equality of opportunity, without some being held back by poverty while others are promoted by wealth that they haven't actually earned for themselves.'

'That's what Marx actually meant,' Mary smiled triumphantly, and Abe coughed politely.

'I'm afraid Mary had too much time on her hands while sitting in married quarters waiting for her husband to come back alive. She took to reading *quite* the wrong sort of literature.'

'Anyone for apple pie?' Esther offered in an eager attempt to break the embarrassing silence. 'Nell made it, and she's an excellent pastry cook.'

'As I can attest,' Jack smiled back warmly at Mary in an effort to convey the impression that she'd discovered a fellow believer who normally had to keep his opinions to himself.

As the lengthening shadows began to steal the natural daylight from the sitting room in which they sat drinking tea, they were reminded that darkness fell early a month before Christmas, and while Abe continued to demonstrate to Bertie that he'd foolishly left the right flank of his advancing force of tin soldiers exposed to enemy cannon fire, and Mary sat singing a silly children's song to an entranced Lily, Jack packed his bag for the week, then came reluctantly back into the room and announced that he would have to be leaving soon. Abe and Mary offered to share the journey with him, since from Fenchurch Street they would need to take a bus to their accommodation in Aldgate, and by the time that they did so it would be dark. There were hugs and kisses all round, then the three of them walked down Bunting Lane together, after a final wave to Esther, who stood in the glow from the lamp that she'd lit in the sitting room.

The train had barely pulled away from Barking Station when Mary smiled knowingly across at Jack from the opposite seat in which she sat holding Abe's hand.

'I trust that you enjoyed my singing, Jack.'

Not sure if this was an acknowledgment that she had indeed recognised him, he hedged his answer.

'Very much, and I could see that Lily did too.'

'I meant the songs I sang in the Club. That *was* you up at the bar with Liam Brennan, wasn't it?'

Jack did his best to look shocked, but Mary was having none of that.

'You're among friends now, Jack, so don't be evasive. You weren't there just for the musical evening, were you?'

Jack glanced across at Abe, who smiled encouragingly.

'We gather from what you said earlier this afternoon that you'd like to see some changes in the way that this nation of ours is governed.'

'Who wouldn't?' Jack replied in an attempt to sound reluctant and guarded.

'Have you become a member of the Club yet?' Mary asked.

Jack shook his head.

'Would you like to?' was her next question. 'I know the right people to ask.'

'Are you a member?' Jack asked Abe, who shook his head with a wry smile.

'In my situation, Jack, it's best just to keep your head down.'

'Which regiment were you in?'

'The Grenadier Guards,' Abe replied. 'First Battalion, proud Englishmen, but with the usual spattering of Welsh and Irish.'

'There's talk of creating a separate Irish Guard regiment out of those of my fellow countrymen who fought in my husband's battalion,' Mary added.

'You're Irish yourself, aren't you?' Jack smiled. 'I remember the songs you sang at the Club.'

'All the way from County Meath, where the kings of Ireland had their throne before the English moved in,' Mary replied. 'I was born just north of Dublin, in a place called Dunboyne, which was where Colonel Blood came from. He very nearly stole your Crown Jewels, but he was so highly regarded by King Charles that he spared his life, even though Blood had originally intended to assassinate him. There's a song about him that I sometimes sing at the Club; here's the last two lines for you.' She tilted back her head and opened her mouth with a smile as she sang,

'Since loyalty does no man good,

Let's steal the king and outdo Blood.'

'That's enough, Mary!' Abe admonished her. 'I don't wish my new brother-in-law to think of us as revolutionaries. I didn't fight for Queen and country to hear that sort of Fenian rubbish from the woman I deserted for!'

Too late, my friend, Jack concluded.

'Let's not jump to too many conclusions,' Percy warned Jack later that evening, as they sat in front of the fire doing their best to digest the fish pie that Beattie had cooked for Sunday tea. She was now sulking in the kitchen, after Percy had asked whether the fish that had gone into it had surrendered due to old age.

'But we can't ignore it either,' Jack insisted. 'This woman Mary Carmody is the singer in the Home Front Club, and she not only has wild Fenian loyalties of her own, but her songs go down very well with the club members. She's also a startlingly beautiful lady, and she persuaded Abe Jacobs to desert from his regiment while on active service, an action that could result in him being taken out and shot. He seemed very nervous on the train back to London, when she began to reveal her revolutionary sympathies. She's also very keen to get me into the Club, no doubt with ambitions to corrupt me as well. She all but guaranteed to get me membership. We can't pass that up, can we?'

'I'm not suggesting that we pass it up, Jack,' Percy replied, 'I just have a feeling deep down where your aunt's tea is waging a war that it's all a little obvious. Real spies and revolutionaries don't give themselves away so easily — it's almost as if they're trying to put us off the scent and divert our attention into the wrong corners.'

'So we just ignore all this — is that what you're saying?'

'Of course not; let's not fall for it hook, line and sinker, that's all. We need to keep our eyes open on just about every front, and I'm beginning to suspect that this Home Front Club is a diversionary tactic designed to take our eyes off the ceremony at St Paul's, where the Queen will be most vulnerable. I also suspect that Markwell's now kicking himself for letting slip that someone had fed him the proposed itinerary for the Jubilee celebrations. When I asked Parker at Stepney, he confirmed that no general circular had yet been issued to all stations, so how did Markwell know?'

'Search me,' Jack replied, somewhat deflated that his latest revelations had not met with more enthusiasm. 'But surely we need to alert someone to what I've discovered?'

'Of course. I'm meeting with Melville himself on Tuesday — perhaps he can point the way, because it's all getting a bit murky.'

Chapter Fourteen

Percy stamped his shoes down on the frost-hardened grass of Tower Green, in search of some feeling in his frozen feet, then looked all around him for any sign of the man due to summon him to meet William Melville of Special Branch. Detective Inspector Enright, old fashioned thief-taker and head-kicker, was beginning to tire of all this cloak and dagger stuff, and only the thought that he was merely one small cog in a mighty machine that was preserving the English way of life prevented him from striding off in the direction of the Middle Tower and back out into Lower Thames Street. At least that way he'd get the circulation back in his toes.

A Beefeater strode towards him with a purposeful look, and Percy was about to argue his right to stamp his feet on royal grass when the man smiled.

'Sorry to keep you waiting. The building behind me — the "Queen's House". Superintendent Melville's expecting you.'

Once inside, Percy was relieved of his heavy topcoat by some functionary or other and shown into a low-ceilinged room in which a large open fire was burning cheerfully in a miasma of pine smoke. Melville was seated to one side of it cradling a balloon of brandy, and as Percy approached the facing chair Melville poured him a generous measure from the decanter on the side table and nodded for him to sit down.

'You wanted to see me?' Percy asked.

Melville frowned. 'I was advised that *you* wanted to see *me*. So what's your problem?'

'*Our* problem, I suspect. Have the precise details of the Jubilee celebrations been circulated yet?'

'Only at the highest levels, not to the divisional police stations. Have they leaked out?'

'Certainly, the Inspector at Bow Street — a shifty chap called Markwell — seemed to know all about them. It was he who told me that the Queen will be a sitting duck at the foot of the steps up to St Paul's while the A of C waves his incense bottle over her head, or whatever. Tell me he was talking out of his arse.'

'No, somebody else's arse, as it transpires. The tame penguin from Her Majesty's Household — an army bloke called McNeill — who's in charge of the Queen's wishes, or so it would seem, insisted that the old biddy's so bad with arthritis these days that she'd never make it up the steps, and is graciously disposed to sit it out in her carriage while the Archbishop does his party piece. When it was pointed out to him that it might rain, his response was that the Queen wouldn't allow it to.'

'If there's a problem with the steps of St Paul's, why not Westminster Abbey?'

'Seems that she's getting bored with the place, and in any case would rather be seen among her loyal subjects in the East End.'

'She might be in for a rude shock,' Percy chuckled hollowly. 'Did anyone point out that what was being proposed was a massive security risk?'

'Naturally. I wasn't there, of course, but I'm reliably advised that he replied that Her Majesty was so well loved by her subjects that the risk was non-existent.'

'That's absolute bollocks!' Percy protested.

'Indeed,' Melville replied with a smile, 'but unfortunately the man speaks it fluently.'

'Can we not change his mind?' Percy asked, but the responding look on Melville's face rendered the question obsolete.

'Apart from anything else,' Melville explained, 'the details have now been circulated at the highest levels around the Cabinet, and the equerry's not keen to lose face by having his lunatic scheme amended in any way. However, it's a bit concerning to learn that the plans have been leaked already. Obviously they would have become public knowledge sooner or later, but the clear inference is that this chappie in Bow Street has a friend in high places. I only found out the details because the Home Secretary took me into his confidence, and I doubt that he'd also have told some bobby in Westminster. Any idea where he could have got it from?'

'There's an Assistant Commissioner at the Yard — name of Doyle,' Percy told him. 'He tried to get me on his team by promising me a leading role in what he chose to call a "new order" of policing in London in the foreseeable future. He hinted that it might come via some sort of uprising like that being threatened in Russia at present.'

'And what was his asking price for this?'

'That I bypass my immediate boss and report all discovered examples of corruption in the Met directly to him.'

'Hmm,' Melville replied thoughtfully. 'That might be in order to keep him fully appraised of how much we know.'

'He also seemed to know that I was working for Special Branch,' Percy added.

Melville nodded. 'I'll detail someone to dig for the dirt on him. He may only be a starry-eyed idealist, *or* he's being blackmailed into it for some indiscretion of his own. We'll know the answer to that within a couple of days, and while we're at it we'll have a closer look at this chappie in Bow Street. What was his name again?'

'Markwell. Chief Inspector Lionel Markwell.'

'OK, we'll add him to the list for special scrutiny. Is that all you have to report at this stage?'

'By no means,' Percy insisted. 'My nephew Jack's discovered the existence of some subversive club or other in the West End, attended by selected police officers and army types. He's within an ace of becoming a member of it, if that meets with your approval.'

'Provided that the information flow's one way,' Melville nodded. 'Do you get the feeling that his being able to identify and infiltrate this club so soon is a bit too convenient? That he's being worked in both directions?'

'That was my first thought,' Percy conceded, 'but then it's going to rather a lot of trouble to set up a fake club just to get information out of one person, isn't it? He's managed to work up a friendship with an Irish sergeant down in Bow Street — name of Brennan — and it was Brennan who introduced him to the club. Surely he could simply have pumped Jack for information by himself?'

'Good point. Give Jack the go-ahead. And now we'd better vacate these palatial surroundings, before the royal ghosts drift in out of the cold.'

'Beg pardon?'

'This building was once home to several noble English ladies on their way out of that front door straight onto Tower Green. Anne Boleyn, Lady Jane Grey and Margaret Pole, to name but three. Their ghosts are reported regularly in the narrow corridors upstairs.'

'I don't believe in ghosts,' Percy told him. 'But I do have more to report. Jack's wife Esther has a brother, recently returned in dubious circumstances from his stint with the Grenadier Guards out in the Sudan. He claims to be a deserter, which is a bold move on one's first meeting with a brother-in-law who's a police officer. As if that weren't enough to raise the hairs on the back of your head, he's got a woman in tow who's a welcome entertainer in this club I mentioned a moment ago and she's offered to smooth Jack's application for membership. Either the pair of them are being spectacularly incautious or it's a ruse to draw Jack out where they can either get information from him, or silence him, or both.'

'I'll get the Army Office onto that immediately,' Melville promised, 'if you can supply the names today.'

'He's Abraham Isaacs. Jewish, with Lithuanian parentage that might link up with those Russian types seeking to overthrow the Tsar. My history tells me that the Lithuanian Jews have a score to settle with the Romanov family.'

'And the woman?'

'Name of Mary Carmody. Bog Irish, apparently, and fervently Fenian when she sings songs in that club.'

'At least she doesn't take her clothes off in the process, one hopes,' Melville smirked. 'But leave it with me for the time being. And now I really have to be off.'

'I was hoping you could tell us what you want us to do next,' Percy prompted. 'We can't hang around Bow Street for much longer without looking suspicious, and if it's true that Her Majesty is going to make herself a target for every lunatic in the Northern Hemisphere when she sits taking the sun in an open landau outside St Paul's, then we need to beef up the security down there. I thought that Jack might be best occupied drawing up a chart showing available police manpower in each station in the East and West Ends, which we can then compare with what we think we're going to need on the day.'

'Sounds sensible. And what were you thinking of doing?'

'No real idea, at this stage.'

'Well whatever it is, do it inside the Yard, where you can be approached again by this Doyle chappie. And tell your nephew to join that club as soon as. Now, our next meeting — any ideas where we might stage it?'

'We've done Westminster Abbey and the Tower,' Percy reminded him. 'At the risk of tempting Fate, how about St. Paul's?'

'As good as anywhere, given that we're likely to be followed anyway. Bring your nephew with you next time. Next Monday, 2 pm.'

Jack sighed as he looked up at the stone lintel above the entrance to Mayfair Police Station, where he could almost guarantee a frosty reception when he informed them of why he was there. It was a bitterly cold Monday morning, and he allowed his mind to drift to Uncle Percy, and the cosy office at the Yard in which he could keep out of this wind that threatened to blast through everything it met, leaving slices of human ice behind in its wake. At least by stepping inside the police station he'd be out of the wind, he reminded himself as he waved his police badge under the nose of the constable behind the charge desk and asked to speak with his Inspector.

Inspector Dalton was guarded at first when Jack announced that he was there to check his manpower roster list but softened somewhat when advised that it might lead to additional men being drafted in from other divisions within the Met in time for the proposed Jubilee celebrations.

'I was a sergeant here ten years ago when we had the last one, and a lot of my men were drafted down to Buckingham Palace,' he told Jack. 'Is the same going to be happening this time? Only we barely had enough men to line the streets with when all the gawpers came traipsing down Regent Street, and the buses couldn't move for 'em. We were lucky nobody got killed.'

Jack thought carefully before giving his tactful answer. 'It looks as if the main event this time will be around St Paul's, although the Queen *will* be coming in from Windsor the day before. But once that second day dawns, it may be that some of your men will be required in the East End.'

'A lot of them live out that way anyway,' Dalton replied, 'so I don't suppose there'll be any strong objections. Just give me plenty of notice, that's all.'

It was the same in Kensington, where Inspector Grainger was delighted to learn that for his station it would all be over on the first day. However, he was less impressed when the suggestion was put to him that he might be called upon to draft men into Whitechapel or Stepney.

'You have to understand,' he warned Jack, 'that these men didn't join up in order to belt scum over the head with billy clubs. On the whole they're a very refined bunch who're more used to investigating burglaries in the posher houses up near Hyde Park. They'll be very reluctant to slug it out with work-shy drunks in seedy pubs.'

'They might learn something to their advantage regarding the true nature of East Enders,' Jack glowered. 'I was attached to Whitechapel for my first two years, and basically they're hard-working and law abiding. The problem is that the relatively cheap housing attracts the wrong sort; but if they're in the pubs while the Queen's at St. Pauls, they shouldn't be a problem for your men, should they?'

'All the same,' Inspector Grainger frowned, 'I'd rather you be the one to tell them that they're likely to be going slumming for a day.'

Jack opted to leave it at that. He'd have enough to worry about when he showed his face back in Whitechapel.

'So what are you wasting your time, and our money, on now?' Assistant Commissioner Doyle demanded as he leaned in through the open doorway of Percy's office. Percy smiled as warmly as he was inclined as he nodded down at his desk.

'We've been given the detailed route for the Queen's Jubilee procession next June, and it seems to be centred on a ceremony at St. Paul's, so I'm conducting a survey of available manpower, in order to determine whether or not we need to draft more men into the East End for the occasion.'

'Good idea, but don't strip the West End too thinly. The first day terminates at Buckingham Palace, where there's to be a State Banquet with all the invited dignitaries.'

So you've been slipped the details as well, Percy thought to himself as he shook his head. 'Obviously I won't, but it's going to be a bit of a squeeze. We might have to pull in all the Specials, but it won't be cheap.'

'Might be best to use the Specials in the West End, and save the real bobbies for the East,' Doyle suggested. 'I take it that's what that nephew of yours is about, to judge by the anguished enquiries I'm getting from the stations he's visited already, wanting to know if we're going to strip them of men. Not much of a diplomat, is he?'

'He's a damn good copper, though,' Percy responded in Jack's defence.

'All the same, you might want to keep a closer eye on him while you polish your trouser bottoms in here,' Doyle replied coldly. 'He's getting into bad company in Bow Street.'

'He's officially finished with Bow Street,' Percy objected.

Doyle placed a finger on the side of his nose in a time-honoured gesture that discretion was required as he slid into the office and took a seat. 'All the same, he seems to still have friends there. Has he said anything to you about a social club that the men down there are in the habit of attending?'

'No, not really,' Percy lied, aware of this non-too subtle attempt to find out how much he knew about the Home Front Club.

'Well, you might want to pump him about it. Can't have able officers like him being led astray, now can we? Concentrate on the East End anyway, Percy, because that's obviously where the greatest security threat lies, assuming that the Queen goes ahead with this insane itinerary that one of her hired loonies has dreamed up. And don't forget what we discussed a little while back — those who show the greatest loyalty to the Met today may well find themselves in positions of considerable influence in the months to come.'

'I trust that my loyalty's well above suspicion, sir,' Percy protested.

Doyle smiled unpleasantly as he rose from the chair and made his way out. He paused in the doorway, looked back and replied, 'At present your nose's clean, Percy. Just make sure that it stays that way.'

'I thought I told you never to come back here!' Inspector Ingram bellowed as Jack appeared in his doorway on the Thursday morning, having left it until last for no reason other than cowardice.

Jack winced inwardly but smiled. 'From memory, you told me to bugger off back to the Yard, but I don't recall you telling me that I couldn't return when it was in your best interests.'

'Meaning?'

'Meaning that Whitechapel will be the police station closest to the action on the second day of the Diamond Jubilee celebrations next June, and you're almost certainly heavily undermanned.'

'It doesn't take more than I've got to surround St. Paul's with blue uniforms,' Ingram growled, thereby revealing his own privileged knowledge of the second day's detailed plan. He was also the first Inspector Jack had spoken to during his miserable four-day tour of police stations who seemed not to regard himself as short of men — was he hoping that a depleted force would make it easier for some assassin to strike?

'And what about the approaches to St. Paul's?' Jack said defiantly. 'The procession will probably be keeping close to the river, so I calculate that we'll be needing your men from Monument onwards in the east, and Blackfriars to the west, all the way up Cannon Street, Cheapside and as far as the Museum, where Holborn will take over, always assuming that they have enough manpower of their own.'

'We can manage,' Ingram insisted.

'You can, unless we take men from you to prop up Stepney or Holborn, both of which are pleading shortage of manpower.'

'You wouldn't dare! And who's this "we" you keep referring to anyway?'

'The Home Secretary and Special Branch are the ones who've authorised this manpower audit,' Jack told him smugly, at which Ingram's face twisted in contempt.

'Idiots, the lot of 'em! Pampered lackeys of a system that's long overdue a shake-up.'

'Authorised representatives of the Queen and the elected Government,' Jack reminded him, which seemed to take the wind from Ingram's sails but not the colour from his face.

'But you have to ask yourself how well they're actually doing the job,' Ingram countered. 'The East End is almost ungovernable, and it's only got worse since you were stationed here. Ask your friend Albert Preedy the next time you take him out for a meat pie.'

So you had us followed, Jack thought to himself as he kept a straight face. 'All the more reason why we need to look carefully at how well policed it'll be when the Queen attends St Paul's on the day,' Jack reasoned. 'Which is why I'm here, so could I please see your muster lists? The sooner I do that, the sooner I'll be out of your hair.'

'I'll hold you to that undertaking,' Ingram growled. 'But you'll find that we can rise to any challenge.'

That sounded hollowly in Jack's ears as he consulted the lists that were brought up to him by a constable who looked as if he ought still to be in school. For normal policing there was sufficient manpower, admittedly, but given the influx of extra thousands from other parts of London, any one of whom could be a stealthy assassin, it would be tight. And Jack knew from what he had read in Yard reports recently that the struggling, teeming masses of the East End were no longer content to be regarded as some sort of sideshow to be visited by patronising middle-class gawpers who regarded it as an entertaining day out to go 'slumming' among the great unwashed, the unemployed, the desperate and the resentful. There had already been violent protests by East Enders marching into the more salubrious areas of the West End with their banners demanding a living wage for a day's work. If too many of the well-heeled middle-class decided to combine a show of solidarity for their Queen with yet another upturned-noses expedition into the darker corners of Cheapside or Newgate, Ingram's men would find themselves grossly undermanned for the full-scale riot that might ensue.

Jack could either let that happen, in a grim 'told you so' gesture to Ingram and his men, or he could do what his conscience told him was the right thing and report all this to Uncle Percy, with a strong recommendation that more men be drafted into Whitechapel. His mind drifted back to his own early days on patrol down here, and how he would have fared had all this happened when he was a constable in his first year, with little to no experience of crowd control. He owed it to the poor buggers who'd replaced him, and if Ingram cared little for what his men had to face, then at least Jack could do his best to preserve them from the worst day of their working lives. There was also the distinct possibility, given Ingram's obvious enthusiasm for some sort of revolution, that Whitechapel was being deliberately left undermanned, to make it easier for the attack on the Queen that seemed increasingly likely to be destined to take place on the steps of St Paul's.

Those possibilities were still dominating his mind on that Thursday evening as he stood outside the front door of the Home Front Club, waiting for Liam Brennan. The police coach pulled to a halt, the horse's breath forming clouds ahead of it in the icy air, and Brennan stepped down with an apologetic smile.

'Sorry that you had to wait out here in the freezing cold, Jack. If you were a member, you could just have walked in unchallenged, so perhaps this evening would be an appropriate time to arrange that. First of all, let's hurry inside and get something warm inside us.'

Half an hour later, having each ordered beefsteak and mashed potatoes at the bar, Jack and Liam strolled down the carpeted front hall, drinks in hand, into the room in which pre-ordered meals were served. The conversation was general in nature, given Jack's reluctance to reveal precise details of the manpower deployments that he'd spent the previous four days investigating, and on the whole it meandered around the many benefits of membership, and the facilities that the club had available.

'How much is the annual membership subscription?' Jack asked casually.

'It's free to men like you, still on active service.'

'You make it sound as if I'm in the army,' Jack smiled.

'You are, in a way,' Brennan told him as his smile faded slightly. 'We all have our duty to perform for the nation, and when the call comes you'll be expected to do your bit.' He leaned back in his chair and gave a barely perceptible 'thumbs up' sign to a man who was hovering in the doorway.

'What "call" is that, exactly?' Jack asked as the man moved from the doorway up to their table bearing some sort of ledger.

'First of all the call of membership,' was Brennan's smiling reply as the ledger was placed on the table between them, and Brennan was handed a pen. 'We had a committee meeting the other evening, and the membership application that I made on your behalf has been approved. You're very privileged, because there haven't been too many new admissions lately. All that's required is your signature, in that third square along the newest row.'

He turned the ledger round for Jack to read and handed him the pen. Jack looked down and along the row, and learned that his membership had been proposed and seconded by two men whose names were totally unfamiliar to him. Then his eye roamed upwards, and just in time he managed to suppress any expression of surprise or horror.

Three columns above the one containing his name was the formal record of the recent admission of another member.

Michael Black.

Chapter Fifteen

Esther stood on a chair and reached up to place the gold paper angel on the top of the Christmas tree that she'd spent the whole day painstakingly decorating in the corner of the sitting room while Nell kept Lily, Bertie and Miriam occupied in the kitchen making gingerbread men. Then she squealed in fear as she felt a hand creep up her skirt and she leapt off the chair out of instinct. As she came down awkwardly while attempting to turn to locate the source of the outrage, she lost her footing and landed heavily on the carpet, feet in the air, narrowly missing the heavily decorated tree in the process.

'Jack Enright!' she spluttered, half in protest and half in laughter. 'If you creep up behind me like that ever again, I'll kick you so hard in the "you know what's" that there'll be no risk of any more children. What are you doing home so early on a Friday anyway?'

'Got the day off, didn't I? Where did the tree come from?'

'Out of the ground, obviously. There are a few straggly pines on the other side of the railway line, so Billy risked life and limb to go over there and cut one down for us. Do you like the decorations? I kept the children occupied all week making them.'

'There's a cherub on the second branch from the bottom that looks pregnant, and one of the Father Christmases has what looks like a satisfied grin on his face, but otherwise it looks fantastic,' Jack said, smiling.

Esther tutted. 'Trust you to think grubby thoughts like that in respect of a religious tradition. *Your* religion, that is. We Jews only had Hanukkah lamps, and I was five before I learned that the Christians cut down trees and decorated them. Since then I've always been drawn to them, and this year I thought we'd do our own, rather than gaze longingly at your mother's. Presumably you'll be home for Christmas?'

'Of course, but are you suggesting that we do the family thing here, rather than at Mother's?'

'I think it's time, Jack. Your mother's still not looking her old self, and if we allow her to take over as usual, she'll put herself into the grave with the fuss and stress that she normally puts into all the arrangements. Sooner or later the generations do a changing of the guard, and it's high time that the Enright tribe based itself here for family events.'

'Including Sunday dinner?'

'That was a ritual that your mother invented to ensure that she got to see something of you once you slipped out of her hands and fell under the wicked influence of your Uncle Percy. It's hardly a family tradition stretching back generations.'

'Have you broached the subject with Mother?'

'At least three times.'

'And?'

'The first time she snorted and refused to discuss it, the second time she employed words such as "tradition", but the third time she was lying back in bed after another funny turn and was prepared to concede the wisdom of my offer.'

'Is she OK?' Jack asked in alarm.

Esther nodded reassuringly. 'This time wasn't as bad as the first, and she knew what to expect and was sensible enough to lie down and send for the doctor. That was Tuesday, and she was back on her feet yesterday.'

'So it's all agreed?'

'I've still got my fingers crossed, but when you go back on Monday be sure to invite Uncle Percy and Aunt Beattie, and

I'll write inviting Lucy and her family. Once we have the balance of those attending, she won't be able to back out of what she conceded in her moment of weakness.'

'What about Abe and Mary?'

Esther's face broadened in a wide smile. 'Could we really? You wouldn't mind? Only I imagine that they'll be all by themselves, and I don't know if Abe's ever experienced a Christian Christmas, while Mary will obviously be missing her own family, wherever they are. Ireland somewhere or other I imagine, given her accent.'

'Of *course* we invite Abe and Mary,' Jack agreed. 'While we're about it, what about Billy? Nell will, I assume, be helping out here, and I'd hate to think of poor old Billy sitting all alone in his gardener's hut, surrounded by gravestones.'

'You really *are* a big softie at heart, aren't you?' Esther said. 'Let's go and see how the gingerbread men are coming along in the kitchen, and I'll put the pot on for tea. Since you're so lovely you can have a biscuit to go with it.'

The weekend continued in this happy domestic vein, and on the Saturday Jack made a point of visiting his mother in time for dinner, if only to discreetly learn more regarding her state of health.

'Why all this fuss, just because I have the occasional giddy turn?' Constance demanded as she forked another helping of lettuce with a frown of displeasure.

'At least you're not calling it indigestion any more,' Jack observed with a smile.

'What does it matter what you call it?' Constance said irritably. 'It's still holding me back from things I have to do.'

'Such as?' Jack challenged her. 'You have enough domestic staff to ensure that you don't need to do things around the house.'

'In my position,' Constance replied imperiously, 'one does not need to soil one's hands with domestic duties. I was referring more to my social duties. The Ladies' Guild, the bridge club, the soirees at the vicarage and so forth. That wife of yours is determined to take over my secretarial duties in the Ladies' Guild, that's obvious, and now she's stolen Christmas. Did she tell you?'

'Indeed she did, and you should be grateful, rather than resentful,' Jack chided her. 'You above all people should appreciate how much responsibility she's taken on — and with four children to look after.'

'Has she seen any more of her brother?'

'Not since they came to visit last Sunday, so far as I'm aware. They'll be there on Christmas Day, anyway.'

'I gather from Esther that he's living in sin with some Irish woman he met in Africa. Was she a missionary or something?'

'As far as I'm aware she was related to someone in his Guards regiment, and they met in Cairo.'

'Not the most ideal of backgrounds, I would have thought,' Constance sniffed, 'but there you go. Times are changing, Jackson, and not for the better, I fear. In my day one needed a formal introduction before even speaking to a lady. But perhaps she's no lady.'

'Really, Mother!' Jack protested. 'You have the poor woman condemned before you even meet her. And if it helps to sweeten your opinion of her, I gather that they were introduced by a fellow officer of Abe's.'

'What sort of name is that — "Abe"?' Constance frowned. 'Is it short for something more socially appropriate?'

'Yes — his full name is "Abraham".'

'Then that's what I'll call him, if we ever meet.'

'He'll be there on Christmas Day.'

'With his hussy?'

'With "Mary", yes. I hope you'll behave civilly towards her.'

'That will depend upon how she disports herself. Would you like the rest of this salad, dear, or shall I instruct Cook to feed it to those dreadful pigs two doors up in the Brayshaws' back garden?'

Later that night, as they lay in bed Jack expressed his apprehension to Esther. 'I think Mother's got quite the wrong idea about Abe's lady friend Mary. I assume you were unwise enough to tell her that they were living in sin?'

'I thought it was best to be honest with her from the beginning, rather than let it slip out like some dreadful secret. I hope you didn't tell her that Abe's a deserter?'

'What do *you* think? You know Mother — everything has to be proper and "appropriate", as she's fond of calling it. And I think she's still in a huff about losing Christmas Day to you. Still, she may have a point about Mary.'

'How do you mean?'

'Well, what do we really know about her?' Jack observed. 'We only know what they choose to disclose, and even *that's* a bit on the shady side. She's out there, married to an officer — or at least, one hopes it was an officer and not the regimental drummer or something — and after what must have been a brief acquaintance on the dance floor she ups and leaves her husband and takes up with a man she hardly knows.'

'You're getting as bad as your mother; do you know that?' Esther chuckled. 'You and I met during an inquest into the murder of a prostitute. And we were never even formally introduced. Did you ever tell your mother *that*?'

'Of course not. And at least we had the decency to "walk out" together for two years, then get married, before we did the deed. It's just that I'm a bit uneasy that your brother's being taken for a ride by a beautiful woman who may, for all we know, have a shady past. Perhaps, when they come over here for Christmas, we should invite them to stay here with us, then you can gently pump her for more information.'

'I'm not a police officer, Jack. I don't "pump" people for information.'

'For someone who's not a police officer, you have a remarkable history of getting involved in my cases, mainly on the insistence of Uncle Percy. I'm just suggesting that you'll be well placed to learn more about her, that's all.'

It fell silent for a moment, then Esther sighed. 'It's another of your cases, isn't it? You're investigating Abe, and you daren't tell me, so you come at it sideways and ask me to find out more about the lady in his life.'

'We're *not* investigating Abe, honestly.'

'And Mary?'

The silence said it all, and Esther rolled over, then sat up in bed and looked down at Jack accusingly. 'What's she suspected of, Jack?'

'Nothing, why?'

'I know you well enough, Jackson Enright, to know when you're lying to me. Now — what's she suspected of?'

'I can't tell you.'

'Then I can hardly be called upon to interrogate her, can I?'

'I'm not asking you to interrogate her. I just thought, since she's so important to Abe, and he's so important to you, that you might feel more comfortable if you knew a little more about her, that's all. Pardon me for caring.'

'Don't get all huffy, Jack,' Esther urged him as she leaned down and kissed him, 'not when you're going away again tomorrow. That reminds me — are we expected at your mother's for dinner?'

'No, thank God. I think my visit today was enough to satisfy her, so I'll keep doing that every Saturday, then hopefully the tradition will fall by the wayside. Uncle Percy and Aunt Beattie are pleading head colds this week, and at least they have this dreadful weather to give them an excuse.'

'I rather enjoy the cold nights,' Esther purred, 'since it means we have to snuggle up together for warmth.' She wriggled down alongside him and wrapped her arms around him. 'Let's just fall asleep in each other's arms, and I promise I'll ask the right questions of Mary.'

At the appointed time on Monday morning, Jack and Percy puffed their way up the last few steps that gave access to the front entrance of St Paul's, and looked back down. Percy grinned. 'That was enough of a struggle for me, so I can well understand why a seriously overweight old lady thirty years older than me might baulk at walking up here while maintaining her dignity.'

'That doesn't make our job any easier,' Jack complained as he looked down to his left at the houses that sat almost alongside the venerable old pile at the top of Ludgate Hill. 'A half decent marksman with a serviceable rifle could pick her off at his leisure from up there, whether she's wobbling up the stairs or sitting in her carriage. Are we sure we can't persuade the Queen to change her plans?'

'What, you and I together, you mean?' Percy replied jokingly. 'I'm advised by this man walking up to meet us that there have been several attempts to change the minds of those who organise these things for her, and that all of them have fallen on deaf ears.'

'Which man were you referring to?' Jack said with a puzzled frown as he surveyed the handful of people mounting the front steps.

'The old man with the walking stick. That's Melville, unless I'm very much mistaken.'

Jack watched with fascination as the bent old man made his way painfully up the steps, stopping after every two or three in order to regain his breath, but never straightening up. Percy was faintly amused to learn that even the head of Special Branch preferred to don disguises, while Jack was still asking himself why the nation's security was entrusted to a hunched old cripple when he made yet another pause for breath one step below them and hissed his instruction.

'Not here, and not now. A coach will collect you from your house in Hackney at nine am on Thursday. Be there — both of you.'

With that he hobbled on past them, and Jack stared after him in amazement.

'Was that him? He's as old as the cathedral himself, by the look of him.'

'Get used to surprises like that Jack, and welcome to my new world. At a guess we're invited to dinner with someone even more important on Thursday. For the time being, where's the nearest tea shop?'

Later that day, having left Jack behind in their office at the Yard, Percy approached the tenement in Lowder Street, Wapping, where Jack had first interviewed Lizzie Black. It had been agreed that Percy would be the better of the two to make this visit, since it might involve the sort of intense interrogation that he delivered best, and matters had gone beyond polite enquiry. Michael Black had never reported back for police duties since the night he'd presumably stood aside while Bartrams' warehouse was looted of army uniforms, and now he appeared to be a member of the Home Front Club, according to what Jack had learned. Some important questions required honest answers, and Percy was not likely to be seduced from his mission by the woman who claimed to be Black's wife.

Percy wrinkled his nose against the smell of human urine and boiled pigs' trotters as he mounted the crumbling stairs to the landing on the second floor of the tenement and hammered on the door. Then he hammered again when there was no reply and was seriously contemplating making his next enquiry with the sole of his boot when the door across the landing opened and an unshaven face appeared in the doorframe.

'You bin sent by the landlord? If so, yer too late. They done a scarper last week.'

'Who done — did — a scarper?' Percy asked.

The man coughed, then spit on the floor of the landing in front of his door before deigning to reply. 'Them what lived there. Lizzie an' 'er bleedin' kids what was always runnin' up an' down them stairs.'

'Lizzie Black?'

'Never knew 'er proper name, but 'er man were a copper, afore 'e pissed off an' left 'em.'

'And they left last week, you said?'

'Yeah — was they owin' the rent?'

'No idea,' Percy told him as he raised his police badge high in the air for the man to squint at across the landing. 'Is there anyone else living there now?'

'You a copper?'

When Percy confirmed that he was, the man coughed and spat a second time, then closed his front door with a loud bang after his parting words.

'Let me see — 'ow can I put this? Piss off!'

The week passed uneventfully as Percy and Jack made one gallant effort after another to organise what they had designated as their 'Master Manpower Plan' for the policing of half of London during the crucial two days of the Diamond Jubilee celebrations. From time to time Chief Superintendent Bray wandered in to demand to know what they were doing, and to remind them that any major transfer of manpower from one police station to another would require his final approval. Then on Wednesday morning they were summoned to the office of Assistant Commissioner Doyle, who glared at Jack as they sat in front of his desk, clearly of the belief that he was more easily intimidated.

'Have you finished that manpower audit yet, Sergeant?'

'Not quite, sir,' Jack replied in a respectful tone, fully aware that Doyle might well have an unhealthy interest in what they were engaged upon.

'And what are you doing with your time, Percy? If your nephew here is in need of a helping hand, surely you'll be better employed in assisting him?'

'I'm searching for possible security weaknesses.'

'And have you found any?'

There was an awkward silence, during which Jack crossed his fingers in the hope that Percy's affability would not fracture.

'I'm afraid I report directly to Superintendent Melville at Special Branch, sir, and — through him — to the Home Secretary.'

'And the ears of an Assistant Commissioner of the Yard are not deemed trustworthy enough to receive any information on possible lapses in operational efficiency?'

'It's a bit more than that, with respect, sir. We know of at least three distinct acts of corruption at street level among Met officers, each of which might have implications for the Queen's safety during her forthcoming Jubilee celebrations.'

'And they are?' Doyle demanded.

'Solely for the ears of Superintendent Melville, sir.'

'This manpower survey of yours, Sergeant,' Doyle continued unabashed, and seemingly unfazed, as he glared round at Jack. 'I trust you aren't going to send West End men into the East End? We can't afford to have any resignations at a critical moment.'

'I'm aware of that, sir,' Jack replied deferentially, 'and so far as possible I'm arranging to move men only one station down the social scale. Stepney will be reinforced from Holborn, Holborn from Mayfair, Mayfair from Kensington, and so on. But at some stage we're likely to need to rely on every "Special" we can call out.'

'For the East End, and specifically St. Paul's?' Doyle asked.

Jack shook his head. 'No, sir, with respect. We'll need our most seasoned men at St Paul's, and I'm proposing that they be drafted in from Stepney. Stepney will get reinforcements from Holborn, and so on, as I already explained, then the final gap will be left in the numbers at Bow Street. That's where I propose that we station the Specials, at least on the first day, while the Queen's in residence at Buckingham Palace.'

'So the weak spot in all this will be in the West, on the first day at least, while "full strength" deployment will be at St Paul's, on the second. Have I got that right?'

'Yes, sir, since that's where we perceive that her Majesty will be in the greatest danger,' Jack replied.

Doyle nodded. 'You may be right at that, Sergeant. Clearly the two of you seem to be on the right track, so I won't delay you any further, particularly since I want you both out of that office by the end of January.'

'Why's that, sir?' Percy enquired cautiously.

'The entire Yard's scheduled to move to new headquarters in the next year or two, and we need to slowly phase out the use of offices in this building, to make the transition smoother when that day comes.'

'And we're being allocated an early office in this new building?'

Doyle smiled unpleasantly as he shook his head. 'No, you simply have to vacate that office by the end of January. By all accounts you'll be finished by then, and I'll ensure that your plans are implemented to the letter.'

'And what about us?' Percy demanded.

'If you're of sufficient remaining value to Special Branch, presumably they'll find some office for you somewhere in their little empire. Good morning, gentlemen.'

Jack waited until they were back in the privacy of what had now become their temporary office before speaking. 'That's outrageous and unfair! Downright rotten! We do all the hard work, solve all his problems, then we're out on our arses! You into greengrocery, and me back to Chelmsford. And after we obviously got it right.'

'You think so?' Percy said with a self-righteous smirk.

'That's what Doyle said,' Jack reminded him.

'That's what he *said*, certainly, but that's not what he *meant*. He wants us out of here before we can come up with another plan.'

'We don't need another plan, if we've got it right this time,' Jack insisted, and Percy's face finally returned to its customary serious expression.

'That's just the point, Jack. Doyle doesn't want us to come up with another plan, because he thinks that we've got it wrong, and he wants us out of here before we get it right. He's happy for us to focus on St. Paul's, and we have to ask ourselves *why*.'

Chapter Sixteen

Jack watched, entranced, as Manning — the butler with a serious looking revolver strapped under his armpit — served the coffee and sandwiches and then slid quietly into the rhododendron bushes. They were having a picnic around a table on the rear lawn of the Home Secretary's private residence in Buckinghamshire, and somehow it all seemed to fit with the bizarre series of events that had begun shortly after breakfast on a far from normal Thursday.

First of all, a coach had pulled silently up to the front garden gate of Percy and Beattie's house in Hackney, and its door had opened seemingly of its own accord. Once they climbed in, Jack had been formally introduced to Superintendent William Melville, Head of Special Branch, and he'd found it impossible to reconcile the appearance of the tall, straight-backed military type sporting a neatly trimmed moustache with that of the bent old man who'd accosted them on the steps of St Paul's the previous week. His companion was a swarthy looking individual with the Irish name of Reilly, but who had a funny way of speaking English, and Jack formed the instant conclusion that he wouldn't trust the man further than he could throw him.

There had been little to no conversation during the two hours in which the coach had rumbled resolutely through the outer western London suburbs before coming to a halt outside a palatial mansion into which they had been ushered by a liveried footman, to be met in the front entrance hall by British Home Secretary Sir Matthew Ridley. Had the Queen herself taken their heavy topcoats and hats, Jack would have not been surprised, such was the unreality of it all.

'I regret that I won't be able to offer you and your nephew dinner today, Percy,' Ridley explained as he smiled across the table, 'since while the House is in session I'm expected to be in my office in Whitehall most afternoons. However, hopefully these sandwiches will be a compensation of sorts, and this way we have at least an hour to learn where your investigations so far have taken us.'

'Melville already knows most of this, since it was in my written report to him two weeks ago,' Percy announced as he selected his second sandwich, 'but basically, we've been able to confirm the acts of corruption within the Met that you suspected. I investigated the Holborn one personally, and there can be no doubt that Sergeant Hector Cameron was responsible for the theft of police uniforms and wagon that facilitated the Hatton Garden gem raid. He was clearly open to bribery, on account of the fact that he has a young son in need of the sort of medical assistance that you can't buy on a police sergeant's salary. He's still in his post, and his somewhat weak Inspector's protecting him for commendable reasons of sympathy and loyalty for a colleague. But not, I think, as the result of any corruption. Jack here investigated two other cases you alerted us to, and I'll let him reveal his own findings while I savour this excellent chicken sandwich.'

Jack cleared his throat, somewhat overawed by the occasion, and mindful of the cool stares of Melville and Reilly. 'I have every reason to believe,' he began somewhat pompously, 'that corruption has set in at the Whitechapel police station, under the guarded control of the Inspector there — a man named Ingram; George Ingram. Thanks to him, and as the direct result of his connivance, there was a change of personnel on fixed point duty outside the Wapping warehouse of Bartrams, from where we suspect that army uniforms were stolen before the place was set on fire. The constable who should have been rostered on — a man called Michael Black — seems to have been heavily in debt to some soldier he'd been playing cards with previously, and of whom, according to his wife, he was very afraid. Shortly before failing to report for duty, he gave his wife a substantial amount of money, but refused to say where it had come from. Then he disappeared from sight, but I think I know where to find him.'

'So who *was* on duty that night?' Ridley enquired.

'A constable called Edward Ainsworth,' Jack replied. 'A man who enjoyed an expensive lifestyle, and who liked the ladies. He was last seen with one, heading towards St Katherine Dock the day after the warehouse fire, and his body was fished out of there, beaten to pulp, almost two weeks later.'

'And you reckon that the man behind all this was his Inspector in Whitechapel?' Melville asked. 'I think you said his name was Ingram?'

'That's right,' Jack replied eagerly. 'He all but threw me out of Whitechapel when he could see where my enquiries were leading, and Uncle Percy here — sorry, Inspector Enright — can tell you more about him. Over to you, Inspector.'

Percy cleared his mouth of sandwich and nodded. 'This same bloke, Ingram, was a mere sergeant at Stepney when a load of illegal firearms, mainly army rifles, were found in a house on his patch, by two constables called Greenway and Padley. When they kicked the door in, they arrested a man called Hiscock, at least according to the information you gave me at the start of all this. But the curious fact that I discovered when I went through the books in Stepney — which now has a new Sergeant who's too thick to be corrupt — was that there was no record of Hiscock having been arrested in the first place. The duty sergeant on the front desk that night was Ingram, and my guess is that he never formally booked Hiscock in, but simply slipped him out of a side door when no-one was looking.'

'As I recall,' Melville interrupted, 'the weapons themselves were conveyed to Scotland Yard, from where over half of them were stolen. Did you manage to get any more information on that?'

'Indeed I did.' Percy frowned. 'You will recall that the two constables who first located them were called Greenway and Padley. I'm afraid that Constable Greenway didn't live long to celebrate his success, since a few nights later he was lured up a dark alley and done to death.'

'And the other one — Padley?' Melville urged him.

'By some miracle that owed more to blatant corruption than coincidence, when Padley was transferred to the Yard he was placed on "stores" duty that made him directly responsible for the arms cache from which eighty or so army rifles disappeared on his watch. I can only assume that the rifles belonged to whichever subversive group was using the Stepney house as a store, and that they were the ones who stole them back while Padway looked the other way.'

'Presumably this man has been interrogated?' Reilly asked in his first contribution to the conversation, sounding as if his Irish ancestry came by way of Eastern Europe.

Percy grimaced as he continued. 'We now come to the bit that I'm sure you don't want to hear. I was in the process of consulting Padley's record, in the hope of locating his current whereabouts and duties, when the file was all but ripped out of my hands by my own ultimate superior officer, Chief Superintendent Bray. The reason he gave was that my remit only covered Met stations, and not the internal workings of the Yard, and I'd like to believe him. But I'm bound to report that the corruption may have crept even higher up inside the Yard.'

'Higher than Chief Superintendent?' Ridley said with worried creases in his brow.

'Indeed,' Percy confirmed. 'You recall that my basic remit was to sit and wait for someone to approach me with a view to corrupting me? Well, you were right. I've been basically offered high office in some sort of post-revolutionary police force, in return for turning a blind eye to what I've discovered, by none other than Assistant Commissioner Doyle.'

'I'm not surprised,' Melville observed quietly. 'It had to be someone fairly high up, and it seems that all this low-level corruption is a prelude to something much worse.'

'To do with the upcoming Jubilee?' Jack asked.

Melville nodded. 'They've so far corrupted only at a low level, although by these means they've managed to acquire guns, police uniforms, a wagon and God knows how many army uniforms. Not only can these commodities be put to good use when the time comes, but they now have a little coterie of corrupted police officers who can be relied upon to either look the other way or positively assist when some sort of anarchistic attack's made on the Queen.'

'We've begun to get a few provisional lines on that as well,' Percy ventured, and all eyes turned to him. 'We know that the Jubilee festivities will last for two days, and that the Met's under strength in both parts of London in which they'll be taking place. The first day will centre around Buckingham Palace, and some sort of State reception of all the crowned heads who've been invited. The responsibility for policing that will fall on the West End stations and chiefly Bow Street, whose Inspector — a man named Lionel Markwell — was far from reluctant to share with me his views on how the nation should be run. Those opinions do not incorporate any sort of elected democracy headed by a monarch — more like a military dictatorship, in which he no doubt envisages himself in a prominent position. He's obviously ex-military himself and has staffed his station with former soldiers.'

'And the police in Bow Street have an unhealthy relationship with soldiers from the local barracks,' Jack chipped in. Embarrassed by the silence that followed, he felt obliged to explain. 'They've formed this club in a very salubrious set of premises in the West End. The membership's free to serving police and army, and it must be costing someone a fortune to finance it, so you'd have to ask "who" and "why". They call it the "Home Front Club", and it's fiercely patriotic on the surface, but with a very uncomfortable Irish undertone. I've managed to get myself elected as a member, and I discovered quite by accident that another member admitted a week or two ahead of me is the same Michael Black who deserted his post in Wapping in order to facilitate the Bartrams raid, and who hadn't been seen since by his wife when I interviewed her. And according to the Inspector here, even the wife's now disappeared.'

Melville whistled softly. 'That's a *remarkable* breakthrough, Sergeant. By the sound of it, you've infiltrated the very centre of what may be the nest of those seeking to wreak their evil on Day One.'

'But is that their real target?' Percy enquired. All eyes turned to him again as he shared his thoughts further. 'The Queen will be far more vulnerable when she sits in her carriage at the foot of St. Paul's steps, surely? Any lunatic with a half-decent gun could pick her off there. It may be that we're being decoyed into concentrating on Buck House when the real danger is at St. Paul's.'

'Or the other way around,' Melville argued. 'It's too obvious, surely? We're being tempted into pouring manpower into the East End, when for all we know the real plot involves the West End, and Day One.'

'It would help if we knew who we were dealing with,' Percy grumbled. 'From what you told me during our first meeting, the threat could come from anywhere in Europe, or indeed from some lunatic bunch here in the British Isles. The Irish would seem to be favourite from what we've unearthed so far, but as you were at pains to advise me, they could just be the hired muscle for some other lot.'

Melville leaned down from the table and extracted several sheets of paper from his valise. He placed them face up on the table between them, then turned them to face Percy, before inviting him to look more closely. 'Have you by any chance come up against any of these little charmers during your investigations?'

Percy looked hard at the photographs in front of him, then his eyebrows shot up as he pointed to a particularly unflattering one of a ferrety-face individual with hair that looked like aggressive thistle spikes. 'This bloke — he's one of the two who warned me off further conversation with Sarah Cameron — the wife of Hector Cameron, the Holborn sergeant who allowed all those police uniforms to get themselves stolen.'

There was a snort from Sidney Reilly, who seemed far from delighted. 'That is Leonid Jetnikov. You are lucky that you live.'

There was a brief silence before Melville offered to enlighten them. 'As you will have gathered for yourselves, my colleague

Mr Reilly has never been closer to Ireland than Liverpool. I will not reveal his real name, but you are entitled to know that he is Russian by birth, and that he was recruited by me in return for his being eased out of Odessa when his Jewish ancestry became somewhat inconvenient for him. Although he is no lover of the Romanov family, neither does he wish there to be some sort of working-class pogrom in the land of his birth, since it would not be for the benefit of those of Hebrew extraction.'

'So who exactly *is* this ferret who offered to engage me in fisticuffs?' Percy enquired, and Reilly spat noisily onto the grass to the side of his chair before replying.

'Leonid Jetnikov is killer — a man who will take life with bare hands in return for money,' he explained. 'We believe he comes to London to assist the followers of Ulyanov who wish to kill the Tsar and replace him with their own government of the people. He cares not for people, but he works for money.'

'Just as we suspected,' Percy grinned. 'Russians are behind all this, using the Irish as their infantry.'

'Let's not jump to conclusions,' Melville counselled him. 'Someone may be using the Russians in their turn.'

'Which brings us back to where we started,' Ridley observed gloomily. 'We don't even know who the chosen target may be.'

'The Queen, surely?' Jack suggested.

Melville treated him to a condescending smile. 'Another conclusion that may prove to be false. The eyes of all Europe will be on the Jubilee, and even if they only succeed in assassinating one of the cavalries, or even his horse, it will constitute a major event, and a powerful reminder of what "they" are capable of — whoever "they" are. We've already identified two potential interest groups — the Fenians and the

Russians — but we knew about them before we even began our investigations.'

'So we've learned nothing after all our efforts of the past few weeks?' Percy said with a sour expression.

Melville replied with a reassuring smile, 'Far from it, Percy. You and Jack here have done the job we set you on, by confirming that the recent incidents in the Met were born of corruption and not mere incompetence. And Jack has presented us with a ticket of introduction inside the network of malcontents who may be calling the shots. What we have to decide now is how to respond to what we've learned.'

'We clearly need to confirm whether whatever they're planning is for Day One or Day Two,' Percy reminded them, 'and my money's on Day Two, at St. Paul's.'

'Yet this club that Jack's penetrated seems to consist of those who'll be well positioned on Day One,' Melville reminded him. He turned to Jack. 'Whatever else we agree on, we'll need Jack here to persevere with his membership of that club. Are you agreeable to that, Sergeant?'

Jack nodded. 'I've come this far, and I'm not disposed to call it quits at this stage. But I remind you that I have a wife and four children.'

'All of whom will be well provided for, should the need arise,' Melville assured him with a smile.

'Now just wait a minute!' Percy interrupted. 'Apart from a wife and four children, he has an uncle, and you're looking at him! He may be a useful temporary pawn for you people, but he's the nearest thing to a son that I'll ever have. There's no way on God's earth that I can sit by silently while you order him onto the enemy's guns in some suicidal attempt to flush out the ringleaders of a plot who employ known killers as expendable infantry.'

'Very touching,' Melville replied coldly, 'but we haven't heard from him yet.'

Jack went cold all over as he became of four sets of eyes fixed on his face. His first thought was of Esther and the children, then he asked himself what their lives would be like if some foreign power conquered England and began treating his nearest and dearest like slaves. Finally he looked Melville firmly in the eye and asked, 'What are you proposing that I do next?'

'Run away while you still can,' Percy muttered, before Reilly grabbed his arm and hissed that if he did not remain silent, he wouldn't survive the picnic. Melville allowed that point to sink in, then smiled at Jack.

'I think that the young man here realises, more than his uncle does, that they're both too far into all this to be able to withdraw without consequences. What we're asking, Jack, is that you join the revolution. Become what is known in my profession as a "double", working ostensibly for both sides, but in reality for only one.'

'Get further involved with those in the club, and pretend to go along with their plans while reporting them to you, you mean?' Jack asked as his throat began to dry.

Melville nodded. 'Precisely. Apart from your club membership, you also have family links to two people we need to keep a careful eye on.'

'Abe and Mary?' Jack said, to another nod from Melville.

'As requested, we did some background digging on the pair of them, and an oddly matched pair they turned out to be. Abraham Jacobs — *Captain* Abraham Jacobs of the Grenadier Guards — far from being a deserter, is officially still in Cairo, where the Army Minister assures me he's engaged in important strategic planning. When Sir Matthew here challenged him at Cabinet level regarding what he knew to be a lie, Salisbury called him off and told him that what went on within the Army Office was no business of the Home Secretary. It isn't the first time that Special Branch have been frustrated in their enquiries by officious types dealing with overseas matters, and the sooner we have a combined Secret Service presiding over *all* matters of national security, the better for the nation.'

'And Mary Carmody?'

'Much easier. She's a straightforward high-class tart. Never *was* married to an English Guards officer, and please God never will be. Employed by interests alien to the nation in order to seduce your brother-in-law into deserting his post and joining whatever cause is paying her no doubt exorbitant fee.'

'So Abraham Jacobs is one of those planning to desecrate the Jubilee with some sort of assassination?' Jack's heart leapt into his mouth at the likely effect on Esther of being told that.

Melville shook his head. 'Probably not, since if he were we'd have been advised by the army, and he'd have been shot as a deserter. As it is, the army won't even accept that he's a deserter.'

'Perhaps he's been allowed to desert, in order to join the conspirators, by someone high up in the army who's in with them too?' Percy suggested, but Melville shook his head.

'I can't believe that because I don't *want* to believe that. If it's true, then England as we know it is well and truly doomed.'

It fell gloomily silent until Percy opted to earn his sandwiches, and he looked across at Melville. 'Assuming that Jack's mad enough to go along with your suggestion, is there anything else you require me for, apart from organising his funeral?'

'Of course,' Melville replied. 'We want you to go "double" as well, Percy. Let Assistant Commissioner Doyle think that you'd like nothing better than a leading position in the brave new

Metropolitan Police Force that will govern the capital and grind the peasants into the mud once the trumpet sounds for the revolution. In the meantime, carry on with your manpower plan, in the hope that, even if we don't foil any plot, we'll at least be fully manned when the uprising begins.'

Two hours later Percy and Jack alighted from the coach at their front gate and stood for a moment gazing up at the house.

'You should never have agreed, Jack,' Percy muttered. 'And I meant what I said about you being my substitute son.'

Chapter Seventeen

Christmas and the New Year were a welcome distraction, and Jack and Percy took as much of their leave entitlements as they could get away with, partly to relieve the pressure on their brains from all the skulduggery in which they seemed to have got themselves immersed, and partly because they instinctively knew that the coming year — 1897 — would not offer them much opportunity for extended leave.

Constance seemed to have gracefully accepted that the old family home in Church Lane had hosted its last Christmas dinner, and that future Yuletide over-indulgences would be at the Bunting Lane home of Jack and Esther. However, not to be outdone, she insisted that her daughter Lucy and her family stay with her when they made the trip from their well-appointed house in Holborn with their own children, and that her own cook and housemaid be added to the domestic staff available for the massive feast that required four separate tables to be set in the sitting room.

Everyone imaginable was there for the best part of a week, with Uncle Percy and Aunt Beattie installed in Jack and Esther's bedroom, while Abe and Mary were afforded what had been Lily's room until she was ordered to share a room with Bertie, which inevitably had the effect of converting it into an almost permanent war zone. Jack and Esther were reduced to sleeping on the floor in Tommy's nursery, with Miriam, who was a few weeks away from her second birthday, tucked in between them.

It was happy, overfed, boisterous and chaotic, but never before had so many Enrights been gathered in the one place to see out the old year and welcome in the new. Constance was in her element, ordering the domestic staff around as if the house were hers, dominating the table that also contained Jack and Esther, reminiscing about all the previous Christmases and making dire predictions about the ones to come if Jack didn't 'buck up his ideas and get a respectable position in the city somewhere.' There seemed to be no sign of any lingering illness, and certainly no evidence that she was sticking to the diet prescribed by Dr. Browning.

Abe and Mary had already become honorary Enrights and gave every indication that they were happy to be included in the expanded family fold. From time to time Jack caught Abe looking at him with a slightly intense expression but he put it down to brotherly curiosity regarding the man his sister had married. As for Mary, she slowly became the life and soul of the lighter moments, happily singing a few of her favourite ballads from her home country, and seemingly unfazed by the absence of any piano accompaniment. But Esther reported back to Jack, more than once as they lay under the blankets on the bedroom floorboards padded with spare sheets to deaden the effect of the gaps, that she found Mary 'difficult to figure. There's always a distance in her manner, somehow, that I can't quite describe, and although we get along fine I can't imagine that we'll ever become warm friends.'

By unspoken agreement Jack and Percy kept their distance from each other, partly to avoid being accused by Constance of 'talking shop', and partly because the year to come would see them almost joined at the hip as they resumed the task of preparing the Metropolis for what might well prove to be a massive outrage on the chosen two days in June — the twenty-first and twenty-second — on which the Queen would unknowingly be exposing herself to anyone who cared to go down in history as an assassin.

Eventually the guests departed according to their individual timetables and commitments, and Sunday the third of January dawned bright and cold, with no guests remaining in residence, and nothing left to remind them of what had been except a huge collection of leftover food that Nell was instructed to convert into pasties, pies and anything else that might tempt their jaded appetites.

'I was hoping that when the New Year came you'd be back here with us all the time,' Esther complained as they gazed mournfully out of the kitchen window at the thin layer of overnight snow that had converted their rear lawn into a virgin landscape that Lily and Bertie were competing to convert into trails of boot prints.

'Hopefully I'll be able to scale it back a bit in a few weeks,' Jack lied, 'and then I'll be back to Chelmsford. If it's any consolation, Aunt Beattie's cooking's going to taste even bleaker after all that rich food we've been enjoying. Thank you again for a wonderful Christmas, darling.'

'Thank your mother, and Nell,' Esther replied as she hugged him closer to her. 'Thank God your mother didn't appear to over-exert herself, and Nell was well worded to keep the heavy lifting and so on for herself. As for food, there are enough chicken pasties and turkey pies in the larder for you to take a few hampers down with you.'

'I'll be travelling by passenger train, not freight,' Jack joked, then it fell silent.

'You really *can't* tell me what you're working on with Uncle Percy?' Esther wheedled, and Jack shook his head.

'I really can't, but as I said I hope that it'll tail off a bit towards the spring, then I'll be home fulltime, I promise.'

His promise sounded even more hollow that evening, as he joined Percy in the all too familiar seat in front of the sitting room fire, having delivered a heavy satchel full of assorted pastries to a delighted Aunt Beattie.

'At least we'll have a half decent supper,' Percy muttered as he puffed away on his pipe. 'That said, I've had enough turkey to last me a lifetime, and supper will only bring back memories of happier days when danger didn't lurk inside a gas oven.'

'Let's hope it won't be a "Last Supper",' Jack joked apprehensively. 'I'm not sure who we should fear the most — the ones who're after the Queen's life, or those allegedly on our own side who'd love to see us out of the way.'

'Hopefully the letter the Home Secretary gave us this time will do the trick,' Percy suggested. 'I'm certainly looking forward to sticking it under Ingram's nose, not to mention Bray, but what we don't know is whether or not Doyle will take the hint.'

'You think he's the one to watch inside the Yard?' Jack asked.

Percy nodded. 'He's just at the right level, and he's Irish by birth. Most of the stuff that we've uncovered inside the Met couldn't have been so easily ignored or overlooked if Doyle had his eye on the ball. Either he's totally incompetent, or up to his uniformed armpits in the plot.'

'So we begin back at the Yard?'

'Initially yes. Then I'll have to act as the resident bad smell in Whitechapel for long enough to force Ingram into devising a workable manpower plan for St Paul's on the fateful day. That should be a *real* treat.'

'And me?'

'I don't suppose it would be too suspicious if you were to adopt a similar role in Bow Street? You need to keep in close contact with everyone in that club, and that might be best done while you're based in the West End. Then, at the same time, you can assess the security arrangements insofar as the Met will be involved, although if it goes to form we can also expect entire battalions of Household Cavalry, Foot Guards and assorted Artillery on both days.'

The following morning they presented themselves back in Whitehall, and Percy stood with a smirk on his face while Chief Superintendent Bray read the scathing letter from the Home Secretary that upbraided him for even considering the possibility that 'two officers personally allocated special duties by me on the authority of Cabinet are to be summarily ejected from your current accommodation. They are to be allowed the best remaining facilities inside the existing Scotland Yard building, and any failure to comply with this instruction will be reported directly to the Prime Minister, whose reaction is likely to be very unfavourable to your future career prospects. Please sign and detach the bottom-most portion of this letter, and have it delivered to me at my office in the House.'

'Level Three, Room 327,' Bray all but spat when he'd finished reading it. 'He doesn't say what those "special duties" are, but presumably you're about to tell me?'

'Far from it,' Percy smirked. 'It must be obvious, even to you, that what we're engaged on is not a matter suitable for general publication. All you need to know is that it concerns the readiness of the Met for all aspects of the Queen's security during the Jubilee in June. Not just the outlying stations, but the Yard itself.'

'You suspect me?' Bray bristled.

Percy shook his head. 'Not necessarily. But I might revise that opinion if I don't get some reliable information on the current whereabouts of Constable Bernard Padley.'

'He's on indefinite sick leave,' Bray replied without blinking.

Percy smiled knowingly as he turned and took Jack's elbow in a gesture that they should leave while they were winning. 'All that loss of property clearly affected Padley's digestion,' was his parting shot at a red-faced Bray.

'He seemed to know all about Padley without consulting any records,' Jack observed as they settled into facing desks in their new office, which was noticeably better appointed than their previous one. 'Don't you think that looks suspicious?'

'Of course it does,' Percy replied as he checked inside his desk drawers for pen and ink, 'but that only suggests that he's totally embarrassed by those rifles going for a walk on his watch. He's a pompous old fool, and he's clearly anxious to maintain his rank, but that doesn't make him a traitor.'

'I'm not sure I share your faith in him,' Jack replied, 'but no doubt you'll eventually be proved right, as usual. So how do we do this? I kept my previous manpower lists from the West End stations, so I can carry on where I left off. Are we to assume that the bobbies will be forming the usual thin blue line facing the crowds, and holding them back, while the first line of defence around Her Majesty will be platoons of cavalry and foot guards?'

'May as well, until we get more detail,' Percy agreed. 'I'm not sure how many bobbies you get to the square yard, but presumably somewhere in Bow Street — or perhaps even here inside the Yard — you'll find the detailed allocations for the bunfight ten years ago, and you can compare that with what's likely to be available this time.'

Jack was into his third frustrating day trying to work out how many blue uniforms he'd have available to line the Mall, Trafalgar Square, Charing Cross and down to The Embankment when a constable tapped on the half open door and stuck his head inside the office.

'Which of you's Jack Enright?' he enquired, and Jack raised his head from the paperwork to acknowledge his identity. 'There's a tottie o' some sort down in the front entrance, askin' fer you. She looks a bit suspect, an' kinda nervous, an' she won't let on what 'er business is to anybody but you, so the sergeant down on the front desk'd be mighty obliged if yer'd deal wiv 'er.'

Jack sighed and rose from his chair, conscious of Percy's cheesy grin. 'I've no idea who she is,' Jack insisted, 'so take that leer off your face.'

He descended to the tiled ground floor, where a vaguely familiar figure sat on one of the benches allocated to witnesses waiting to be interviewed. There was something about her that rang a bell in his recent memory, but he wasn't kept guessing for long, since as soon as he appeared at the foot of the stairs she scuttled towards him with an apprehensive backward glance towards the front door, as if she feared that she was being followed.

'Remember me?' she pleaded. 'I'm Lizzie Black — yer come up ter my place when I were livin' in Lowder Street, down in Wappin'. Yer was lookin' fer me 'usband Mickey, an' yer said as 'ow, if I needed any protectin', I could come ter you.'

'Of course I remember,' Jack confirmed as he noted that the woman was shivering, despite the excessive temperature at which the building was maintained. 'Come with me, and we'll find somewhere where we can talk.'

In a side interview room on the ground floor he motioned her into a seat and decided to give nothing away to begin with. 'Has Mickey returned?' he asked.

She shook her head, adding, 'At least, not 'imself. But 'e sends money every week, so I know 'e's still alive. But I think 'e's in trouble, 'cos these blokes come ter me room, an' told me to get out, else I were a gonner.'

'Some men called at your lodging and ordered you out of there on threat of death?'

Lizzie nodded. 'Yeah, like I just said. I don't know why, or what I've done, an' what's gonna be 'appenin' ter me an' the kids if the money ain't comin' in no more.'

'Do you know who these men were?' Jack asked hopefully.

'Only that they was two o' them what'd bin watchin' the 'ouse from time ter time, like they was waitin' fer Mickey ter show up. An' one week one o' them turned up wiv me regular money.'

'From what you've told me, Mickey had been sending you the money each week, that right?'

'Yeah, it musta bin 'im, 'cos who else'd take the trouble ter look after us?'

'But Mickey never showed up himself, or tried to contact you?'

'No, never.'

'These men who ordered you out of your present accommodation, did they suggest anywhere else where you should move to?'

'Yeah, they gimme this piece o' paper wiv sumfin' written on it, but I can't read, so yer'll 'ave ter tell me what it sez. I tried ter ignore that, an' when I first moved out I went ter live wiv me sister in Stepney. But they come an' found me, an' said that if I didn't move ter this place by the end o' this week, I'd be 'orsemeat, but if I did what I were told, then they'd keep comin' wiv the money.'

Jack glanced down quickly at the crumpled and grease-stained piece of paper that Lizzie thrust into his hand. 'It's an address, right enough,' he advised her. 'Another lodging house in Wapping, by the look of it. "Fifteen, Carter's Rooms, Pennington Street." Do you know it?'

'Yeah,' she nodded with a smile. 'It's just at the back o' London Dock, where me bruvver used ter work 'til 'e 'ad 'is accident. But I ain't got no key fer the place.'

'I suggest that you just turn up there and ask the Superintendent for the key,' Jack told her. 'Something tells me that he'll be expecting you.'

'Will yer come wiv me?' she asked with a pleading look in her eyes, and a hand on his wrist. 'I'll make it worth yer while, if yer get me meanin'.'

'No, best if I don't,' Jack replied gently as he moved his hand back from where hers had been lying on it. 'But come in here and see me again whenever you need to.'

'Thanks,' Lizzie muttered as she leaned forward without warning and kissed him on the cheek. 'An' if yer find Mickey, yer'll be sure an' tell 'im where I've moved to?'

'Of course,' Jack reassured her. 'And good luck.'

Back upstairs, he recounted the strange conversation to Percy, who thought for a long moment, then voiced his opinion. 'Sounds to me as if "they" don't want Michael Black to talk to his wife about what he's involved in. That certainly explains why she wasn't there when I called just before Christmas. If they've been watching her place, they were probably planning on intercepting him if he managed to get too close to his old home, and of course there was always the risk that he'd guess that she'd moved in with her sister. "They" clearly don't mean her any harm, and whatever Black's got himself involved in, one of its terms is that his wife and children will be provided for financially, but that he can't go near them. That sound plausible to you?'

'Very plausible,' Jack agreed. 'And, as you no doubt recall, it shouldn't take too much effort on my part to meet with Michael Black and assure him that his family's fine. But to do that I'll need to stick my head further into the lion's mouth, so to speak.'

'Just don't get it bitten off in the process,' Percy warned him. 'I'm relying on another consignment of pastries from the Christmas leftovers.'

'I sent your nephew packing when he stuck his nose where it didn't belong, so now he sends his uncle?' Inspector George Ingram demanded angrily as Percy was admitted to his office.

'He sent nobody,' Percy smiled back with a challenge in his eyes. 'But the Home Secretary's sent me, if you'd care to pick up that telephone on your desk and confirm that. I can give you his home number, since it's still fairly early in the day, and when I last had dinner with him he had to cut it short in order to be in the House for its afternoon session.'

'Is that supposed to impress me?' Ingram snarled.

'I don't think anything would impress you that came from a desire to preserve the Queen and the nation from foreign threats.'

'Your meaning?'

'My meaning, Inspector, is that someone with no idea of what they're doing has decided that Her Majesty will — on the Twenty-second of June, as I have no doubt you're already aware — sit in her carriage at the foot of the steps of St. Paul's while the Archbishop of Canterbury conducts an open-air service. Regardless of how long that service is intended to take, she'll be a sitting duck, and I have every reason to believe that you don't have enough men to protect her.'

'It's not the job of the police to protect the Queen on these occasions,' Ingram countered. 'That's why she has all those tin soldiers in fancy uniforms.'

'Carrying sabres and ceremonial pikes!' Percy reminded him angrily. 'Modern assassins carry guns, let me remind you.'

'Not my problem,' Ingram replied coolly. 'All we're required for is crowd control around the perimeter, and as I pointed out to your nephew we have enough men for that.'

'Do you think so?' Percy challenged him. 'Well, Detective Sergeant Enright brought his findings back to me, and in my opinion you have only seventy per cent of the men you'll need, so we'll be drafting more in from Stepney, and possibly Holborn. Even the West End if necessary.'

'And what do the West Enders know about policing the East End?'

'More than you do, apparently,' Percy fired back. 'I'm not here with a request for co-operation, Inspector, but a *demand* in the name of the Home Secretary that you hand over the day to day administration of Leman Street to me by the end of May.'

'Show me your authority for that,' Ingram challenged him.

'I'll return with that authority within the week,' Percy growled, 'and when I do it may well be combined with your formal dismissal from office. Or do you consider yourself too well protected in certain quarters of the Yard?'

'What are you getting at?'

'I think we *both* know what I'm getting at, but my orders come direct from the Cabinet.'

'Via Special Branch, no doubt?' Ingram enquired with an amused smile. 'Understand this, Enright — there are forces at play here that make Special Branch look like a vicar's bible class. Get in the way and your widow will regret it.'

Percy allowed himself a slow smile. 'At least the gloves are off now, and we needn't walk around each other like two prize fighters who can't be bothered to exchange blows. I'll return with my authority, and a couple of members of my vicar's bible class to escort you off the premises.'

'Let me know when, and I'll arrange for tea and cakes,' was the last riposte Percy heard as he stormed down the staircase and out into Leman Street.

Jack smiled politely at Mary as he entered the bar area unaccompanied, ordered a beer and stood and watched as the pianist arranged Mary's music on the hanger in front of him. It was another musical evening at the Home Front Club, and the room was moderately full already with off-duty soldiers in all their dress uniform finery and police officers in dinner jackets. It was also Jack's third visit to the Club as a member, and the previous ones had been uneventful.

Mary began with the haunting Irish folk ballad 'She Moved Through the Fair', and while the audience was listening with rapt attention Jack was conscious of a man of roughly his own age leaning alongside him at the bar, drinking what looked like a large whisky. Mary finished her first song, then invited the assembled company to join her in a rousing version of 'The Black Velvet Band'. As the noise grew, the young man leaned closer to Jack in order to be heard by him, but no-one else.

'Well, yer bin lookin' fer me, an' now yer've found me. I'm Michael Black.'

'How did you know I was looking for you?' Jack replied as casually as he could.

'Yer don't need ter know that, but 'ave yer seen Lizzie lately? Since that time yer was around our place, that is?'

'I'm telling you nothing until you tell me how you knew I visited her,' Jack insisted, and Black made a backward jerk of the head to indicate the noisy company behind them that was engrossed in loud and largely tuneless song.

'*They* told me — them what's runnin' this show what yer've joined. Yer was followed, like I was every time I tried ter get 'ome ter tell Lizzie what I were still alive.'

'I saw Lizzie only this week,' Jack reassured him. 'She and the kids are fine, and they're getting money from you every week that Lizzie thinks you're sending to her.'

'Which I am, in a way,' Mickey smiled. 'Me wages fer what I does fer this lot, though I'd much rather be at 'ome. But they tells me that I'll be done fer if I tries ter see Lizzie again afore this job's over.'

'What job?' Jack asked hopefully, but Mickey had obviously been well warned about 'loose lips'.

'I can't be seen ter tell yer owt, but yer'll soon learn fer yerself, like Bernie Padley did.'

'Here's here?'

Mickey nodded. 'Joined last week, but 'e's pissed off that 'e can't visit 'is old mam in Shoreditch. Still, they reckon that she's bein' well cared for an' all, just like Lizzie.'

'So how did you come to be in this lot?' Jack asked as he gestured to the barman for their drinks to be refreshed.

'I were a fool, that's 'ow,' Mickey replied as he nodded in thanks for the new drinks order. 'I aluss 'ad a bit've a problem wiv me gamblin', then one night I found meself playin' against this army bloke what seemed to 'ave kings and queens up 'is arse, an' afore I knows it, I'm thirty quid down an' scared shitless 'cos I couldn't pay. But the soldier give me a week ter pay, then when I turned up after me week were up, expectin' ter finish up wiv a bayonet in me guts, lo and be'old the bloke told me that 'e'd cancel me debt an' gimme fifty quid if I'd disappear from me work down at Whitechapel. Needless ter say I agreed, an' the next thing I know'd I were bein' took ter this doss'ouse in Gerrard Street an' told that I weren't allowed ter go 'ome 'til I'd done anuvver job.'

'What sort of job?'

'Don't know yet, does I? An' like I said, I wouldn't be allowed ter tell yer, even if I knew. All I knows is that we spends most days down in Waterloo Barracks, on the parade ground there, bein' made ter walk an' run up an' down like we was in the army or summat. Borin', but we gets ter come in 'ere of an evenin' an' enjoy the facilities.'

'How many of the people in here this evening are in the same position as you?'

'Not all of 'em,' Mickey replied as he cast his eye over the company, 'since some of 'em's obviously army. But there's a few former coppers like me — that bloke what's walkin' up ter the pianner fer a start — used ter be a sergeant up in Mayfair, or so 'e told me. 'E sez 'e's bin told that we're gettin' ready ter fight off an invasion from Russia, but then 'e talks nonsense most o' the time.'

Jack looked towards where Mickey was indicating and recognised the master of ceremonies who was preparing to regale the company with more of his Gilbert and Sullivan favourites, just as Mickey placed an urgent hand on his arm.

'By the sound o' things, you ain't spendin' yer days down at the barracks, that right? I've never seen yer there.'

'That's right,' Jack confirmed, 'although that day may not be far away.'

'If yer still free ter walk around durin' the day,' Mickey enquired tentatively, 'could yer see yer way clear ter poppin' round ter Lizzie, an' makin' sure her an' the children are alright?'

'Of course,' Jack agreed, far from certain whether it was a promise he could keep and hoping that Mickey wasn't about to enquire if they were still living in their old room in Wapping. 'And now I have to be going, before I'm recruited into your new army.'

'You've nothing to reproach yourself about,' Percy assured him as they sat on either side of the fire, awaiting the supper that neither of them felt hungry for. 'We might have known that your membership of that club came with a price tag, and that they'd proudly show you off as their latest recruit to those in there already who must be beginning to doubt their wisdom in agreeing to dishonour the uniform in return for reward. Michael Black clearly failed to report for duty outside Bartrams, allowing them to install Edward Ainsworth in his place, in return for the cancellation of a heavy gambling debt, and we can only assume that Bernard Padley was escaping from something even worse if he was prepared to lose a consignment of rifles from a store in circumstances that would clearly point to his involvement.'

'What's puzzling me,' Jack replied, 'is why I'm not already a virtual prisoner, like the others. There's been no approach to me to act dishonestly, or to join the squad doing daily exercise at the barracks, so what's the price of my membership, and when will I be advised?'

'We can only hope that it won't be yet,' Percy replied thoughtfully. 'In fact, what I imagine they'll want from you, in due course, are the exact manpower deployment details for

Day One in the West End. The longer you can string that out the better.'

'But how will they know when I've finished?'

'You may be approached in the Club for that information. Either that, or it's time I got more cosy with Assistant Commissioner Doyle. It looks as if we're both about to cross the line into the other side's camp. As I recall, that's what Melville and the Home Secretary wanted us to do, but I'll need to speak to him first.'

'How do you normally contact him?'

'I don't — he contacts me. But this time we'll have to take the initiative.'

'How?'

Percy thought for a few moments as he 'reamed' the inside of his now empty pipe in order to clean out the residue of ash, which he tipped into the open fire before sitting back in his chair and thinking out loud. 'As far as I know, his office isn't part of the Yard, but is somewhere inside the Home Office outbuildings on the north side of St James's Park. But you can be sure that "they" will have it well watched, and Melville wouldn't thank either of us for being spotted going in there. Somehow we have to get a message to him, and we obviously can't trust the network in here.'

'So what you need is for someone unlikely to look suspicious or out of place to go in there with a message that you need a meeting with Melville?' Jack said, a horrible thought beginning to form inside his head.

'Either Melville or one of his apes, yes. The first few contacts I made were through some bloke who enjoyed wearing disguises.'

'What's it look like inside that building in St. James's Park?' was Jack's next question, and Percy spread his arms wide.

'How should I know, since I've never been in there?'

'Are they likely to employ women?'

Percy's mouth opened in appreciation. 'You're ahead of me, Jack my boy, if you have in mind sending Esther in there, looking like a clerk or something. I'm sure they employ them in there somewhere, and a smartly dressed woman walking into a Government office wouldn't be likely to attract any attention. All she'd need to do is leave a note from me, addressed to Melville, at what passes for their front desk. In that note I'll ask him for a meeting, then wait for someone to contact me with the time and place. Too easy.'

'I didn't mention Esther,' Jack smiled.

'Your face did,' Percy grinned back.

'How do you know she'll agree? She's responsible for four children every day while I'm away.'

'That's what mothers-in-law are for,' Percy assured him. 'Added to which she's got that big girl with the red hair who seems to be her fulltime domestic. What was her name again?'

'Nell, but we can't take Esther's consent for granted. I'm sure that Mother would be happy to rule over the house while Nell takes Lily and Bertie to school and back, but it's been a while since we got Esther involved in anything like this.'

Anything like what?' Percy demanded. 'We're simply asking her to deliver a letter in central London, and she'd probably be glad of the day out. If you slip her some extra money, she can even go shopping in Oxford Street.'

'I hand over all my money as it is,' Jack advised him, 'and I'm the one who has to pluck up the courage to ask.'

The sitting room door opened, and Beattie announced that supper was ready.

'Is it turkey pie yet again?' Percy asked resignedly.

Beattie shook her head. 'We've eaten all that. Tonight it's my new fish recipe.'

'A good opportunity to polish up your courage, Jack,' Percy grimaced as they rose dutifully from their seats by the fire and walked into the kitchen with all the enthusiasm of men trudging in manacles towards the gallows.

'I might know that the two of you wouldn't once consider what it's like for me living here in isolation until you needed me for some devious scheme of your own,' Esther pouted as Jack put the idea to her over a late supper on Friday evening. 'Of course I'll do it, and of course I'll take the time to visit Oxford Street, always assuming that your mother will agree to hold the fort here for the day. It'll cost you a new hat.'

'I don't need one,' he smiled.

'I meant for *me*, you idiot!' she grinned.

'And do you trust Nell to take the children to school and back?'

'Of course, since she's done it lots of times before, although I'll get her to take Billy with her. He seems better able to control Bertie than she is, mainly because your older son gets no male influence these days.'

'I'll ignore that unworthy slight and ask that while you're in London anyway you visit another lady who's missing her man.'

'Who said I miss you?'

'You did, more than once in the past, and to judge by the kiss I got when I came home, you still do. But this woman hasn't seen her man for some weeks and needs to be reassured that he's still in the land of the living and missing her and the children.'

'And where does she live?'

'Wapping — a street just behind London Dock.'

Esther shuddered. 'I might have known there'd be a catch. I *hate* that place.'

'I'm not asking you to do anything dangerous,' Jack argued. 'It's just that there's a fellow police officer involved in something I can't tell you about, and he's not allowed to contact his wife and children until it's all over. She needs to be reassured that he's all right, and *he* needs to be reassured that *she's* been reassured, if that makes sense.'

'Insofar as anything you say makes sense, yes. And I can certainly relate to the misery of a woman with children who doesn't see her man very often, so I'll hold my nose, grit my teeth, and do it. But the new hat will now come with matching gloves.'

'You asked to see me, sir?' Percy asked as he stuck his head round the door of the office that housed Assistant Commissioner Doyle.

'Indeed I did, Percy — come in,' Doyle smiled back. 'Tea?'

'Thank you, although I can't stay for long, given the bed of nails that I spend every day laid out on, working with my nephew to make the manpower stretch over two very demanding days in June.'

Doyle called out loudly, and when the constable occupying the desk in the corridor entered with a look of resignation, Doyle ordered tea and biscuits for two. 'And make sure that there are plenty of ginger nuts, since they're Inspector Enright's favourites. Now then, Percy, how goes life on that bed of nails you just referred to? Any closer to a final manpower plan?'

'It's only February, sir, and the Jubilee's in June. In any case, with the greatest respect to your office, I report directly elsewhere.'

'Yes, Melville in Special Branch,' Doyle reminded him. 'But given that the task you're engaged on is a routine police matter, my rank in here gives me a right to know how you intend to allocate my men. Where do you perceive the main danger to lurk?'

'Clearly, in the East End on Day Two,' Percy replied, happy to reveal that he had spotted the attempt to divert attention from Day One. 'To be specific, the time when Her Majesty will be sitting in open view in her carriage at the foot of St Paul's steps.'

'Pretty obvious, I would have thought,' Doyle replied thoughtfully as he cleared papers from his desk to make room for the tray of tea and biscuits that had just been delivered. 'Are you sure you're not missing anything important on Day One?'

'That's Sergeant Enright's responsibility, sir. He's tearing his hair out trying to stretch a totally inadequate number of blue uniforms along the route into Buckingham Palace, then out again on the morning of Day Two.'

'And the State Banquet?' Doyle enquired.

Percy frowned. 'Haven't even thought about that, sir. I think we've both been assuming that Palace security will be sufficient to take care of that.'

'Don't you think that we should be planning for a force of elite officers to be allocated the task of policing the inside of the Palace during that banquet, bearing in mind the number of visiting heads of state who'll be there?'

'You may be right, sir, but where are they to come from?'

'Would you be prepared to let me organise that?'

'Of course, but it will only serve to reduce our already depleted numbers on the outside.'

'Not necessarily, Percy. You're not the only one who's being relied upon to guarantee the Queen's ongoing safety, and not the only one who takes instruction from outside the Yard.'

'Special Branch?'

'You don't need to know, Percy. What you need to do is to ensure that whenever you and your nephew have completed your manpower distribution plan you let me have the details, so that I can ensure that none of the men you've delegated to "outside" duties are among those I wish to use inside the Palace.' When Percy's face expressed his indecision, Doyle pressed home his agenda. 'I realise that you regard your first priority as being that of reporting back to Melville, Percy, but how do you know he's got the best interests of the nation at heart?'

'He's head of Special Branch, that's why,' Percy insisted by way of justification, 'and to have achieved that position he must have passed a lot of loyalty tests.'

'And you wouldn't draw the same conclusion regarding an Assistant Commissioner at the Yard?'

'It's not that, sir,' Percy explained with a slightly red face. 'It's just that — well, Melville is better placed to see the whole picture, and ... well, to be frank with you, sir, he has reason to believe that the threat comes from outside the realm.'

'That must be obvious to anyone,' Doyle replied with a frown of his own. 'You don't need to have access to all the information that lands on Melville's desk to know that nobody *within* this country would wish Her Majesty any harm. The problem is that Melville's very selective about who he shares his information with, and some of us are not convinced that he has his eye on the ball. Should he be wrong, then we may all be heading for a national calamity of massive proportions — perhaps even total anarchy. But those of us who're in a position to prevent him dropping the ball at the vital moment will finally get the recognition we deserve for being the true guardians of the nation and will be rewarded with seats at the high table when the dust's settled. I believe that you deserve to be one of those people, Percy.'

'What do you want of me?'

'Simply that you share with me the information that you've been instructed to pass on to Melville. You *and* your nephew, who I may say seems more amenable to being on the winning team, to judge by his eagerness to acquire membership of a certain West End club. Presumably he's told you about that?'

'Only in general terms, sir,' Percy replied, maintaining a mask of apparent concern that he hoped conveyed the impression that he felt that something was being kept from him.

'You needn't worry about him, Percy, since he seems to know which side his bread's buttered. In due course he'll have no reservation in letting those who run that club know what the manpower allocations are for the West End; so far as concerns the East End, I'm well aware of your suspicions regarding Inspector Ingram, and if you're prepared to share your East End proposals with me, I'll have him transferred to somewhere harmless — perhaps across the river — then you'll have Leman Street to yourself.'

'I can't ask for more than that,' Percy conceded, 'and I'd certainly feel happier if you gave me operational control of the East End for Day Two of the Jubilee.'

'Consider it done, Percy, and just remember to keep me advised. You can obviously continue to report to Melville, but before you do that, just make sure that I have the same inside information.'

'I think Doyle's bought it,' Percy announced with a grin as the new coal crackled and spat in the fireplace between him and Jack. 'He's made it clear that he has no problem with me reporting to Melville, but he wants the same information from me at the same time.'

'Will you go along with that?'

Percy's grin widened. 'He'll certainly be getting *some* information from me, but whether or not it's the same information that I give Melville will depend. For example, I can have one manpower plan prepared for the reality of Day Two, while slipping Doyle another one that gives the impression that we're far less prepared than we are.'

'And do you expect two plans from me regarding Day One? Preparing one's proving to be almost beyond me, to be perfectly honest.'

Percy shook his head. 'Doyle seems to think that the people who'll want to see your plan will be those in that club of yours. And there's something else you should know in that regard. Doyle all but confided that he's got a special force lined up to police the inside of the Palace during the banquet that's being planned for that first evening.'

'Surely the Palace has its own security, drawn from the various Guards regiments?'

'Correct — so what's Doyle up to, and where is this "special force" of his coming from?'

Jack's eyes lit up as the penny dropped into the slot. 'Mickey Black told me that he and a few other bobbies who've gone absent without leave spend their days in military type drill in the Waterloo Barracks! They must be the lot that Doyle's talking about!'

'How many?'

'No accurate idea, at this stage. But how soon before I get the offer that I can't refuse, and get to learn the price of my club membership?'

'Hopefully that won't be long, Percy suggested, 'but I need to contact Melville before all this gets out of hand, so the sooner you get Esther to deliver the message the better. Here's the note, already written — take Friday off, give her the note for Melville, then when we come back on Monday you might wish to take yourself back to Bow Street. That way you'll be easier to approach.'

Chapter Eighteen

Esther threw another handful of crumbs from the remains of her cheese sandwich to the eager pigeons that cooed appreciatively round her boots and smiled as she breathed in the fresh air from her bench seat a few yards down from the Marlborough Gate entrance to St. James's Park. Then she gazed appreciatively to her left, where in the distance she could just make out the rigid roofline of Buckingham Palace through the trees that were just coming into bud.

Her first two missions had been accomplished, and in her capacious shopping bag was a box containing the new hat with matching gloves, both in her favourite blue, which she had purchased at a reasonable price from the John Lewis store in Oxford Street. The letter had been handed over at the front desk just inside the imposing Government building with its Georgian pillars in Marlborough Road, and hopefully it would now be in the secure hands of the man to whom it had been addressed in Percy's immaculate copperplate hand. Now there was only one task left before she could take the bus back to Fenchurch Street Station and home, and she sighed as she regretted having left it until last. Had she undertaken it first, then this seat in the Park would be her final memory of a day out in London; as it was, she now had to make the depressing trip down into the sordid backstreets of Wapping in order to keep her promise to Jack.

As she alighted briskly from the bus platform at the stop by the junction of Nightingale Lane with the Ratcliff Highway she kept her head well down, conscious of the leering stares of two lounging labourers on the corner. She scuttled hastily down the wide expanse of roadway along which tobacco carts were plying their way towards Whitechapel, wrinkling her nose against the sickly-sweet odour of their cargoes that blended with the stench from the recently dropped horse dung. She took the first side street to her right, then turned left into Pennington Street in the hope that number fifteen was at the end of the street closest to her.

With a sigh of relief she found it several alleyways up on her left and walked down the dank approach to the outside door of the communal kitchen where, if the lodging house was anything like the ones she had known in the Spitalfields of her youth, she would find the Superintendent. Instead she found his wife, who looked Esther's relatively fine clothes up and down with suspicion before advising her that she'd find Mrs Black on the fourth level up, and that 'Yer can't miss it, since 'er noisy bleedin' kids'll be blockin' the stairs as usual.'

There were two fairly ragged children of around eight years of age sitting gloomily at the top of the third landing, who confirmed that 'Mam's one floor up, but she's not expectin' nobody.' On the top landing at last, Esther tapped smartly on the door, and a few moments later it opened to the sight of a scrawny woman with greying auburn hair who smelt heavily of yesterday's sweat and was carrying a mewling baby under her arm.

'Mrs Black?' Esther enquired politely, and the woman's eyes narrowed defiantly.

'You from them "child neglect" busybodies?' she demanded aggressively.

Esther shook her head. 'No, I'm here with a message about your husband.'

The woman's eyes widened, and her mouth relaxed. 'Yer'd best come in,' she told Esther with a gesture to indicate the open doorway, and as Esther slipped past her she heard her bellowing down the staircase from the top balcony, 'Liza! Jimmy! Get yer arses up 'ere afore I comes down an' grabs the pair o'yer be the scruff! Sorry about that,' she smiled at Esther as she nodded towards the vacant chair, then perched herself on the end of the unmade bed with the infant still in her arms, 'but the little buggers get in the way o' the other folks what lives 'ere, an' I'm constantly gettin' complaints. Now, what were that about Mickey?'

'I haven't seen him myself,' Esther hastened to advise her, 'but my husband has, and he asked me to come here with a message that your husband is fine and well but won't be able to come home for a little while longer.'

'What's 'e workin' at?' Lizzie Black asked. 'Is 'e still a copper?'

'As far as I know,' Esther replied. 'My husband met him in the course of his work, since he's a police officer himself.'

'Yer name's not Enright, by any chance?' Lizzie demanded bluntly.

'Yes. But please call me Esther.'

Lizzie looked thoughtful for a moment as she gazed appreciatively at Esther's full-length wool coat and polished lace-up boots. 'I don't reckon as 'ow I've ever met anyone o' that name afore. Yiddish, innit?'

'Jewish, yes. Is that a problem?'

'O' course not. I've got lotsa friends what's Yiddish — leastways, I *used* ter 'ave 'til I got dumped in 'ere, where I don't know nobody 'cept them what moans about the kids.'

Right on cue the two urchins from the stairwell slouched through the open door, and Lizzie yelled for them to shut it, which they did before taking sullen seats on the bare floor, making no attempt to conceal their curious stares at their new visitor with the 'posh' clothes.

'Yer Dad's still in the land o' the livin',' Lizzie advised them bluntly, receiving no responding facial expressions of either relief, or even vague interest, from either of them. 'That's what this lady 'ere tells me.' She looked back at Esther. 'But 'e still won't comin' 'ome in the foreseeable future, that what yer tellin' me?'

'I'm afraid not,' Esther confirmed. 'But I'm told that you're still receiving money regularly?'

'Yeah, that's right,' Lizzie nodded. 'A bit more than 'e used ter bring 'ome, actually, so 'e musta given the gamblin' away at long last. This bloke brings it every Friday, regular as clockwork. Would yer like a cuppa?'

'No thanks,' Esther replied politely. 'I have to be going now, since I only came to pass on the message.'

'Will yer come an' see us again?' Lizzie enquired pleadingly. 'Only that way, I'll know that Mickey's still alive.'

'Yes, of course,' Esther replied in a moment of weakness as she felt a wave of pity for the woman and her children. 'It won't be every week, mind — just now and again.'

'Whenever,' Lizzie smiled as she reached out a work-reddened hand to touch Esther on the wrist. 'If possible could yer get a message ter Mickey that me an' the kids is fine, an' that Tommy's almost walkin'?'

'Of course,' Esther promised as she rose to leave. That seemed to be the signal for the two older children to scuttle out ahead of her, yelling like marauding pirates as they scampered barefoot down four flights of stairs and out into Pennington Street. Esther smiled as she walked past where they had settled on an upturned cart that they'd converted into a make-believe fairy castle, and fiddled in her handbag for her purse, before handing each of them a penny.

Then she walked gratefully back towards the bus stop, thanking God for bringing Jack Enright into her life.

Four days later, and over a week after being offered free range in the East End, Percy strolled into Leman Street Police Station and held up his police badge for inspection by the fresh-faced sergeant on duty behind the metal grille.

'You our new Inspector?' the young man enquired eagerly. 'I'm Albert Preedy. You're Jack Enright's father, aren't you?'

'Uncle,' Percy corrected him. 'But may I take it that we've met before?'

'When you were down here on that "Ripper" business, with Chief Inspector Abbeline,' Albert replied eagerly. 'I had tea with him not long ago, and he told me that the stiff that was pulled out of St Katherine Dock was Teddy Ainsworth.'

'That should make my job here a lot easier,' Percy smiled. 'I assume that Inspector Ingram's no longer here?'

'He left last Friday, thank God,' Albert smiled. 'Meaning no disrespect, but he could be a right bugger some days.'

'So can I,' Percy advised him with a frown, 'so keep your nose clean while I'm here, although it won't be forever. Only until the Queen's Jubilee in June.'

'Jack told me about that. From what he said it seems that we're going to be busy.'

'Busy, *and* overstretched,' Percy replied. 'I'll need all your roster books, assuming that Inspector Ingram didn't set fire to them on his way out.'

'No, they're still where they should be,' Albert grinned back. 'But they make glum reading — we're three men short on every shift, and it's got to the stage where we have to decide which patrol to abandon. We try to rotate it, so that we don't get any complaints when folks rumble what's going on, but even so...'

'I'm hoping to get you more men,' Percy told him, 'but they may be drafted in from Holborn or Stepney, and that won't be until the Jubilee itself, when we'll need every man we've got out on the streets — even those who've just come off a night shift.'

'You'll make yourself as popular as a fart in a colander,' Albert grinned, then remembered himself. 'Sorry, sir, I'll get the records you need sent up to your office. Second floor, two down on the left. It's been left clean and tidy.'

'I remember where it is,' Percy smiled, 'although the last time I was in it I was threatening Inspector Ingram that he'd soon be out on his arse. I keep my promises, as you can see, so keep your nose clean on my watch.'

After a thoroughly depressing day perusing a roster sheet that was inadequate, even for everyday policing of one of the most violent areas of East London, Percy decided to call it a day as the lengthening sun's rays that managed to penetrate his grime-encrusted west-facing office window reminded him that dusk began early in late March. With a sigh, he left things where they were on his desk, told the 'late shift' sergeant who was just taking over from Albert Preedy to leave his office untouched, and walked up to Commercial Road in order to catch the bus that would leave him with only a short walk from its eventual terminus at Hackney's Victoria Park.

As they clattered and lurched through Bethnal Green, Percy became aware of a stately looking clergyman, complete with dog collar, walking unevenly down the swaying gangway towards where he was seated with his back to the horse end of the carriage. To Percy's considerable annoyance the man took the outside seat next to the window seat that Percy was occupying, even though there appeared to be several vacant double seats still available.

'Going far?' the clergyman enquired.

'Home,' Percy muttered, both annoyed and constitutionally unwilling to give away unnecessary information.

The man sighed. 'Thanks to men like you, prepared to risk life and limb in the constant war against crime and evil, we can all look forward to going home every day. Take this Bible, my son, since you will find that it contains words of guidance for you.'

Before Percy could tell the man where to stick his Bible he'd risen from his aisle seat and headed for the rear platform with considerably more agility than he had demonstrated when he got on. Curious as to why a man of the cloth would be alighting at the roughest location in a rough neighbourhood he opened the Bible that the man had left with him. Written on the inside of the flyleaf was a simple instruction: 'Marble Arch, 2 pm next Tuesday'.

'Do you have a couple of hours to spare from whatever it is you're working on?' Liam Brennan enquired of Jack one day as they sat in their shared office on the Tuesday of the second week of Jack's return to Bow Street. Jack looked up from the pile of paper and rubbed his eyes.

'Anything's better than ruining my eyesight trying to make all these figures fit,' he smiled. 'What did you have in mind?'

'A brisk stroll down to Birdcage Walk, to the Wellington Barracks where many of our club members are based during the day. The Grenadiers are in residence there at present and will be joined by the Coldstreams ahead of the Jubilee bunfight that you're working on. It might be useful to you to get a general idea of the calibre of men who'll be guarding Her Majesty during the public parts of it. We can get a spot of dinner in the Officers' Mess afterwards.'

As they strode down through St James's Park, Jack was reminded of Esther's enthusiastic description of her day in London in order to deliver the messages from Percy and himself. The buds had begun to burst into life on the scattered oak trees and the wildfowl on the ponds were well into their spring nesting ritual. It was a bright cool day, and the stiff walk was a good opportunity to exercise cramped muscles that had sat for too long behind desks.

Brennan showed some sort of pass to a uniformed official at the gate behind the largely ceremonial Guardsmen in their distinctive bearskin hats. They were waved through, Liam in his sergeant's uniform and Jack in his well-worn charcoal grey suit, and after a further short walk they passed under an arch and found themselves on one side of a parade ground, up and down which a dozen men were panting backwards and forwards while a drill sergeant barked out less than sympathetic commands.

Jack looked more closely at them as they came to a sagging halt, men bent double in the effort to regain their breath before being ordered back at a run to where the drill sergeant was barking a further command as he stood with a notebook and pencil. Brennan grinned as he saw Jack's bemused expression.

'The best half dozen will form the final team.'

'Two questions,' Jack replied. 'First of all *what* team? And secondly, what happens to the ones who don't make the final selection?'

'Second question first,' Liam replied as he kept his eyes firmly on Jack's face. 'The ones who don't make it will go back to their original jobs as uniformed police officers.'

'Really?' Jack replied sarcastically. 'I can see at least one who won't be able to do that. The one struggling to keep up with the rest — the one in the grey vest and trousers? That's Michael Black, formerly based in Leman Street, who deserted his post weeks, if not months, ago, and who'll be facing serious criminal charges if he's ever located. I have no doubt that, if you make enquiry, the remainder of this sorry bunch will be found to have disappeared from sight at a time when they were suspected of corruption while employed as officers inside the Met. You seem to have recruited a bunch of deserters.'

'And yet you, as a serving Scotland Yard officer, have done nothing to have them apprehended, despite knowing of their origins?' Liam smiled back at him. 'Our judgment was correct, it seems.'

'Meaning?' Jack asked as his scalp began to prickle.

'Meaning that in only a few weeks time — by the end of May at the latest — you'll be required to take command of this lot, when they undertake the task that they're being kept ready for. All this exercise nonsense is just a front — an excuse, if you like — to keep them available until we need them.'

'Need them for what?' Jack demanded.

'Later,' Liam replied as he took his elbow to lead him off the parade ground. 'Let's have dinner first.'

'Then what?' Jack persisted.

'Then Chief inspector Markwell wants to see the pair of us. It's time to earn your membership, Jack.'

Chapter Nineteen

Percy jumped hastily aside as the coach rumbled past him in the narrow, rutted roadway under Marble Arch, threatening to launch a cascade of dirty water all over his boots from where it had collected under the slight hollow following the incessant late spring rain. He cursed quietly, narrowly avoided a large lady carrying a basket of bread, and almost collided with the stonework. He was consulting his watch for the fourth time when a carefully concealed doorway in the centre of the side of the archway opened, and a man beckoned him inside.

At the top of a narrow flight of stone steps, Percy was amazed to find himself in some sort of small reception area with a desk, behind which sat a man in a red and blue livery. The man rang a small handbell on his desk, and out from a room inside what was clearly the centre of the arch itself walked William Melville, a broad grin on his face as he contemplated the look of confusion on Percy's countenance.

'You're about to tell me that you had no idea that this place existed?' he said, and Percy nodded.

'Something like that. People pass under here by the thousand every day, and I've been a copper for thirty odd years, yet this place has remained a secret all that time?'

'Yes and no,' Melville advised him. 'It belongs officially to the Honourable Company of Constables of the Royal Parks, but they're mainly "ceremonial only" these days, and it will shortly become the smallest station inside the Metropolitan Police. In the meantime, we find it a convenient meeting place close to our office just up the road there, where your message was dropped off for my attention. Step inside my closet and we'll have some tea.'

He wasn't exaggerating about the limited space inside the office, underneath which could be heard the rumble and rattle of traffic and the occasional shrill call of a visitor calling an errant child to heel before they got run over. There was just enough space for a desk with a chair on either side, but once the tea had been served and the door closed behind them, Percy couldn't shake off the feeling that he was conducting a clandestine meeting inside a wardrobe.

'Now, why the urgency?' Melville asked.

Percy's face set in displeasure. 'It looks as if we're nearing the point of no return, and I wanted to make absolutely sure that we have your authorisation for what we're both about to do, but Jack in particular.'

'You mean he's been handed the gun with which to do the deed at St. Paul's?' Melville said with a look of amusement.

'Almost,' Percy told him. 'He's been told that he's been selected to lead a team of men inside Buckingham Palace during Day One of the Jubilee celebrations.'

'So what's your problem?'

'*His* problem, primarily, is that the small group in question consists of deserters from the Met, at least one of whom — Michael Black — was complicit in the Wapping warehouse fire in which we believe all those military uniforms went missing. They've got these men hidden away at the Guards' Wellington Barracks down the road there at Birdcage Walk, keeping fit and awaiting further orders.'

Melville sighed. 'You really aren't cut out for this Intelligence work are you, Percy? You see everything in terms of challenge — a brick wall with only one side. Can you not for one moment accept that, far from being a barrier, it's an open door?'

'But surely these ne-er-do-wells are being prepared for some sort of outrage during the Jubilee?' Percy protested, still unable to think sideways.

'Of *course* they are, and Jack just received his ticket to a ringside seat. Provided that he lets us know, at the last minute, what's being planned, we can nip it in the bud with our own people.'

'But that will place him in extreme danger, will it not?'

'Of course it will — isn't that what he joined up for?'

'He joined as a young, idealistic and starry-eyed constable of the Metropolitan Police at the age of nineteen,' Percy reminded Melville in a voice trembling with anger. 'He's now just approaching his thirtieth birthday, with a wife and four kids, and you expect him to throw himself in front of an assassin's gun?'

'Let's not exaggerate, Percy,' Melville frowned in irritation. 'We're simply asking that he keep in with this mob, passing regular information on to you, and ducking behind the parapet when the lead starts flying. My only concern is that all this is a little too obvious, as if we're being led by the nose up a blind alley while all the real action is planned for somewhere else.'

'Like St. Paul's, you mean? I've maintained all along that this will be where the Queen's at her most vulnerable, which is why I'm working my arse off trying to stretch an under-strength East End police force into something resembling a safety ring of blue uniforms. To be perfectly honest with you, I don't trust the army types to do a proper job, armed only with their tin soldier toys.'

'And it never occurred to you that the East End might be the red herring in all this?' Melville queried with raised eyebrows.

'It's so obvious that the Queen will be at her most vulnerable then that I think that the enemy are relying on us going down the wrong track and wasting our limited resources on Day Two when all along their real target has been Day One.'

'Not for the first time, you're telling me that I'm wasting my time,' Percy grumbled, but Melville shook his head.

'On the contrary, you're fulfilling a most valuable role in all this. For as long as you're seen to be racing around guarding against an attack on the second day, the forces of anarchy will think that we've bought the ruse. That's why this door that's been opened for Jack's so important. They may be under the false illusion that they've bought his loyalty and may even try to use him to feed you disinformation — to keep you focused on Day Two, that is. If they've *really* made a serious error of judgment, then they may even be relying on Jack to play a part in whatever they're really planning. But let's go cautiously here.'

'In what way?' Percy enquired, well out of his depth with all this thinking and double thinking.

'We can't jump too eagerly at the chance Jack's been given. He has to string things out a bit — appear reluctant to prove disloyal to his oath of allegiance. I hope he hasn't agreed already?'

'No,' Percy assured him. 'That's why I've come seeking your advice, and perhaps as well that I did. For how long do you want Jack to appear reluctant? He's already been interviewed by Markwell at Bow Street and been given a week to think about it.'

'Make him drag it out for a fortnight,' Melville instructed him, 'then he can agree with feigned reluctance, making it look less suspicious. Given his excellent record within the Met I'm surprised that they chose him, to be perfectly honest with you.'

'That's another thing,' Percy added. 'It's all too convenient that his wife's long-lost brother Abraham turned up when he did, with that tart of a woman Mary Carmody in tow. We haven't been given the information we need on the circumstances in which that man deserted his post — in fact, the army won't even admit that he has. For my money, Jack and his wife were deliberately targeted from the very beginning, and if Jack hadn't been seconded onto your team I wouldn't be surprised to learn that they intended to get him involved in something underhand in the course of his police duties, then go to ground like all the others did. And we don't know why some of those who opted to play the enemy's game finished up dead.'

'They clearly weren't regarded as good enough for this little elite team that's being kicked into shape for the big day,' Melville suggested. 'And so far as concerns Jack being targeted from the outset, and with the greatest respect to him, of what subversive value would a Detective Sergeant in an Essex backwater have been? He clearly became important when they somehow learned that he was working for Special Branch alongside you.'

'Why didn't they try to subvert me instead?' Percy thought out loud, and Melville smiled.

'Feeling unimportant again, are you? I thought that Assistant Commissioner Doyle had given you the come-on. Have you heard any more from him?'

'Not recently. Do you want me to take the initiative?'

'And say what, exactly?' Melville challenged him. 'Best let him come to you — that way it doesn't look too suspicious. We don't want to seem over-eager.'

'And in the meantime?'

'Keep doing what you're doing. Give every appearance of trying to build a wall of blue around the steps of St. Pauls on the Twenty-second. Do it as if you meant it, and as if you're convinced that the second day is the vulnerable one. Share all your information with Doyle, so that he reports back to whoever's pulling his strings that we've bought the entire subterfuge. We'll need to meet every week now, and this time and place are convenient for me. So — while I still appear to have some biscuits left — that would seem to be all for this morning.'

'What's *really* going on, Jack, and why is that poor woman being kept virtually a prisoner in that awful doss house in Wapping?' Esther demanded as they sat around the Sunday dinner table. 'What's her husband really up to, and how come you're involved? Uncle Percy again, isn't it? Not content with dragging you back into London, he's somehow got you involved in God knows what skulduggery that also includes Mickey Black, whose wife doesn't have a clue what he's up to. Am I to be treated like her? The "Enright Code of Silence" yet again? I'm surely worth better than that.'

Jack sighed, and was sorely tempted to reveal all, until he stopped himself with the reminder that if Esther knew what he was really involved in, she'd not only be scared to death, but would lecture him on his responsibilities towards her and the children. A bit like he'd been lecturing himself lately, but he didn't need to hear it from her as well.

'You must know by now that I can't disclose any details of cases that I'm working on,' was his first tame excuse, and it got the treatment it deserved.

'Until you want *my* assistance in solving them,' she reminded him. 'How many times in the past have I proved to be the most valuable member of the team, the vital cog in the wheel? I was good enough to be given confidential information then, but this time I'm seemingly only your message girl.'

'That's not fair,' Jack protested. 'This latest job really *is* top-secret, as you'll have to agree when the details finally become public knowledge, as they undoubtedly will. For the time being I can't tell you anything, that's all, any more than Lizzie Black can be told what her Mickey's up to.'

'Are you working with him?'

'In a manner of speaking, but I really can't say any more.'

'At least I'm not being held prisoner, like she is,' Esther conceded. 'I went to see her again last week, and she tells me that everywhere she goes she's followed, and that when she tried to go and live with her sister she was forced into that dreadful single room on the top floor of that disgusting rooming house that makes the one I was staying in when we first met seem like the Grosvenor.'

'You must stay away from there!' Jack commanded her without thinking.

The colour rose in her face in an expression of defiance. 'And who are you to tell me where I should and shouldn't go, while you spend your weeks prancing around London engaged in matters that you refuse to discuss with me?'

'Look, I'm sorry if I sounded a bit bossy just then, but it really wouldn't be a good idea for you to visit Lizzie Black again. There are people watching her every move, and no doubt taking a good look at her visitors, and I don't want you involved in all this. It's bad enough that I am.'

'And even worse that you won't tell me anything about it!' Esther replied accusingly, then her face softened. 'I'm beginning to agree with your mother, that it would have been better if you'd chosen another profession — or at least a *real* profession, like your father's.'

'If I had done, we'd never have met,' Jack reminded her.

'And if we hadn't, and I'd married a lawyer, or a doctor, or someone more likely to meet with your mother's approval, at least I wouldn't be left at home five days out of seven. I know that the woman's place is in the home, Jack, but there's no law that says that her husband can be somewhere *else*. It's Sunday again, and I'm beginning to dread these Sunday dinners, knowing that in a few hours you'll pick up your bag and head off again for another five days. I love you even more than I did when we first met, and I've just about had it with all these partings!'

She threw her fork down on the kitchen table and burst into tears. Jack got up and hurried round the table to fold her in his arms as he knelt beside her and nuzzled her hair with his lips.

'It won't be for all that much longer,' he assured her. 'Just a few more weeks. It's the beginning of May next week, and this will be all over by the end of June.'

'That's still two months. Eight more weeks! And how can you be sure that it'll all be over then?'

'I can't tell you, but I promise that it will,' Jack assured her. 'And I promise never to get involved in another case that takes me away from you — ever.'

She looked up through her tear streaks. 'You promise? You *really* promise?'

'I really promise. Now please don't let's quarrel like this, when I have to go away before supper time. Let's just go and cuddle in the sitting room.'

'Your week's up,' Markwell told Jack as he appeared in his doorway, 'and frankly I'm surprised that I haven't heard back from you already. You're being offered a wonderful opportunity to demonstrate your loyalty to the Queen, which can only result in a rapid promotion through the ranks.'

'Forgive me,' Jack replied in what he hoped was a suitable tone of deference, 'but it's all been a bit sudden, and I have my family to consider.'

'They're obviously important to you, and I respect that,' Markwell said more softly as he entered the office and took the visitor's chair in front of Jack's desk, 'but this is a matter that concerns the ultimate welfare of every family in the realm.'

Jack allowed his expression to appear unconvinced, and Markwell fell for it.

'Has Liam Brennan told you exactly what will be involved, Jack?'

'Not precisely, no.'

Markwell looked furtively behind him, then lowered his voice. 'We have every reason to believe that an attack will be made on the Queen's life during the State Banquet on the first day of the Jubilee celebrations — the Twenty-first of June. The only security inside the Banqueting Hall in the Palace consists of toy soldiers in fancy uniforms. We need a team of *real* security professionals, and that's why the men you'll be leading are being specially trained to form an elite guard of their own. Once we catch the assassin he'll be carted away by police officers and locked up where we can interrogate him regarding his motivations and loyalties.'

'And my job will be what, precisely?' Jack enquired.

'To command the men, who'll be on standby to effect the arrest.'

'But who's going to prevent the actual assassination?'

'You don't need to know that,' Markwell replied abruptly. 'Just take my word for it that we have the matter in hand. Now, are you prepared to take on this responsible duty for the nation?'

'Can I have another week?' Jack asked meekly. 'I need to reassure my wife that I'll be in no danger and let her know that I'll be missing on the day when she no doubt wants to bring the children down to London to wave their flags for Her Majesty.'

'Very well,' Markwell agreed, 'but that's the final limit. After next Friday, the honour will be offered to someone else.'

By the time that Wednesday dawned, the memory of that gentle afternoon on the Sunday had faded in Esther's memory, and had been replaced by the more familiar resentment. Once Lily and Bertie had disappeared from sight at the end of the front drive, in their school clothes and shepherded by the ever-reliable Nell, Esther pulled on her boots, put on her coat, scooped up Miriam into her pram and tucked Tommy in beside her. Then she headed off the half mile or so down the lane, and persuaded Constance to devote the following day to presiding over the house in Bunting Lane while Esther made another trip into London.

She fed Constance the little white lie that she was visiting an old friend who had recently lost her husband in tragic circumstances, and who was in need of the sort of spiritual upliftment that members of the St Margaret's Ladies' Guild were committed to dispensing, and by ten o'clock on the Thursday morning she was rattling her way down to Fenchurch Street with a light heart and a handful of sweets in her coat pocket for the Black children.

As she got off the bus at Nightingale Lane, there were once again two loafers on the corner to ogle her passing. Had she paid them any great attention, she would have realised that they were the *same* two loafers as on the previous occasions, but she was too intent on keeping her head down in the faintly guilty realisation that Jack had told her not to come back here. But she was intent on defying him, not just for her own satisfaction, but also in the belief that the poor woman would welcome any company in her enforced loneliness. After all, Esther got to see Jack two days a week at least, whereas poor old Lizzie Black didn't even have that comfort.

Three hours later, in a warm glow of self-righteousness, Esther walked back to the bus stop, her mind full of the fact that Jack would be home the following evening. Once again she kept her eyes on the uneven ground ahead of her as she picked her way down Ratcliff Highway, and failed to notice the old lady with the shopping basket who followed her from the shade of a shop doorway and climbed onto the bus platform behind her.

In due course the old lady was replaced by a middle-aged man who kept Esther in his sights all the way back to Fenchurch Street Station, where he nodded to the youth with the school bag who sat three carriages back from hers until the train reached Barking, where he kept two hundred yards behind her and kept on walking down Bunting Lane when she turned into her driveway, slowing down only to make a note of the number on the gatepost as he walked casually by, then turned back five driveways later and hurried back towards the station with a triumphant glint in his eye as he calculated how many pints he could get for the shilling he'd just earned.

Chapter Twenty

'We haven't seen you at the club lately,' Liam Brennan commented casually to Jack as they sipped their morning tea in the tearoom inside Bow Street Police Station. 'Have you been too busy with all that paper that you're pretending will make all the difference on Day One of the Jubilee bunfight? You already know where the real security will be coming from, and Chief Inspector Markwell won't wait forever, you know.'

'I have a wife and four kids to think about,' Jack reminded him. 'From what I've been told, leading that team will take me right into the centre of an assassination attempt, and...'

'You too scared, is that it?' Brennan challenged him.

'Not for myself, no,' Jack replied curtly, 'but I'm the family breadwinner. If you had any family of your own, you'd know what a responsibility that imposes on you.'

'How do you know I don't? Have you been checking up on me?'

'Of course not, why would I?'

'Just wondered. You're right, of course, which leaves me free to take full advantage of the benefits of club membership, particularly of the female variety. But even if you're not interested in those, which I assume you're not, why don't we see you at the club so much these days? What do you do with your time in the evenings?'

'I'm not sure it's any of your business,' Jack replied coldly, 'but if it makes you feel any happier I'll drop by this evening.'

'Excellent. The coach will leave around six, and we can travel there together.'

As promised, Jack was propping up the bar mid-evening when he was joined by Mickey Black, who seemed to be clinging to him after the favour he'd performed in getting a message to Lizzie several weeks earlier.

'How's it all going?' Mickey enquired casually.

'Pretty well, I suppose,' Jack conceded, hoping that the conversation would turn towards what Mickey and his fellow deserters were preparing for. Mickey's next comment made him pay more attention.

'We was told this mornin' that we'll be finished the job they've got in mind fer us by the end o' June, but I'm not prepared ter wait that long. I'm plannin' ter run away, but I'll need somewhere ter keep me 'ead down fer a week or two. I've gorra bruvver what lives in Shoreditch, an' 'e'll see me right fer a day or two, if yer could get a message ter Lizzie ter join me there wiv the kids. She knows the place.'

'What about the others in your team?' Jack enquired.

'Bugger the others,' Mickey smiled. 'This is just me, right? Tell me yer'll do it?'

'Yes, of course,' Jack assured him, 'but it won't be until next week some time, so don't make your run too early.'

'Next week'll be fine — and thanks, pal.'

Esther was surprised that Jack was prepared to let her go back to Wapping, even though she would simply be carrying a message. But it was a happy message, and as she watched Jack disappear down Bunting Lane on the following Sunday afternoon she reminded herself of how lonely she felt watching him walk away and tried to imagine what it must be like for Lizzie.

Happy to be the bearer of good tidings, she made the now familiar arrangement for Constance to come over on Tuesday to supervise the house for the day and set off with a light heart back to Wapping. The usual loungers were hanging around the junction near the bus stop, and she paid them no heed as she walked cheerfully down Ratcliff Highway, not once looking round, and therefore not realising that she was being followed.

As she reached the top landing of the lodging house, she half noted with curiosity that the door to the opposite room was wide open, with seemingly no-one inside. Too late she became aware of the stealthy footfalls behind her, and with a brief yell of protest she felt herself being lifted bodily off the floor with a burly hand under each armpit, and seconds later she was inside the empty room, the door barred behind her, screaming to be let out, but realistically knowing that her protests were in vain.

On the following day, Jack was irritated to look up and see Chief Inspector Markwell once again darkening his open doorway, this time with a smirk wide enough to join one ear with another.

'Have you made your mind up yet?' Markwell demanded, and Jack frowned.

'You gave me one more week. I don't know about you, but my weeks end on a Friday.'

'When you go home to your family in Barking?'

'That's right,' Jack replied nervously.

'Well, while you're deciding whether or not to join us, you might like to be advised that when you go home tomorrow, you'll find one less person there waiting to greet you.'

Jack froze, then shot Markwell a murderous look. 'Have you kidnapped one of my children or something?'

Markwell smiled. 'Let's just say that your dear lady wife will be our guest while you fulfil the role allocated to you in ensuring the Queen's safety.'

'You bastards!' Jack yelled.

'Clearly, the time for diplomacy and polite walking around each other has expired,' Markwell responded with a sneer. 'You have my assurance that your wife will come to no harm, provided that we receive your co-operation in what is to come. No more questions, no more less than subtle attempts to probe the activities of the Home Front Club, and no more pretence of compiling manpower figures for the Twenty-first of next month. Understood?'

'What about my children?' Jack demanded, outraged and fearful. 'Even if you assure me that you don't mean them any harm, who's going to look after them while I'm down here in London?'

'Your mother lives down the road, does she not? And she brought up two of her own in her time. That's not a skill that you lose over time.'

'She's a sick woman!' Jack protested.

'Then what about the girl who takes your two eldest to school and back every day? And that young man of hers?'

Jack's next objection froze in his mouth as he took in the implications.

'You obviously know a great deal about my family life, and I think I can guess where that information came from. Which tells me *precisely* who's behind all this, and if I get my hands on him, brother-in-law or not, I'll...'

Markwell raised his hand in the air by way of a request for silence. 'Never mind the wild speculation, Sergeant. I imagine that you have a few domestic arrangements to make in your wife's absence, so I won't keep you.'

As he disappeared from the doorway, Jack leapt from behind his desk and headed full pelt down the stairs to the front door. He dived onto the platform of the first bus heading towards Whitehall, and within half an hour he was gasping for breath as he burst into Percy's office in the Yard with the dreadful tidings. Percy looked shocked at first, then his rational brain took over.

'The chances are that they mean what they say, Jack, and they need your co-operation. I'll obviously send men over to the address of this Lizzie Black, in case Esther made it that far, but my guess is that they'll have her secreted away somewhere where we won't think to look. You'd best get back to Barking immediately and check that everything's in order, then you'll have to make arrangements for someone to see to the kids while you come back here on Monday and do what they require of you.'

'I can't just sit down here in London while Esther's in danger!' Jack protested, and Percy tried his best to be both logical and supportive at one and the same time.

'The only way she'll be in danger is if you don't go along with what they're demanding,' he reminded Jack. 'And wherever they're holding her, it's almost certainly here in London. So what choices do you have?'

'You're a great help!' Jack yelled as he ran from the office and headed for Fenchurch Street. Two hours later he was doing his best to explain to the children, who were home for dinner, and a very concerned grandmother, that Esther would be away in London with him for a little while, and that Constance and Nell would need to look after the children in their absence.

'Typical of the irresponsibility of young people these days!' Constance complained. 'They bring children into the world, then expect other people to look after them. I have my responsibilities with the Ladies' Guild and my weekly commitments at the bridge club to think about, remember? This is *quite* unacceptable.'

'Please, Mother,' Jack pleaded. 'This is very important — you've no idea just *how* important, believe me.'

'Very well,' Constance agreed with visible reluctance, 'but don't think that you can call upon me every time the pair of you feel like gallivanting around in that wicked city. I've always maintained that if you'd pursued a *proper* career, instead of...'

'Yes, thank you, Mother,' Jack cut her off before she launched into her usual recriminations. 'I need to grab some more things, then head off back to London, so if you'll excuse me...'

'You haven't had any dinner,' Constance objected, as Jack kissed her gratefully on the cheek and raced from the kitchen with a parting shot of 'I'm not hungry, honestly.'

He was just slipping out of the scullery door with fresh clothes stuffed into an old portmanteau when Nell called out to him from the open kitchen door, then scuttled through the scullery to join him on the back step.

'The missus is alright, isn't she? Only it's not like her to stay away from the children.'

'She's alright, Nell, trust me,' Jack replied as he looked down into her wide blue eyes with a serious expression. 'But just make sure that when you're taking the children to school and back, or when they're out playing, you have Billy with you as well.'

With that he took off down the drive as fast as his legs could carry him.

Esther had spent barely two hours in the empty room, alternating between staring out through the grime of the locked window, whose frame had been nailed down to prevent any possible escape down four floors, and pacing the floor while quietly cursing her own folly in ever setting foot in Wapping again. Then she heard the turning of the outside lock, the door opened, and there stood the last person on earth she had expected to see.

'Is this your doing?' she demanded. 'Is this how you repay our hospitality?'

'Shut up,' Mary Carmody demanded. 'Think yourself lucky it's me who's been put in charge of you, and not those oafs who locked you up in here, since they have no respect for a lady such as yourself.'

'So what happens now?' Esther demanded with a defiance that she didn't feel. 'And can I at least visit the outside privy, assuming that this place has one?'

'Of course. You can go now before we leave.' Mary smiled obligingly.

'And where are we going?' Esther asked as she moved to the doorway.

'A short journey, by coach,' Mary told her. 'Shall we go?'

As she closed the door to the backyard privy behind her, Esther toasted her good fortune in having Mary in charge of her transfer, because the two ruffians who stood alongside her with knowing leers would surely have taken advantage of her, given any opportunity. As it was, they stood sullenly to the side as Esther rejoined Mary, and the little party made its way out into Pennington Street, where a coach sat waiting. Inside the coach, Esther was blindfolded, and the coach rumbled off slowly.

She did her best to memorise the number of turns to the right and left as they weaved their way through busy thoroughfares, but soon gave up the daunting task and took to wondering what was to become of her, how the children would react when she didn't come home, and what Jack would do to find her once he realised that something had happened to her. The coach eventually came to a halt, and the surrounding sounds of the street suggested that they were still somewhere in the city. The blindfold was not removed as she was assisted down the step and hustled along through a doorway, up two flights of stairs and down a corridor. Another door opened, and she was led through it to the sound and smell of a recently lit fire. Then the blindfold was taken off, and as she shook her head and blinked to clear her vision she saw a familiar male figure seated in an armchair.

'Well, Abe,' she said sarcastically, 'I think I preferred it when you just pulled my hair.'

Chapter Twenty-one

The next few weeks were the most frustrating that Jack could ever remember. Percy had ordered an immediate police raid on the lodging house in Wapping where it was known that Lizzie Black lived with her children, but Lizzie could only advise them that she'd seen nothing of Esther since her visit the previous week, and they'd left it at that, since the other residents of the tenement, true to form, claimed to have seen and heard nothing. They could not even be sure that Esther had even got as far as there; all they knew was that somewhere in this massive city she was being held, presumably against her will, and in circumstances they could only speculate about.

Every day Jack's first thought on waking — not that he slept very much — was the one he forced himself into. That she was still alive, and not being brutalised. His equal concern was for her mental and emotional health. He knew that she was strong enough to withstand mere captivity, always assuming that she was not being physically abused, but she must be tortured with concerns regarding how the children would exist without her. She'd been farsighted enough to leave his mother in charge, but every weekend, as he hastened home to reassure them that they still had one remaining parent at least, he could see the strain on Constance, and dared not tell her the brutal truth as she constantly moaned and complained about Esther's prolonged absence. The children seemed to accept the situation, although he could see in the looks that he occasionally caught from Nell that she at least could tell from his anguished face that something was seriously wrong.

He would dearly have loved to remain at home, if only to spare his mother, but he was left in no doubt, on a daily basis, that he was expected to attend at Bow Street Police Station and appear to be working. After the second week he abandoned further work on his manpower chart, now firmly convinced that whatever was being planned — whatever he was an unwilling party to — would take place inside Buckingham Palace, and almost certainly at the State Banquet being planned for the evening of the Twenty-first of June.

Percy was almost equally convinced, although he made a continued pretence of drawing up detailed duty rosters across six police stations. For one thing, if nothing transpired on the Twenty-first, his master plan would need to be activated on the Twenty-second, and for another it was necessary to keep Assistant Commissioner Doyle thinking that the Enrights were doing nothing to rock any revolutionary boats.

The weekly meetings with Melville continued, but became increasingly acrimonious as the head of Special Branch refused to activate any programme for discovering Esther's whereabouts and securing her release. 'Whatever's being planned,' he reasoned, 'we have the inside position on it thanks to your nephew's bravery, and we can't afford to do anything to block it while they still have time to plan something else.' After their third consecutive weekly screaming match it was agreed that there would be no more meetings, since 'the big day' was now only two weeks away.

Jack was still staying with Percy and Beattie through the week, and they agreed that she was to be told nothing. This was perhaps a wise policy, but it made it harder and harder to think up reasons why Jack was eating almost nothing after a lifetime of healthy appetite, and why Percy would jump down her throat if she made any suggestion that they cheer up. On weekday evenings Jack would wander down to the club and try not to get drunk on the cheaply priced drinks. He wisely stuck to beer, and only once came close to abandoning his assumed air of quiet confidence. That was when he turned around from his perch at the bar to find a crestfallen Mickey Black at his elbow.

'I'm truly sorry, my friend,' Mickey muttered, 'but they threatened ter kill Lizzie an' throw the kids inter one o' them orphanages.'

Jack took a deep breath, swallowed hard and forced a wan smile to his lips.

'Don't worry yourself about it, but for obvious reasons I can't send anyone to find out if they carried out their threat.'

Mickey slid away from the bar as Jack made a point of turning his back on him, downing his pint and loudly ordering another one.

While Jack was turning into a mental wreck and losing weight at a rate he would never have thought possible, Esther was trying to come to terms with the fact that she'd become a prisoner at the hands of her own brother. At least she was being well treated, with regular meals, a bedroom of her own and laundry facilities. She was also allowed occasional shopping trips under the close guard of two surly looking guards, and by this means she managed to acquire fresh clothing when required. Her regular trips to the communal lavatory one floor down were chaperoned by Mary, who treated her with muted, slightly sullen, respect.

The well-established suite of rooms had large windows, and from the room allocated to her Esther could just make out, in the far distance, the tall spire of Christ Church, Spitalfields. She knew it well from her childhood, and it had also been the place where she and Jack had walked regularly, hand in hand, on Sunday afternoons during their courtship almost ten years ago now. From the window in the sitting room, which pointed in the other direction, she could make out tall crane derricks and ships' masts, and by her calculation she was somewhere in Aldgate, just south-west of Whitechapel, and up-river from where she had been seized in Wapping. But knowing where she had been taken brought her no closer to securing her freedom, and as the days passed she became more and more frustrated and anxious regarding the children she'd left back in Barking.

She lost no time in complaining bitterly to Abe about the way he was treating her, and the suffering he was causing, not only to Jack, but also to his own nephews and nieces. Abe appeared unconcerned until Esther finally lost her temper and hurled a pepper pot across the supper table at him, hitting him squarely on the cheek.

'You're an utter bastard, Abraham Jacobs — a disgrace to our parents, who brought you up to better than this.'

Mary made a grab for Esther's arm, but Abe instructed her sharply to leave Esther alone.

'She has every right to speak to me like that, and believe me, Esther, I'm not enjoying this.'

'Then why are you doing it?' she yelled back. 'What on earth is going on?'

'You're here in order to ensure that Jack does as instructed,' Abe replied calmly. 'And if it's any consolation, he clearly loves you so much that he's prepared to abandon his duties, betray his oath of office and join in a conspiracy against the English throne.'

'I can't believe that of Jack for one moment,' Esther protested. 'His work is his life.'

'And so are you, sister dear,' Abe smiled back. 'You should feel very special, and if nothing else comes of all this, you have the satisfaction of knowing that you're the most important thing in your man's life. Not every woman can say that.'

'Not every woman's being held prisoner indefinitely by her own brother!' Esther retorted, and Abe smiled again.

'It won't be for ever. Today's the fourteenth of June, and a week today it'll all be over, and you'll be free to go home.'

'And Jack?'

'That will depend on how he conducts himself.'

On the morning of the Twenty-first of June the Queen's Diamond Jubilee celebrations began with a triumphant procession from Windsor Castle to Buckingham Palace through the rapidly expanding western suburbs of her Empire's capital. Tenements that were already beginning to crumble from shoddy and hasty workmanship, blackened by the soot of British industry, were ablaze with colour, as Union Jacks and other banners recently sold at exorbitant prices by opportunistic street traders were festooned from upstairs windows, factory balconies and shop awnings.

As the regal procession approached Knightsbridge, a platoon of the Household Cavalry clattered out to meet it, and Her Majesty's coach was flanked on both sides by men on glowingly groomed mounts, their cuirasses flashing gold in the midday sun, and their white feathered plumes waving in the breeze of their jogging passage down Grosvenor Place through cheering ecstatic crowds, then left into Buckingham Gate before wheeling majestically through the gates of Buckingham Palace.

The deafening cheers and shouts of goodwill were faintly audible even through the closed windows of the almost empty

Bow Street Police Station, whose uniformed officers were fanned out along the royal route, as Jack looked up from his desk to see Liam Brennan standing in the doorway holding up a police sergeant's uniform on a hanger.

'Time to dress for the party, Jack,' he smiled.

'I was wondering when you'd get around to telling me what role you expect me to play in whatever you have planned,' Jack growled. 'Is that by any chance the uniform that was stolen from Holborn last year?'

'Never mind where it came from, it fits you,' Liam advised him without breaking the smile. 'Now get changed into it and come with me.'

The police wagon trundled through the back-garden gate of Buckingham Palace once the tin soldier on the gate had read the letter authorising their passage, and Liam looked behind him as he lifted the rear canvas flap.

'The rest should be close behind us,' he commented, and Jack was curious.

'What "rest", exactly?'

'The men you'll be commanding during the banquet this evening. Every squad of police officers needs a sergeant to keep it under control.'

'In connection with what, precisely, and will you now be releasing my wife?'

'No idea what's happening to your wife, but I can tell you what *will* happen to her if you don't do what you're told.'

'And what's that?'

'You'll find out soon enough. In the meantime, enjoy the scenery. Not everyone gets to visit the kitchens of Buckingham Palace.'

Esther knew only that she'd been told to prepare herself to leave her enforced accommodation late that afternoon. When she enquired why, Mary simply smirked and remarked sarcastically, 'We assume that you don't want to go and wave your little flag for your fat Queen, so where else would you like to be dropped off?'

'Barking,' Esther replied curtly. 'And where's Abe?'

'He's otherwise engaged, and Barking's too far. Will you settle for Hackney?'

'Uncle Percy's, by any chance? But won't he be on duty?'

'Him and just about every other copper in London. But they're wasting their time. Now, get your coat on — the coach's downstairs waiting.'

Inside the Palace kitchens it was heaving, steaming, yelling chaos as the chefs, cooks, kitchen hands and assorted underlings went about their appointed tasks, glowering accusingly at the small group of uniformed police officers cowering in one corner in an effort to avoid being burned, scalded or trodden on as dish after dish was loaded into the bain maries to keep them at an even temperature until they were needed. The chicken and asparagus salads were already loaded onto the trolleys that the *esculiers* would push into the Banqueting Chamber, and from which the gaudily-liveried waiters would collect the dishes that they would place on the tables.

The men, notionally commanded by Jack, had been fed earlier that afternoon, and were now grouped in a corner, wondering what they were to be required to do next. Jack was unable to advise them, since he had been given no more information than they had and was about to go in search of further instructions when a red-faced chef appeared through the steam and peered into his face.

'You Sergeant Enright?'

'That's me.'

'Yer wanted in the cold larder — now.'

'Beg pardon?'

'The cold larder — down there on the right — an' keep yer 'ands off the merchandise.'

Thoroughly at a loss, but grateful for what sounded like an opportunity to go somewhere cooler, Jack told his men to remain where they were, and picked his way carefully between the heavily laden metal benches until he stopped at the door labelled 'Cold Larder'. As if aware of his presence, the door was pushed open from the inside, and Jack came face to face with his brother-in-law Abe, dressed in his full Grenadier Guards Mess Uniform.

'What the…?' was all he had time for before he was pulled roughly inside the larder and told to shut up by a man who looked the absolute opposite of the genial, if quiet, man who'd shared his Christmas fare in Barking. Then Abe produced a revolver.

'Why shoot me in here, and spoil all this food?' Jack joked nervously.

'It's for you, you idiot!' Abe advised him sharply. 'Hopefully you'll be the only man in your contingent who's armed.'

'Armed for what?'

Abe nodded towards the back of the door. 'In a few minutes' time you'll be called into the Banquet Chamber to make an arrest. When you do, make sure above all else that your prisoner remains alive, since we need to confirm who commissioned him.'

'For what?'

'To assassinate one of the guests at the banquet.'

'Not the Queen?'

'Shut up and listen. I'll be foiling the assassination attempt, then calling for a police squad to take him into custody. We believe that there'll be an attempt on the assassin's life by that shower of plebs under your command, and your most crucial job is to prevent that happening. Hence the revolver. Now go back out there, keep the weapon hidden, and await the call. By the way, Esther's been released, and hopefully is now with your Aunt Beattie.'

Jack thanked him, and did as instructed, keeping the weapon tucked inside his uniform jacket as he rejoined his men with a lighter heart and several fervent prayers of thanks. The pace quickened in the kitchen as several dozen sides of roast beef went under the carving knife, and dozens of steaming tureens of vegetables began to re-emerge from the bain maries.

Inside the Banqueting Hall the top table, with the Queen in its centre, resembled a living portrait of all the senior world leaders, allocated their places in accordance with their current order of importance in world affairs. On the Queen's immediate right was Archduke Franz Ferdinand of Austria, heir presumptive of the Austro-Hungarian Empire, while to her left was the Prime Minister of New Zealand. Her Majesty would have much preferred to talk sheep with the man on her left, but it seemed that Franz Ferdinand was anxious to practice his English as he engaged his distant cousin in polite conversation that she smiled her way through while awaiting the soup course.

The first course platters having been swept off the table as if by sleight of hand, the waiters formed a queue at the trolley for the lobster bisque bowls that were being loaded by those in charge of them. The waiter who had been serving Her Majesty took his bowl at the same time that Abe Jacobs slid deftly past the laden trolleys and took his place in the rank of Grenadier Guards who were lining the back wall. Without seemingly taking his eyes off the Queen immediately in front of him, Abe watched out of the corner of his eye as the diminutive middle-aged waiter moved slowly down the raised platform carefully carrying a single bowl of soup towards Her Majesty. At the last moment he gave his real intentions away as he drew back one hand beneath his white serving cloth to reveal a long broad knife.

Abe waited until the knife was poised behind the back of its intended victim, then leapt forward with the agility of a panther on a young deer. The arm bearing the knife was bent back until it snapped, and the would-be assassin gave a grunt of displeasure when most men would have shrieked in agony. The two men fell to the ground, where Abe swiftly pulled the man's arms up his back, and from nowhere came an Army uniformed colleague armed with a set of police wrist restraints. The man was pulled roughly to his feet and led away as the call went out for police to formally arrest him and take him into custody. From the door that led to the kitchen Jack appeared at the head of his small police contingent, looking confused, and the man was handed to him while Abe turned back to the stunned looking Queen with a polite smile.

'My apologies, Ma'am. He was about to serve the soup from the wrong side.'

Back in the kitchen, Jack nodded to Michael Black and the uniformed colleagues alongside him.

'With me, all of you. Take him outside and summon a paddy wagon.'

Out in the darkness of the Palace yard, the only light coming from the uncurtained kitchen windows, Jack drew his revolver and hung back until Black and four others punched the man to the ground and began kicking him.

'Leave him be!' Jack commanded.

'We was told ter kill 'im.'

'And I'm telling you to leave him alone!' Jack yelled back. 'I'm armed,' he added as he flourished his revolver in the air.

'But there's six've us,' came a voice from immediately behind him as a hand shot up to wrestle the gun from Jack's grasp, 'an' yer've only got the one gun.'

'But there are ten more here!' someone shouted, and from out of the shadows strode a ring of uniformed officers, all armed, and with gun barrels pointing at the group. Then the source of the shouted challenge became obvious, as Assistant Commissioner Doyle stepped into the light and nodded to Jack.

'Well done, Sergeant. My men will take over from here.'

Jack stood stock still, bewildered by all the swift and unexpected turns of events.

'How do I know whose side you're on?' he enquired as Doyle's men began carrying the assassin away.

'You don't, but you usually do what your uncle tells you,' came the familiar voice, and Uncle Percy stepped into the light with a broad smile. 'Esther's safe at home with your Aunt Beattie, but we need to lose no time in rescuing her, before she's talked into eating something.'

Chapter Twenty-two

'Her Majesty's sent this excellent bottle of Bordeaux to wash down our dinner,' Home Secretary Ridley smiled at those around the table as Manning passed among them doing the honours, 'so the least I could do was to order beefsteak for our celebratory dinner.'

'It's not likely to go far among the four of us,' Melville grumbled.

'There are eleven other bottles in the case she sent,' Ridley advised him. 'It was left over from the banquet that nearly got ruined.'

'I hope the beefsteak isn't from the same source,' Percy chortled, and was gratified that everyone appeared to enjoy the joke.

'It has indeed to be hoped not,' Ridley agreed, 'since that was a week ago. She also sent her thanks in a short note in her own fair hand, in which she expressed her delight that her nation is so well served by loyal servants of the Crown.'

'But she was never the target all along?' Jack asked, still confused, but as happy as a child on its birthday with the way things had turned out. He'd been given the entire week off, Esther had been most loving and attentive after their reunion, his children had been told that he was a national hero, and even his mother had deigned to observe that he had at long last done something to honour the family name, conveniently overlooking his bravery medal some years in the past.

'We were meant to believe that the Queen was the target of Fenians again,' Melville explained, 'because had we known what was really afoot we'd have taken diplomatic steps to have that murderous arsehole Jetnikov expelled from the country.'

'That Russian bloke?' Jack enquired, and Melville nodded.

'Russian certainly, but working for the Germans, according to what we got out of him when we applied a certain amount of pressure to his broken arm.'

There were several suppressed shudders around the table, and it fell silent for a moment as they began the soup course. It was Percy who decided to ask the obvious question. 'Why would a Russian be working for the Germans?'

'Jetnikov works — or rather *worked*, since he won't be available for employment until he's released from Pentonville well into the next century — for anyone who'll pay him, and his paymaster this time was our old friend Kaiser Wilhelm.'

'But if the Queen wasn't the real target,' Percy persisted, 'then who was?'

'The bloke sitting next to her — the heir presumptive to the Austro-Hungarian Empire, Franz Ferdinand.' He smiled back at Percy's still uncomprehending face as he added more explanation. 'As I once remarked, Percy, international cloak and dagger isn't your strongest suit. The Kaiser wanted Franz Ferdinand to be assassinated by a Russian so that he — Wilhelm — could beat his breast in anguished outrage, and attack Russia while earning himself a few more friends in Austria, which would have been correspondingly weakened. He's been looking for the excuse for years, so I'm informed.'

'So *that* was why Jetnikov had to be kept alive,' Jack piped up. 'If he'd been killed, no-one would have known who'd put him up to it, and this Kaiser Whatshisname could march on Russia in righteous revenge.'

'Kaiser *Wilhelm*, Jack,' Melville corrected him. 'Remember the name, since we expect him to cause more trouble for us in the years to come, when hopefully you'll be one of our number, since your grasp of double dealing would seem to be more keenly developed than your uncle's.'

Jack preened himself at the praise, but Uncle Percy wasn't about to take that lying down.

'So keen that he was completely hoodwinked by his own brother-in-law.'

'A man he'd only just met, remember,' Melville replied in Jack's defence. 'But Captain Jacobs — or *Major* Jacobs, as he now is — also fooled the entire network that tried to inveigle him into their fold, using Mary Carmody as the lure.'

'So he wasn't fooled by Mary?' Jack enquired, and Melville shook his head.

'Far from it. We had reason to believe that Russian dissidents would try to enlist the Fenian roughnecks to do the dirty work in return for money for their cause, and Mary Carmody was their first-choice whore when it came to seducing officers and gentlemen. When intelligence officers in Cairo spotted her cosying up to Captain Jacobs, he was called in and given instructions to go along with it.'

'So seeking out Esther to catch up with her after all those years wasn't part of some devious scheme?' Jack asked, much relieved.

'Indeed not, but he was more than surprised when he learned that his little sister had married a fine young police officer who appeared to be incorruptible. He reported that fact back to his masters, and their instructions were to get you into the Home Front Club, where you might prove useful, as indeed you were, as matters turned out.'

'So who was calling *his* shots on our behalf?' Percy enquired. 'No, let me guess — Doyle.'

'Doyle was certainly his main contact within the Met, and Doyle in turn reported to me,' Melville explained, and Percy snorted with indignation.

'He certainly had me fooled, and I no doubt owe him an apology.'

'I don't see why,' Melville objected. 'It was his job to make you so suspicious of the entire Met that you lost no effort in exploring every nook and cranny inside it. We really *did* need to know the extent of the corruption, in an effort to see who was behind it.'

'You'll probably take back the compliment you paid me regarding my intelligence skills,' Jack conceded as his beefsteak appeared on the table in front of him, 'but I'm still confused about who was behind all this.'

Melville looked across the table at Ridley, who nodded and supplied the answer.

'It operated on three levels. On the ground floor were the Fenians, who believed they were working with the Russian revolutionaries, to foment rebellion and working-class anarchy within the nation. They were told to move in and corrupt as many Met officers as they could, and stage outrages such as the Hatton Garden gem raid and the Wapping fire. One of the more depressing aspects of all this is how successful they were at that, and we're indebted to you for flushing out those responsible.'

'Why were some of them then murdered, while others were kept on, and what will happen to men like Michael Black?' Jack enquired.

'The ones who were murdered by their own paymasters were no longer of any value to them, and there was always the risk that they'd talk if caught,' Melville explained. 'The remaining ones had obvious reasons for hiding themselves away and were recruited into that little team that was standing by to kill Jetnikov after he'd assassinated Franz Ferdinand, which he would have done had it not been for your brother-in-law. It was he who instructed that you be inducted into the Home Front Club to lead that team, since he was banking on being able to persuade you to keep Jetnikov alive.'

'So Abe Jacobs was part of the Irish lot?'

Melville nodded. 'So he led them to believe. Mary Carmody's been a key member of the Fenian movement for some years now, so when she approached your brother-in-law, he was instructed to appear as if she'd succeeded in seducing him into her little network. So yes, he was operating at the ground floor level, infiltrating the Fenians, many of whom we now have under lock and key.'

'You didn't say what was to happen to Michael Black,' Jack prompted him. 'I know he was a disgrace to the uniform, but I feel sorry for his wife and children.'

Melville smiled. 'All we could realistically accuse him of was desertion from his post. He was very helpful to us with inside knowledge of how the club was operated, so we closed it down with immediate effect, and Black goes back to foot duties in Whitechapel next week, with a big black mark on his service record. It's unlikely that he'll ever make sergeant.'

'What about Padley?' Percy enquired.

'On remand in custody on a charge of grand larceny,' he was advised. 'He'll probably get ten years, but he should be happy in jail, given his preference for male sexual partners that got him blackmailed into the subversive fold in the first place.'

'Markwell and Ingram?' Percy persisted as he reached for more potatoes.

'Currently in custody awaiting charges of corruption, to which they've both indicated a willingness to plead guilty, rather than be charged with treason and hanged. And before you ask, Sergeant Cameron has been reduced to the rank of Constable and transferred on a permanent basis to Records, inside the Yard. Despite his undoubted corruption, he had some passable excuse, given his son's medical difficulties, and this way he can at least be more regularly on hand to assist in the boy's nursing, and we've come to some arrangement over the cost of all that. Again, he was most forthcoming regarding the Fenian involvement in the theft of the uniforms and police wagon.'

'So how did the Fenians come to get involved with that Russian bloke?' Jack asked, still trying to take it all in.

Melville took a sip of wine before explaining. 'They were plotting to assassinate the Queen, obviously, since the heir presumptive to the Austro-Hungarian Empire was of no great propaganda value to them. Their previous attempt ten years ago failed dismally, so they put the word out that they were looking for someone who could do the job properly for a substantial fee. They were approached by Jetnikov, whose provisional target was indeed Her Majesty, but when the word leaked out through the revolutionary channels, our Russian friend was offered double by agents of the Kaiser if he'd transfer his murderous talents to Franz Ferdinand.'

'There's clearly no honour among scum like that,' Percy muttered, and Melville chuckled.

'Still the old-fashioned copper at heart, eh Percy?'

'Always will be,' Percy growled, 'and the thing that bothers me is that none of this has been made public. In my book we should loudly broadcast every success we have in suppressing lawbreaking, in order to deter others.'

'The Queen was most insistent that we draw the curtain of silence over the entire business,' Ridley explained. 'Apart from the embarrassment of the infiltration of our security network, we don't need to stir the waters with Germany just at the moment. She's accepted that her grandson is a disgrace to the dynasty, and a dangerous near lunatic, but we're seeking an alliance with Russia, and the Foreign Secretary persuaded her that the last thing we need is to accuse them of sending an assassin to her party, mainly by threatening to expose Wilhelm's part in all this if it became public knowledge. Not good for the family image, it seems.'

'Talking of families,' Jack muttered as he pushed his empty plate away, 'was it *really* necessary to have my wife held hostage like that?'

'It could have been worse,' Melville smiled. 'Liam Brennan — who's likely to be taking the drop for treason in the near future — thought that you weren't keen enough to lead what he believed would be a murder squad. It was important to have Jetnikov done away with in circumstances in which it could be claimed that he was seeking to escape custody, and an upright officer such as yourself, with a Queen's Bravery Medal to his credit, would be above suspicion. But when you seemed less than totally committed to the cause, Brennan suggested that they kidnap your wife. In the event, she suffered no more than a few weeks enforced holiday with her own brother.'

'That's not quite how she tells it,' Jack muttered, 'although she was most appreciative when she found herself back at Aunt Beattie's, and unharmed. It may be a while before she invites her brother back home to our place, but I think she understands what it was all in aid of.'

'Now for the sweet course,' Ridley announced as the lemon syllabub was brought in, 'and in more senses than one. Her Majesty was obviously anxious to ensure that you two gentlemen were adequately rewarded, but unfortunately we can't present you with medals or anything, because then we'd have to explain what they were for. So it has to take some other form. Percy first.'

'Early retirement on full pension?' Percy enquired hopefully, but Ridley shook his head.

'You're too valuable, Percy. According to Assistant Commissioner Doyle, anyway. That's why he's asked that you be appointed to head up a new team, with the rank of Chief Inspector. Given your demonstrated enthusiasm for sniffing out corruption within the Met, it will be labelled the Disciplinary Branch. Put more crudely, you'll be kicking constabulary arse with a promoted rank. The added attraction — to you — will be that you report directly to Doyle, thereby sidestepping Chief Inspector Bray, with whom you seem to regularly engage in conflicts of philosophy.'

Percy grinned widely, then paused to think for a moment, and looked sideways. 'Will Jack be working with me?'

'No!' Jack said firmly, then looked sheepishly down at his syllabub. 'Sorry and all that, but if I were to move back into the Met I'd have to give up living in Barking, and my family are happily settled there.'

'No fear of that, so breathe more easily,' Melville advised him. 'In fact, your daily train journey may well become easier, since I believe that your home station of Barking is on the Fenchurch Street line to Southend.'

'You're sending me to Southend?' Jack enquired nervously. 'That's even further out than Chelmsford. And what about all the work I've got to catch up on there? I've been gone eight months.'

'And you won't be going back, if you accept our offer,' Melville smiled.

'What offer's that?' Jack half croaked at the prospect of having to tell Esther than they might be moving again.

'Tilbury,' Melville replied. 'More specifically, the Port of Tilbury, which is so strategically important to us in terms of exports, imports, the ferry across to the south bank of the Thames, and foreign types coming in hoping to escape scrutiny in the London Docks that we've established our own police force there — the "Port of Tilbury London Police". It operates as a normal police force but reports to Special Branch and the Foreign Office. It's also about to become in need of a new Inspector, when the existing one retires. Interested?'

'*Definitely*!' Jack beamed.

'Good, then that's all sorted, and we can enjoy the coffee and port that I can see Manning entering with,' Ridley smiled.

'There's just one condition — for both of you,' Melville added. 'That is that if ever we need you again for an operation like the one you've just satisfactorily completed, you'll answer the call without question.'

'Of course!' Jack enthused.

'Suits me, since I've got less than two years to go,' Percy grinned, to which Melville gave him a mockingly stern look and a shake of the head.

'Don't get your garden spade out just yet, Percy. There's many a good tune played on an old fiddle, as the old saying goes.'

They walked out into the driveway of the Home Secretary's country mansion, full of an excellent dinner and encouraging future prospects, in order to enter the coach via the step that had been lowered for them. Jack held back deferentially and waved for Percy to go in first.

'After you, old fiddle.'

'I still outrank you,' Percy grinned back. 'And don't ever forget that.'

A NOTE TO THE READER

Dear Reader,

If you enjoyed this novel, my grateful thanks for joining me in the reality of the late Victorian world, which was far from the 'good old days' that the nostalgia merchants sometimes try to sell us. By 1897, most of Europe was a powder keg of revolution and sullen resentment, as the 'have-nots' grew tired of watching the posturing of the 'haves' from behind their economic and social barriers. Across in Russia – where Victoria's grand-daughter Alexandra was to become the final Tsarina of that nation in the Revolution that would remove the Romanovs from their lofty perches – the working class rumble was already building into the explosion that would rock the aristocratic world in 1917.

Another of Her Majesty's grandchildren – Wilhelm 11 of Germany – was beginning to display the bellicose mental instability that would lock three Saxe-Coburg descendents into the Great War, while in England itself the Fenians were staging outrages designed to secure Home Rule for Ireland, and the Suffragettes had long passed the point at which peaceful protest was having any effect.

When launching Jack and Percy Enright into their next challenge I could hardly ignore the reality of the London they were helping to police, and so I opted to throw them right into the middle of it, using as much actual historical fact as was available. Queen Victoria really did have two Jubilees; the Golden Jubilee in 1887 that marked her fifty years on the throne, and the Diamond Jubilee ten years later, when she become the longest reigning monarch of England to that point in its history.

It's a matter of record that a Fenian inspired attempt on her life was made during the 1887 Jubilee, and it was not stretching credulity too far to imagine one a decade later, but from a different source. I crave your indulgence for giving Wilhelm of Germany the idea to bump off Franz Ferdinand of Austria a generation earlier than he did, but even in 1897 it would have served the same purpose of giving him the excuse to rattle his sabre at Russia.

Although Percy and Jack have now proved themselves to be a formidable crime-fighting team, with Jack's wife Esther playing a vital role whenever the services of a highly intelligent but bored mother of four are required, even they seem to be out of their depth when what they are confronting is something more out of the ordinary than East End violence, West End corruption or Essex crime in general. Jack in particular has learned to become wary of simply playing monkey to Uncle Percy's organ-grinder, and is rapidly coming to learn that being the father of four, and the husband of one, must be his greatest priority. Esther is hardly likely to disagree with him, but just occasionally she needs a mental break from boiling nappies and bandaging cut knees. So in they plunge, three lambs to the slaughter of international intrigue and murderous skulduggery.

There has to come an end to all of this one day, and this awaits them in Book 8 – 'The Lost Boys', which is due out early next year.

As ever, I look forward to receiving feedback from you, in the form of a review on either **Amazon** or **Goodreads**. Or, of course, you can try the more personal approach on my website, and my Facebook page: **DavidFieldAuthor**.

Happy reading, ,David

davidfieldauthor.com

SAPERE BOOKS

Sapere Books is an exciting new publisher of brilliant fiction and popular history.

To find out more about our latest releases and our monthly bargain books visit our website: **saperebooks.com**

Printed in Great Britain
by Amazon